IN THE
BALANCE

IN THE BALANCE

A MISS SILVER MYSTERY

Patricia Wentworth

OPEN ROAD
INTEGRATED MEDIA
NEW YORK

Cover design and illustration by Jeffrey Nguyen

ISBN: 978-1-5040-4786-9

This edition published in 2017 by Open Road Integrated Media, Inc.
180 Maiden Lane
New York, NY 10038
www.openroadmedia.com

IN THE BALANCE

ONE

Miss Maud Silver looked along the crowded platform and felt thankful that she herself was in a through carriage. She was very comfortably settled in her corner, with her back to the engine to avoid smuts and the magazine presented by her niece laid face downwards on the seat beside her. She gazed with amiable interest at the family parties which came and went, hurrying into sight and then hurrying on again. Miss Silver's mind, incurably Victorian, found an apt quotation: "Ships that pass in the night—" Only of course it wasn't the night, but ten o'clock of a sunny July morning. Not that that really mattered, because poetry was not intended to be taken in too literal a sense.

> "Ships that pass in the night and, passing, speak one
>   another.
> Only a voice and a call, then darkness again and the
>   silence."

Symbolical of course. She hoped she had the words quite right.

Dear me—what a crowd! Everyone going away on their holidays. She herself had greatly enjoyed her fortnight at Whitestones with Ethel and the children. After the very trying affair of the poisoned caterpillars it had been pleasant to relax in the bosom of an affectionate family. They had sat out on the beach all day, and she had knitted three pairs of socks and a coatee for the baby, a nice plump, friendly child. The holiday had done her good, and the circumstance that there are no caterpillars by the sea had certainly added to her enjoyment.

She watched a stout woman push herself and three children through the crowd with the efficiency of a tank. There was a little boy with something in a basket. He wrestled with the catch, lifted the corner of the lid, and in a flash a black kitten clawed its way out and was gone. Miss Silver said "Dear me!", approved the slap administered by a competent maternal hand, and lost the group as it surged on in pursuit of the kitten.

Nearly everyone seemed to be leaving this train. Miss Silver herself was returning to London. She reflected that it would be an agreeable end to an agreeable holiday if she were to have the carriage to herself for the rest of the way—agreeable but improbable. A tall, thin man with a dreaming face went by. He stood a head and shoulders above the crowd and walked as if he were alone on a windy moor. Two young girls went by, chattering nineteen to the dozen. They wore grey flannel trousers and brilliant pull-overs with no sleeves. Their mouths were plastered with lipstick, their hair shone in bright sophisticated waves. A nurse went by, very stiff and starched, with a child in a sky-blue bathing dress. The little creature danced along, clutching a new tin bucket all ready for the beach, its head a tangle of yellow curls, its arms and legs as brown as oak-apples. No one seemed to be coming in. They all went by.

Miss Silver looked at the watch which she wore pinned with a gold bar brooch to the left-hand side of her brown silk blouse and confirmed an impression that the train was due to start. She wore besides the blouse a coat and skirt of drab shantung, black Oxford shoes, and a brown straw hat with a small bunch of mignonette and purple pansies on the left side. A pair of openwork drab cotton gloves lay in her lap beside a rather shabby black bag. Under the brim of the shady hat there was a good deal of mouse-coloured hair, a set of neat middle-aged features, and a smooth sallow skin. The brown blouse was fastened at the throat with a large cameo brooch bearing a Greek warrior's head in high relief. A string of bog-oak beads ingeniously carved went twice round Miss Silver's neck and then fell to her waist, jingling a little as they touched the double eyeglass which she wore suspended by a fine black cord.

A whistle blew, the train gave a premonitory jerk. Someone shouted. Miss Silver looked up and saw the door beside her wrenched open. The train gave a second jerk. A tall girl in grey came stumbling up the step into the carriage. A third and heavier jerk threw her against Miss Silver, who was at her best in an emergency. The girl was steadied. The door, which had swung loose, was caught and slammed. Lisle Jerningham found herself being pressed into a corner seat by someone who looked like a retired governess, while a voice strongly reminiscent of the schoolroom informed her that it was extremely dangerous to endeavour to enter a moving train—"*and* quite against the company's regulations". The voice came from a long way off, from the other side of that gulf which lay between her and every living soul. On that other side there had once been a schoolroom and a voice like that. "Don't bang the door when you come into a room, Lisle. Sit up, my dear—don't slump in your chair like that. Oh, my dear Lisle, do please attend when I speak." All these things—long ago and far away—on the safe other side of the gulf—

"Not at all safe," said Miss Silver in earnest admonition.

Lisle stared at her. She said, "No." And then, "It doesn't matter, does it?" She saw Miss Silver quite plainly and distinctly, a little old-fashioned governessy woman sitting up prim and straight in the opposite corner, with frumpy clothes and the sort of hat that nobody had worn for years. With the least possible movement she could have touched her, and yet Miss Silver, like her voice, seemed a long way off. She said in a flat, exhausted voice, "It doesn't matter," and leaned back into her corner.

Miss Silver made no reply. Instead she observed the girl attentively. A tall girl, very slight and graceful, with the ash-blonde hair and milky skin which belong more to the Scandinavian than to the English type. An English girl as fair as this would have blue eyes, but the eyes which were now fixed on the moving landscape were of a pure deep grey fringed with lashes which were many tones darker than that very light hair. The eyebrows were golden, narrow and oddly arched, like frail gold wings spread for a flight. This gold gave the face its only colour. Miss Silver thought she had never seen a living person look so pale. The very white skin made the effect more startling.

The girl was wearing a grey flannel coat and skirt, beautifully cut. Everything she had on was perfectly simple, but the simplicity was of the kind which cannot be achieved without money. The small grey felt hat with its blue cord looped in a careless twist, the grey handbag with the initial L, the fineness of the silk stockings, the quality of the grey shoes—all these things Miss Silver observed. Her eye passed to the ungloved hands, noted a platinum wedding ring, and dropped to her own drab lap. Her practised mind summed up its impressions in three words—shock—money—married.

She took up the magazine which Ethel had so kindly provided and began to turn the pages. When she had turned three in rapid succession she went no farther. Her gaze, at first fixed and intent, became abstracted.

After a little she closed the magazine and leaned forward.

"Do you care to read? Would this interest you?"

The grey eyes came slowly to her face. She thought there was a resolute attempt to focus then. They had not really been seeing the flat green fields with their chess-board pattern of hedgerows—all the same size, all slipping by faster and faster as the train gained speed. She was not really seeing Miss Silver now, but she was making an effort.

Miss Silver abandoned the magazine as a gambit, and said directly,

"Something is the matter, is it not? Can I be of any assistance?"

The voice, kind and authoritative, reached Lisle Jerningham—the voice, not the words. She heard the words of course, as she heard the clanking of the train, but one meant no more than the other. The voice reached her. Some of the blankness went out of her eyes. She looked at Miss Silver and said,

"You are very kind."

"You have had a shock." This was a statement, not a question.

Lisle said, "Yes;" and then, "How did you know?"

"You came away in a hurry."

"Yes." She repeated her question rather piteously. "How did you know?"

"This is a London train. You would not be going to London without any gloves if you had not come away in a hurry. And they are not in your bag. That flat envelope shape would not close upon a pair of gloves without bulging."

Again it was the kind, decisive voice which reached Lisle and steadied her. There was something about it which made her feel safe. She said like a distressed echo,

"I came away in a hurry."

"Why?" said Miss Silver.

"They said he was trying to kill me," said Lisle Jerningham.

Miss Silver betrayed neither surprise nor incredulity. It was not the first time she had received a similar confidence. It was in fact her professional business to deal with such confidences.

"Dear me," she said—"and who is supposed to be trying to kill you?"

Lisle Jerningham said, "My husband—"

TWO

Miss Silver looked at her steadily. An unbalanced mind not infrequently displayed itself in such an accusation. She had encountered persecution mania, but she had also encountered murder, and that not merely attempted. In more than one case it was only her own intervention which had prevented the attempt from being successful. She looked steadily at Lisle Jerningham and judged her sane—a normal creature shocked into a temporary abnormality. Shock sometime acts as an anæsthetic. Control is in abeyance, the tongue is loosened, reserve is gone.

These thoughts took no more than a moment. She repeated her former mild "Dear me!" and enquired,

"What makes you think your husband is trying to kill you?"

Not a muscle of Lisle's face had moved. She had spoken in a flat, emotionless tone. It did not vary now.

"They said so."

"Yes? And who were 'they'?"

"I don't know—I was behind the hedge—" Her voice trailed away. Her eyes remained open, but instead of seeing Miss Silver they saw the hedge, a long, dark wall of yew set here and there with berries like little blood-red bells with the green seed for a clapper. She was not in the railway carriage any more. She was standing pressed close up against the hedge with the sun shining hot on her back and the queer stuffy smell of the yew in her nostrils. She was looking at one of those crimson berries with the bloom on it, and all at once voices came to her from the other side of the hedge:

"Of course you know what they say—" A slow, drawling voice.

"My dear, you might as well tell me." A voice that hurried and was amused.

And then the first voice again.

Lisle found herself speaking to the frumpy little woman in the opposite corner. If she spoke, it would stop those other voices.

"I didn't know they were speaking about Dale—not at first. I oughtn't to have listened, but I couldn't help it."

Miss Silver had opened her bag and put away the magazine. She was now placidly knitting the second of a pair of grey stockings for Ethel's eldest boy. The bright steel needles clicked as she said,

"Very natural. Dale is your husband?"

"Yes."

It was a relief to speak. The sound of her own voice drowned the voices which had spoken about Dale. When she was silent they went on speaking all the time in her head, round and round and round like a gramophone record. They were beginning again now, and she could smell the yew with the sun on it.

"It was a very lucky accident for him." A low, drawling laugh.

And then the other voice, hurrying to be cruel:

"Some people have all the luck. Dale Jerningham's one of the lucky ones."

That was when she had known that they were talking about Dale. She said faintly and piteously,

"I didn't know—I really didn't know—not till she said that."

Miss Silver turned her stocking.

"Not till she said what, my dear?"

Lisle went on speaking. She did not think about Miss Silver at all. It was easier to talk than to listen to the voices which went round and round in her head.

"She said that Dale was lucky because his first wife had an accident. They married when he was very young—only twenty, you know, and she was older than he was—a good deal older—and she had a lot of money. They talked about that. They said Dale would have had to sell Tanfield if he hadn't married her. I don't know if that is true—I don't know if any of it is true. Her name was Lydia. They said he didn't love her, but she was very fond of him. She made a will which left him everything, and a month later she had an accident when they were climbing in Switzerland. They said it was a very lucky accident for Dale. They said the money saved Tanfield. I don't know if that is true."

Miss Silver observed her gravely. No expression in the face. No expression in the voice. No colour. No life. There was more here than the death—by accident—of an unknown first wife a good many years ago. She said,

"I am a great admirer of the late Lord Tennyson. It is a pity that he is not more read nowadays, but I believe that he will come into his own again. When he wrote, 'A lie that is half the truth is ever the worst of lies,' he wrote something that we would all do well to remember when we have been listening to injurious gossip."

The words went past Lisle, but the calm, authoritative voice soothed her. She said with a faint note of pleading,

"Do you think it wasn't true?"

"I don't know, my dear."

"She fell," said Lisle—"and she was killed—Lydia—I didn't know her—it's a long time ago. They said it was a lucky accident—"

Miss Silver's needles paused.

"I think they said something more than that. What did they say?"

Lisle put a hand to her cheek in a strange frightened gesture. She wanted to go on talking, but she did not want to talk about the thing that had really frightened her. When she approached it even in thought everything in her went cold and numb. There was no pain yet, but there would be pain when this numb terror relaxed—there would be anguish. Talking kept it away. She went on talking.

"They said her money saved him from having to sell Tanfield, but I don't know if that is true. The money nearly all went in the depression—Dale told me that himself. And they said it was my money he wanted now."

"I see. You have money of your own?"

The dark grey eyes dwelt on her without expression. The white lips said,

"Yes."

"I see. And you have made a will—leaving your money to your husband?"

"Yes."

"When did you do this?"

"A fortnight ago. We have only been married six months."

Miss Silver knitted. Lisle Jerningham fell silent, and heard a drawling voice which said:

"The money's tied up, but I believe he comes into it if anything happens to her."

And the other voice, quick with malice:

"Is she going to have an accident too?"

Pain stirred the numbness at Lisle's heart. Fear stabbed her. Better to say it herself than to listen to the voices. She said on a shuddering breath,

"'Is she going to have an accident too?' That's what they said—an accident—because if he had the money to do what he liked with he could keep Tanfield. And I don't like it very much, you know, because it's so big. I'd rather live at the Manor—it's more like a home. So I said why not sell Tanfield? There's a man who wants to buy it. But Dale said his people had been there always, and we quarrelled. But he *wouldn't*—just because of that! Oh, it was an accident!"

"What sort of accident?" said Miss Silver.

"We were bathing. I'm not a very good swimmer—I couldn't get in. He and Rafe and Alicia were laughing and splashing each other—they didn't hear me call. I was nearly drowned. It was an accident. But that's what they said—"

The voices drowned her own voice with a sudden surge of sound which filled her ears:

"Is she going to have an accident too?"

And then the other:

"My dear, she's just had one—fished up out of the sea like a drowned cat. Dale doing the broken-hearted widower for the second time. Practice make perfect, but this time it was a bit premature. She came round, and he hasn't got the money—*yet*."

"Who was tactless enough to save her?"

There was a drawled "Not Dale."

Lisle's hand dropped into her lap. It was no good, she had to listen.

Miss Silver's voice came to her, saying quietly,

"But you were not drowned. Who saved you?"

"Not Dale," said Lisle Jerningham.

THREE

The train slowed down to the curve by Cranfield Halt.
Sometimes it stopped there, and sometimes it did not. Today it
was going to stop. There were half a dozen passengers waiting
on the open country platform, and four of them precipitated
themselves into the carriage in which Miss Silver had hoped to
continue a very interesting conversation. They pushed between
her and the pale girl who had just been saying such startling
things—a hearty, comely mother and three children from six
to sixteen, all off to town for the day to visit their relations. The
carriage became filled with their voices, their opinions, their
criticisms, their anticipations. They all talked at once.

Lisle Jerningham leaned back in her corner and shut her
eyes. Why had she ever gone down to Mountsford? The Cranes
were not really her friends at all. She hardly knew them. They
were Dale's friends. And in the end Dale had cried off and
made her go alone. Business in Birmingham—Lydia's money.

There wasn't very much of it now—she knew that. Lydia's money . . . She tried to stop thinking about Lydia. Mr Crane was nice—she liked him—big, and jolly and kind. Mrs Crane always made you feel as if you had a smut on your nose. She liked Dale—women generally did—but she had a grudge against him for marrying. She liked men to be single and faithfully adoring. She liked a court. She was devoted to her husband, but she liked other men to be devoted to her. And Dale had broken away and married Lisle, so she didn't like Lisle.

Dale oughtn't to have made her go down to Mountsford alone. She ought to have refused to go—then none of this would have happened. She would never have stood with the sun on her back, and smelled the yew hedge, and heard the voices say, "A lucky accident for Dale."

She jerked her thought away. This time yesterday she was seeing Dale off. And then shopping and lunch with Hilda. And then in the late afternoon the hot train journey down to Mountsford. She had left it as late as she could. She had even left it a little too late, because she had had to hurry over her dressing. She saw herself in her silver dress, with the emerald which had been her mother's. Some people's eyes would have taken a green shade from the green stone, but hers were never anything else but grey. They didn't change. There was something in herself which didn't change either. Even if it was all true, she couldn't change. Even if Dale wanted her dead, she couldn't change.

She wrenched away from that. Dinner. Marvellous food. Mr Crane telling Scotch stories very badly and laughing at them so heartily that it didn't seem to matter whether anyone else laughed or not. A crowd of people whom she didn't know.

A fat man who wanted her to come and see the rose garden by moonlight, and who said "All the better" when she pointed out that there wasn't any moon. Bridge—much wearisome bridge. And at last bed. She had dreamed about Dale—Dale looking at her—Dale's eyes laughing into hers—Dale kissing her . . . She mustn't think about that—

But whatever she thought about, it came back to Dale.

This morning, lovely, with the mist rolling up off the sea, dissolving, thinning away, clearing away from the pale, bright, perfect blue of the sky, and the sun so hot on her back where she stood in the shelter of the hedge.

A lucky accident for Dale—

It was no good. It all came back to that.

In the opposite corner Miss Silver had put down her knitting and had once more opened Ethel's magazine. She looked at the same page which had engaged her attention before. It displayed the full-length photograph of a girl in a silver gown. Underneath, in italics, the legend, "Lovely Mrs Dale Jerningham in her loveliest frock." All round the photograph, in lines of varying length, there meandered a gossip letter which began with an italicised *"Darling"*, and ended with *"Yours ever"* and a large question mark. Anonymity may mean that you are either too well known or not known at all. It has certain advantages, and the writer of this letter exploited them to the full. Dale Jerningham became Dale as soon as his surname had been got on record. "A lucky man, not only because he owns Tanfield Court which costs the earth to keep up, but he has married two quite rich wives—oh, not both at once of course—that would be too much luck even for lucky Dale,

and he really was a widower for a surprisingly long time. His
first venture was poor Lydia Burrows, who was killed climbing
in Switzerland umpteen years ago. The present Mrs Dale was
Lisle van Decken. And has she got plenty of the needful? Oh,
boy! She's as pretty as her picture, or even a little bit prettier.
Father American and dead. That's where the cash comes from.
A Scandinavian grandmother. Hence the platinum hair which
looks too good to be true, but isn't really . . ."

Miss Silver permitted an expression of distaste to change
the set of her lips. Vulgar—very vulgar indeed. She really did
not know what the press was coming to. She looked across at
Lisle and saw her leaning back. Her eyes were closed, but she
was not asleep. The hand in her lap was clenched upon itself,
the knuckles showed bone-white. No, not asleep, only with-
drawn into a desperate unhappiness.

A little later, as the train slowed, the eyes opened and met
Miss Silver's. There was a long moment before the eyelids
dropped again.

Miss Silver unhasped her bag and extracted from it a neat
professional card inscribed:

MISS MAUD SILVER

15 Montague Mansions,	Private Investigations
West Leaham Street,	Undertaken.
S.W.	

She closed her bag again with a decisive snap as the train
slid into the gloom of the terminus. A porter flung the door

open. The woman with the three hearty children gathered her brood and got out. Mrs Dale Jerningham rose to her slim height and turned to follow them.

She had reached the platform and had walked a few steps, when she became aware of a hand on her arm. The little dumpy woman to whom she had talked in the train was walking beside her. She had talked to her, but she could not remember just what she had said. She didn't want to talk to her now. She looked down vaguely and saw that she was being offered a card. She took it and put it in her bag. The voice which reminded her of all the governesses she had ever had said kindly and distinctly,

"If you need help at any time, that is my name and address."

The hand dropped from her arm. Without looking round she went forward to the barrier and gave up her ticket.

FOUR

The sun blazed down on the tennis courts at Tanfield. There were three of them, two under beautiful turf, and the third a green hard court. A high mixed hedge of hornbeam, holly and thorn shut them in. The great mass of the house, except for its high flanking towers, was out of sight.

On the farther grass court Alicia Steyne was finishing a hotly contested set with Rafe Jerningham. The ball skimmed the net and went low and straight past Rafe's backhand. He ran, reached for it vainly, and came down sprawling. Alicia threw her racket in the air and called in her high, sweet voice, "Game *and!*"

Rafe got up and saw her laughing at him. She was as little and light as a child, with dark tossed curls and a vivid, wilful face. All her colouring was brown, but the quick blood gave brilliance to lip and cheek. Her teeth were as white as hazel nuts. She came round the net tossing her racket and laughing.

"Pouf! I can always beat you!" She pursed her lips and blew him a kiss. "And for why? Because I play much, much better than you do. *And* I don't lose my temper."

Rafe laughed too. He was as brown as she—medium size, very slim, very goodlooking in something of a gypsy way. He had slender black eyebrows with an odd kink in them. The brown-skinned, well-set ears were a little pointed like a faun's. There was something that was not quite a likeness between him and Alicia Steyne. They had, in fact, the same grandmother, and the same very white teeth. He shewed them as he said,

"But I don't lose my temper."

"Never?"

"Never."

"Not even secretly! Most men do when a woman beats them."

"Not even then."

She flung her racket down with a sudden impatience.

"Well, I've got a beast of a temper, and I don't care who knows it! Only I don't lose it at games—I keep it for something better worth while."

"Such as?"

A stormy look came over Alicia's face. Rafe went on in a light, teasing voice.

"Like your own way, don't you, and cut up rough when you don't get it—even at games."

She flashed into brilliance.

"That's not true, anyway!"

"Not? Sure?"

"You know it's not true!"

He laughed lightly.

"Well, you do generally manage to get your own way."

The brilliance went out like a blown flame.

"Not always."

She jerked round and ran to pick up her racket. Rafe watched her with a curious teasing look. His thin, mobile lips showed the white teeth again. It amused him to consider that Alicia, who had taken her own way as a right ever since she was a baby, couldn't take it, and would probably never be able to take it, where his cousin Dale was concerned. She could have had him once when she was nineteen and he was twenty, and he had no money and she had no money and Sir Rowland Steyne had a great deal. Well, she had let Dale go and married Rowland. So what had she got to grouse about? It was her own doing, and ten years stale at that. Dale had married Lydia Burrows under some pressure from his family and Lydia's family, and by the time he came in for Lydia's money Alicia was Lady Steyne. It amused Rafe quite a lot.

He wondered what would have happened if Rowland had smashed up himself and his car a month or two earlier. By the time that obituary notices appeared Dale was already engaged to Lisle van Decken. They were married before Alicia could decently enter the lists.

She came back swinging her racket, her eyes bright on his face.

"Why do you look at me like that? I hate you!"

His smile widened.

"I was thinking you didn't look like a widow."

This made her laugh.

"Would you like me to put on black streamers?"

"Not at all. I like you as you are."

"I wonder if you really do, Rafe."

"I adore you."

Alicia shook her head.

"You don't adore anyone. You love yourself and Tanfield. You like Dale—you don't like Lisle. And sometimes I think you hate me."

He slipped an arm around her waist, brought his lips close to her ear, and said in a low, seductive voice,

"You don't believe any of that really."

"Don't I? I think it's all true."

He put his cheek against hers.

"Darling!"

She said, "You hate me—really."

"Yes—like this."

She pulled away from him angrily and then burst out laughing.

"You like making love to me because it's quite safe. I wonder what you'd do if I suddenly fell into your arms."

"Try!"

"Too public." She laughed again. "You *are* a fool, Rafe! Some day, you know, you are going to be taken seriously, and you won't like that at all."

A curious expression passed over his face.

"All right, let's make a start here and now. In sober earnest, why do you say I don't like Lisle?"

She said in a lazy, teasing voice,

"Because you don't darling."

The expression deepened. It was quite evidently distress.

"But I do—I like her awfully. I'd want to like Dale's wife whoever she was, but I'd like Lisle if she wasn't his wife at all. She's my type on the face of it, fair and tall. Why shouldn't I like her?"

"Because she doesn't like Tanfield," said Alicia.

Rafe laughed at her.

"Well, nor do I—so that's a bond, anyhow."

Alicia nodded.

"You don't *like* Tanfield—yes, that's true—you love it."

He shook his head.

"I suppose I did—when I was a kid. A good big lump of masonry like that is the sort of thing a kid understands. One gets a bit more practical as one gets older. No one wants a place this size nowadays—it's just asking for bankruptcy. You've only got to look back into the family history to see what a drain it's been. Five of the last seven Jerninghams married quite respectable heiresses, and who's any the better off for it? I haven't a stiver. Dale would have been on the rocks without Lydia's money. That saved him, but Tanfield has swallowed it, and now it's opening its mouth for anything he can get out of Lisle."

"She hates the place," said Alicia. "She'd like him to sell."

"So would I," said Rafe. "It's the only sensible thing to do. The Manor has been in the family just as long. It's a much more comfortable house, and to my mind a much more beautiful one. If Dale had a grain of sense, he'd close with Tatham's offer—it won't hold good for ever. The trouble is he hasn't got a grain of sense where Tanfield is concerned. We've been here for five hundred years, and he expects us to go on being here for another five hundred—any sacrifice being only an obvious and natural tribute."

Alicia looked startled. Rafe actually *was* serious. She could not remember having ever seen him so much in earnest before. It impressed her a little—against her will. She turned and looked in the direction of the house. The tower windows caught the sun and held it. They were all that could be seen. The long front with its eighteenth-century portico, the two wings running forward to enclose a paved courtyard where stone lions kept guard about a fountained lily pool—all these, though out of sight, were most familiar and present to her mind.

"You make it sound like a sort of Juggernaut."

Rafe Jerningham broke into sudden mocking laughter.

"My sweet, the car of Juggernaut rolled over its devotees. Tanfield Court, I think, may be trusted to stay put."

FIVE

The two big drawing-rooms at Tanfield Court looked out upon a very low terrace from which wide, shallow steps descended to the famous Italian garden. Lisle Jerningham hated it—a couple of acres of arabesques and geometrical patterns, hard, formal, set with cypresses and statues, and flowers which looked too tidy to be real. Beyond its confines Nature, though still dragooned, had been permitted to produce turf and trees—at first the more carefully clipped varieties, but as the distance from the house increased these gave place to spreading branches and unchecked growth. Dale's grandfather had been a lover of trees, and the beeches, coloured sycamores, oaks, and maples of his planting had grown and flourished. There were tall conifers too, gold-tipped, deep emerald and blue—cypress, cedar, and deodar.

Lisle walked among them and waited for Dale to come home. Yesterday was yesterday and a long way past. Her colour had come back, and enough courage to make her think very slightingly about yesterday's panic flight. The sense of shock having passed, she considered her own behaviour with amazement and some shame. Dale had sent her down to the Cranes for the weekend, and she had run away after a single night. He was going to be angry about that, and he was going to want an explanation.

She walked between the trees and wondered what she was going to say. Easy enough if you didn't mind telling lies. She could say that she felt suddenly ill and didn't want to be laid up away from home. Rafe and Alicia, horrified at her yesterday's looks, could very well be trusted to bear her out. But she hadn't been brought up to lie her way out of a fix. Lies were—rather horrid, and lies to Dale unthinkable. The truth then? Unfortunately the truth was rather unthinkable too. How was she going to say to Dale, "I stood behind a hedge, and two women were talking—I don't know who they were. They said that Lydia had an accident because you wanted her money, and they said perhaps I would have one too?"

All at once she was shuddering with the recollection of how cold the water had been coming up over her chin, over her mouth, over her eyes—ten days ago—only ten days ago. She steadied herself against the thought and went out from the trees to get the warmth of the sun. She couldn't tell Dale a lie, and she couldn't tell him the truth.

She turned to see him coming towards her, and at once the whole thing slipped from her and was gone. It always gave her such a quick pleasure just to see him. Right from the first time there had always been a sense of being warmed and lifted up. It was something to do with the way he looked, the way he held his head, the confidence in his voice, the smile which his eyes kept just for her. Dark eyes, but not as dark as Rafe's; a brown skin too, but not as brown as either Rafe's or Alicia's; and where they were lightly and gracefully built Dale had a tall, hard strength. When he put his arms round her she felt how easily their strength could have crushed her, and always until today the feeling had thrilled and pleased her. Now she felt something else. Even while he kissed her and she gave him kiss for kiss there was a small cold tremor of fear which nothing would still. She was glad when he let her go—glad and rather breathless.

"Dale—I didn't stay—"

"I see you didn't."

He wasn't angry yet. Perhaps he wouldn't be angry at all. If only she could think of the right thing to say—But she could only stammer out,

"I wanted to come home."

His hand was on her shoulder. She felt its pressure there.

"Why?"

"Dale—"

She was half turned away, and he pulled her round. His voice was rather rough as he said,

"What's all this about? I rang up last night, and Marian Crane said you'd rushed off after breakfast. When I said "Why?" she said she thought you'd had a telegram. I suppose that's what you told her?"

"Yes."

"Did you have a telegram?"

"No—Dale—"

She wouldn't lie to him.

"Then why did you come away?"

She had not looked at him till then. Now she raised her eyes. They were steady and sorrowful.

"I don't want to say."

"That's nonsense! You've got to!"

"Dale—"

He laughed angrily.

"What's come over you? The Cranes are my friends. You go down for the weekend, and you run away next day. You can't do a thing like that and make no explanation. Did you have a row with Marian?"

Her colour rose—with relief, not embarrassment.

"Of course I didn't! I don't have rows with people." She stepped back, and he let her go. "It was nothing to do with Mrs Crane. I'll—I'll tell you what I can. It was—after breakfast. I went into the garden, and I—overheard two of the other women talking. I don't know who they were—it was a very big house—party—"

"What did they say?" His tone was scornful.

She had a moment of sick wonder as to what he would say if she told him. But she couldn't tell him. Her breath failed her at the thought.

"I don't know who they were—"

"You said that before. I want to know what they said."

Good heavens—why couldn't she tell him and have done with it? Some stupid bit of scandal about his friendship with Marian! He had at no time a patient temper. The thought that

Lisle had run away from some rubbish of that kind stirred it sharply. She saw his face darken, and said, hurrying over the words,

"It was stupid of me, but I didn't feel as if I could meet them afterwards—I didn't want to know who they were. Oh, Dale, can't you understand that? It was a horrid thing to hear, and I didn't want to know who had said it, or—or—to meet them. But if I had stayed I should have had to, and as soon as I heard them speak I should—I should have known who they were. Oh, don't you see?"

The dark look settled into a frown.

"Not yet, but I'm going to. You haven't told me what they said. You heard something which made you treat the Crane's with a good deal of discourtesy. Well, just what *did* you hear?"

Her colour had all gone again.

"It was something about Lydia. Dale, please don't be angry. I wasn't expecting it—and it was a shock. I couldn't stay."

"Lydia?" said Dale Jerningham. *"Lydia?* It was something about Lydia that stampeded you? That doesn't make sense! What did you hear?"

Lisle's voice fell low.

"They said she had—an accident—"

His eyes considered her from under those frowning brows.

"But you knew that."

Her hand went up to her cheek.

"Yes. It was the way—they said it—"

How little could she tell him? How much would she have to tell him? He was waiting, and she forced herself on.

"They said—it was—a lucky accident—for you—"

She had meant to go on looking at him, but she couldn't do it. Her eyes dazzled. She looked away and a pulse beat hard in her throat.

He was very still for a moment. Then he said in a controlled voice,

"So that was it? A pretty old story! I should have thought they'd have done with it by now. I don't really think you need have run away."

She looked at him then, and was frightened. She had seen him angry, but not like this. This was anger iced over with contempt. Most terrifying was the thought that the contempt was for her. Because she had first listened to calumny and then run away from it. Her only comfort was that he asked for nothing more. If he had gone on questioning her she would have had to tell him everything, and her very inmost heart fainted with fear at the thought. Because if he once knew just what shock had sent her on that panic flight, there would be an end between them. She did not think this. She had not yet come to the place where she could think. She only knew it with a deep, unreasoning conviction.

Dale Jerningham walked a little way and came back again.

"You'll have to learn not to fly off the handle every time you overhear a bit of spite," he said. His voice was almost careless now. "People say that sort of thing, you know. They don't expect it to be believed—they don't even believe it themselves—but there's poison in them somewhere, and that's the way it works out. You won't be able to go through the world running from everything you don't like—better make up your mind to that, or I'm afraid we shan't have much of a social life. Marian won't bear malice, but you'll have to think out as convincing a reason for that telegram as you can. Pity I rang up, or you could have said it was from me and left me to do the explaining. I expect I'm a very much better liar than you are."

She looked up quickly at that to see if the words had been spoken with a smile, but in spite of the casual tone his eyes were hard and dark. He said abruptly,

"I've been in trains and offices for two days. I'm going for a tramp." And with no more than that went striding off among the trees.

SIX

Lisle went down to the sea wall. She did not love Tanfield, but she loved this low cliff above the sea. From where she had talked to Dale a green ride led on between the trees until they opened out to show the curve of the bay with its shoaling waters which changed continually under sun and cloud. The cliff had been none too safe fifty years ago, and though the drop was no more than some fifteen to twenty feet, Dale's father had fenced it with a low stone wall broken only where a flight of steps ran down to the bathing beach.

Lisle sat down on the coping and looked out across the water. It was half past five, and the sun slanting over Tane Head. Presently it would go down there and the shadow of the headland spread like spilled ink right over until it touched the very foot of the cliff. But for the moment the water was all clear and bright, and the shadow only a line on the farther side of the bay. The day had been hot, but the wind blew fresh off the sea. At the first touch of it she shivered a little in her green linen dress, and then forgot whether she was hot or cold. Dale was angry. She had known very well that he would be angry. Even if she had told him everything, he would still have been angry with her for running away. Angry—and contemptuous. The contempt hurt more than the anger, and she had no defence against it, because if Dale despised her, she also despised herself. She had run away when she ought to have stayed and outfaced calumny with the strength of her confidence and trust. She looked across the water and her eyes filled slowly with stinging tears. She was bitterly ashamed and unhappy, but behind her pain and misery there was still that something which was fear.

She sat there for a long time, with the shadow creeping nearer across the water and the blue losing colour and shading imperceptibly into grey. Someone came up behind her and stood there for a while before he said her name. As she turned round startled, she saw that it was Rafe. He had pulled on a sweater over his white tennis shirt, and he was holding out a coat all gay stripes and checks of green and yellow and red on a cream ground.

"This is yours, isn't it? What a fool you are to come down here in that thin dress without a wrap—and after the way you looked yesterday."

"I wasn't cold." But she shivered as she spoke.

Rafe made a face at her.

"Are you trying to make yourself ill? Or don't you have to try? Here—put the thing on. What's the matter with you?"

"Nothing."

She was fastening the coat. It felt soft and warm, as if all the gay colours were radiating some warmth of their own. Dale liked colour, and she had bought the coat—for him—with a little un-certainty, because she really liked herself best in softer shades. But now she was glad of the colours. She buttoned up the coat without looking at Rafe or thinking of him.

He pulled her down again on to the flat coping and sat beside her, his back to Tane Head. His eyes were very bright, and the wind caught his hair.

"What's all this about, my dear?"

"Nothing."

"Storm in a teacup? Probably—most things are." He sang in a whispered tenor: '*Car ici-bas tout passe, tout lasse, tout casse.*' "That's the way it goes, and 'The sooner it's over the sooner to sleep.' I can do a lot more maudlin quotations like that. But meanwhile what's getting you? You came home yesterday like a death's head escaped from the feast, and just as you begin to cheer up a little Dale comes home and you go all to bits again. What's up?"

"Nothing."

"Don't be a fool!" He snatched both her hands and swung them up and down. "Quit looking like a hypnotised sheep and tell me what happened at the Cranes'."

"Really, Rafe—"

"Yes, really. I want to know, and I mean to know. Come along—you'll feel a lot better when you've got it off your chest. Did some sweet womanly soul tell you that Dale had been Marian's lover?" His eyes danced maliciously. "It isn't true, you know, but I suppose you swallowed it whole and rushed home to meditate divorce."

If he wanted to rouse her he certainly succeeded. She jerked her hands out of his and said indignantly,

"Of course not! It wasn't that at all!"

"Then what was it? Tell me, honey-sweet."

"Don't be so silly!"

He said in a melting voice, "But you *are* honey-sweet— when you like, and when you are happy. That's why I can't bear to see you unhappy."

"Rafe!"

"Didn't you know? I must be an awfully good concealment-practiser. It shows what brains will do when really used. Do you know, Alicia thinks I don't like you—she said so just now. That shows how terribly well I've practised to deceive, doesn't it?"

He had startled her into a laugh which was partly a caught breath.

"You really do talk more nonsense than anyone I've ever met."

"That's why I'm such a safe confidant. Even if I repeat everything you are going to tell me, nobody will believe a word I say. They'll only think I've made it up."

"But I'm not going to tell you anything," said Lisle. "There's nothing to tell."

He smiled.

"I shall have to ask Dale—and I'd so much rather you told me yourself."

"Rafe—you couldn't!"

"Oh, couldn't I, honey-sweet? You just watch me!"

"Rafe—you really can't! Look here, it wasn't anything. But you can't ask Dale, because—it was about Lydia."

He whistled softly.

"Oh, my hat! Has that cropped up again?"

"What do you mean?"

"Nothing." His tone mocked her.

Lisle leaned forward, her hair lit by the sun, her hands on the coping, taking her weight.

"Rafe, I want you to tell me about Lydia. Nobody will. I can't ask Dale. Will you tell me?"

He laughed. The sound floated away on the wind.

"Why not, my dear? She wasn't a very interesting person, and she didn't live very long, so there isn't a great deal to tell."

"You knew her?"

"Of course I knew her. Being an interesting orphan, I was brought up here with Dale. We both knew Lydia. Her father made a lot of money out of pots and pans of the humbler sort, but her mother's sister was married to the man who had Tallingford before old Mossbags, so Lydia and her mamma used to visit, and both families had the bright idea of marrying her to Dale. He was twenty, but very well grown for his age, and she was twenty-five. He would have Tanfield, and she would have pots of money. The relations fairly cooed."

SEVEN

W_{hy} did he marry her?"

She hadn't meant to ask him that, but it was what she had always wanted to know. There was a portrait of Lydia in the long gallery, the last and least of all the portraits there. A dull, pale girl in a dull, pale dress. Why had Dale married her—*Dale*? She looked earnestly at Rafe.

He said in a lively voice, "Oh, didn't you know? She got him on the rebound. Alicia had just thrown him over and married Rowland Steyne."

Lisle tingled from head to foot. No—she hadn't known. She sat up straight, her hands numb and cold from the stone coping.

He laughed.

"So you didn't know? What a chump Dale is! Now when I get married, which God forbid, I shall spend my honeymoon recounting all my previous love affairs down to the last detail.

You see the idea? I shall enjoy myself, because after all everyone does like talking about himself, and the wretched girl will be so bored that she'll never want to hear about them again. Brilliant—isn't it? Of course Dale's list would be a longer one than mine, because for one thing he has two years' start of me—and then women always have fallen for him. Odd, isn't it, when I'm so much more attractive? And Dale doesn't even notice they're doing it half the time. Did he ever tell you about the Australian widow who threw a water-jug at his head? . . . No? Well, perhaps better not. It's rather a rude story."

Lisle had herself in hand again. She said,

"Don't be silly."

"Honey-sweet, she wasn't my widow. Far from me be it—a terrific female." He rolled about fifteen r's.

She took no notice.

"Rafe—tell me about Lydia—about the accident. You see, I *can't* ask Dale, and if people say things—it seems so stupid if I don't know."

"So people have been saying things?" He laughed again. "They will, and they do, and you can't stop them. I'm not at all sure that your best line isn't the blushing, innocent, nitwit bride."

"Really, Rafe!"

"It's a good lay, and no tax upon the intellect. You know, my sweet, there *is* something rather nice and innocent about you—a please-don't-hurt-me-I'm-only-a-poor-strayed-angel sort of touch which might be quite good at quenching the darts of the poison tongues. And if you've got a good lay, what I say is, stick to it."

"I do wish you'd stop talking nonsense and tell me what I want to know."

"What do you want to know?"

She beat her hands together.

"About the accident—about Lydia."

His voice changed just perceptibly.

"My sweet, there's so little to tell."

"I want to know how it happened—I want to know who was there. Were you there?"

"We were all there, a whole party of us. But as to how it happened"—a shoulder twitched—"well, that's asking. Everyone asked. No one could answer. So there we were, and there we are. I don't think I should ask Dale about it if I were you."

There was indignation in her voice as she said,

"I wasn't going to! I was asking you. And you don't tell me—you keep trying to put me off. And it's no good—I'm going on until you do tell me."

"Desperate challenge!" said Rafe at his sweetest. "Well, strayed angel, what do you want to know?"

"Who was there. You say, 'We were all there.' Who is *we*?"

"Dale, Lydia, Alicia and Rowland Steyne, some people called Mallam, and me. Lydia's dead, Rowland's dead, and the male Mallam is dead. That leaves Dale, and Alicia, and the female Mallam, and me. Why don't you go and have a heart-to-heart with Alicia? She'd love it."

"I want to know what happened. It's no good, Rafe—I shall just go on until you tell me."

He made a queer wide gesture with his hands.

"But I've told you. There isn't anything more. Lydia fell over a cliff and was killed."

She repeated his words in a horrified tone.

"She fell over a precipice? What do you mean? That sounds . . . Was she climbing?"

"*Climbing—Lydia?* My poor child, that *would* have been murder! Any jury in the world would have hanged anyone who took Lydia climbing. We all had one look at her doing a thing like a six-inch anthill and swore off taking her anywhere off the beaten track."

"Then how was she killed?"

"She fell off the beaten track," said Rafe in an airy tone.

Lisle gazed at him. Only one word came to her, and that one stuck in her throat.

"How?"

"Well, that's what everybody wondered. We were all straggled out, you know, and nobody saw what happened. There was quite a wide path—hill going up on one side and down on the other—a long way down. Lots of wild flowers about, and the path winding all the time. The girls were picking the flowers. Lydia might have leaned over too far. She might have turned giddy on the edge, or she might have slipped. Everybody heard her scream, but nobody saw her go. When I got to the place, Dale was looking over the edge and Alicia was having hysterics as far away from it as she could get. The Mallams were arriving from the opposite direction." He shrugged again. "Well, there you have it. I suppose it was the Mallam woman who stuck her claws into you yesterday. Dale told me Marian Crane had asked her down." His laugh had a spice of malice. "Perhaps that's why he found he had to go to Birmingham."

She spoke at once and breathlessly.

"Why do you say that? Rafe, why do you say that?"

"Because she's that sort of woman. As you've met her—"

"I haven't—I didn't—I only heard her speak. I was on the other side of a hedge. She said something horrid about Dale."

"Quite likely. Voice like a wasp in a treacle pot, all drawl and sting?"

She could not help a faint laugh, but a shiver cut it short.

"Yes—exactly like that. Rafe, you *are* clever."

"Of course I am. 'Be good, sweet maid, and let who will be clever.' Another of my apposite quotations. Hits us off to a T, doesn't it?"

Lisle was suddenly cold. She remembered the little woman in the train who had quoted Tennyson—Miss Maud Silver, Private Investigations—and an address in London.

Rafe said, "I shouldn't upset myself over Aimée Mallam if I were you. Another quotation on the way—'Hell has no fury like a woman scorned.' She chucked herself at Dale, and he never knew which side of the street she was on, so there was quite a spot of hell fury knocking about." He put an arm round her and pulled her up. "Come along, it's getting late. Dale will be thinking we've eloped."

They came into the large square hall. It was one of the places that Lisle hated. A mid-eighteenth-century Jerningham, fresh from the Grand Tour, had converted the beautiful Elizabethan hall with its oak stairway and mellow panelling into a cold mortuary chamber paved with marble slabs and watched by chilly statues. Pretentious steps of black and white marble led to a half-landing presided over by a rather horrifying group which portrayed Actæon torn by his hounds. To right and left the stair went on to join a gallery which ran round three sides of the hall. More marble, more statues—a headless Medusa—a bust of Nero—a copy of the Laocoon—the Dying Gladiator. Lisle thought Mr Augustus Jerningham must have had a distressing predilection for the macabre.

As she went slowly up towards the landing, Alicia came down. She had changed into a soft white chiffon dress, wide-skirted and frilled almost to the waist. Except for the narrow black velvet sash, she might have been an eighteen year old débutante. The dark, cloudy curls were drawn back into a demure cluster at the nape of the neck. She smiled up at Lisle and went on down into the hall without speaking.

Lisle went on past the hounds and their slavering jaws, and Actæon with his tortured face, and along the right-hand gallery to her bedroom. She felt a sudden urge to change, to brush her hair until it shone, to put on her prettiest dress. Something in Alicia's smile made her feel like that. She threw off the rainbow coat, dropping it carelessly over a chair and liking herself better without it. The soft green of her linen dress was all right, but the greens and reds and yellows of the coat were too strong for her colouring. They gave her skin a washed-out look and made her hair seem pale instead of fair. She thought, "I was stupid to get it—I'll give it away," and as the words went through her mind she heard Dale call her name.

That meant he wasn't angry any more. She forgot everything else and ran. But he wasn't in his room next door. It opened upon the gallery. She ran out to lean upon the marble balustrade and look down into the hall. She couldn't see Dale, but Rafe and Alicia stood there just below. Alicia's voice came fluting up to her, high and sweet, with every word distinct.

"Pity Dale doesn't teach her how to dress. That *ghastly* coat!"

She drew back, startled and hurt, and saw Dale coming along the gallery. He must have been on the stair, hidden from her by one of the marble groups.

He came up to her, frowning a little.

"Where have you been?"

"Down by the sea wall. Rafe brought me my coat."

And then she wished she hadn't spoken about the coat. She hated it now. She wouldn't keep it an hour longer than she need. She must find someone to give it to—quickly, so that she could say quite lightly and casually in Alicia's hearing,

"Oh, that coat of mine? I've given it away. A horrid thing. I can't think why I got it." Yes, that would be the right tone. That was the sort of thing Alicia said, and Alicia's friends.

Dale was still frowning. He said,

"You'd better hurry up and dress. Alicia's gone down."

He was still angry. Her heart sank sorrowfully. She went into her room and shut the door.

EIGHT

For some little time now Lisle Jerningham had got into a way of reckoning days which a few months ago she would not have believed possible. It was a good day if Dale was pleased with her. It was not such a bad day if she only vexed him a little. It was a bad day if he talked about Tanfield and how there had always been Jerninghams there. It was a dreadful day when he laboured with her to persuade old Mr Robson, who was her trustee, that some of her capital should be devoted to keeping Tanfield in the Jerningham family. At first all the days were good. Then, when she was silly and tactless enough to let him see that Tanfield chilled her to the bone, the good days became fewer and fewer, and the bad days more and more frequent. She had done all she could to please him—tried to hide what she felt about Tanfield—and sometimes everything cleared up and there were happy times again, just as there had been at first. The week before the visit to the Cranes had been a really happy time.

Lisle lay in bed and thought about what a happy time it had been, and tried not to think that the happiness had begun on the day she signed her new will in Mr Robson's office. And yet, why shouldn't she think of it? She had done it to please Dale. Well then, why shouldn't she be pleased? And she had no near relations, so what other sort of will could she make?

"Your father has left you the power of appointment, Mrs Jerningham. Failing children, you can leave the whole estate to your husband. If there are children, you can leave him a life interest in half the estate. You can, of course, make any other dispositions you please. Have I made myself quite clear?"

"Oh, yes, Mr Robson."

Dale had smiled at her over the old man's head with a deep, warm look which was like sunshine to her heart. She heard herself say in a happy, spontaneous voice,

"Then that's what I'd like to do—leave most of it to Dale."

The happiness had lasted all through the week. Looking back into it was like looking into a sunny garden full of flowers. Even the fact that she had very nearly been drowned didn't spoil it, because when she thought of that she could only feel Dale's arms round her as she opened her eyes, and Dale's voice choked with feeling saying her name over and over again:

"Lisle—Lisle—*Lisle!*"

The fears and doubts which had shocked her into talking to Miss Silver in the train had no longer any place. They had gone up like mist and vanished.

If only she hadn't run away from the Cranes . . . Dale had come to look for her. He had kissed her as if he loved her. And then, as soon as he knew that she had run away, the happiness was gone. He hadn't looked at her once all the evening. He had hardly spoken to her, though he had been gay and affectionate with Rafe and Alicia. And when they came upstairs he had given her the curtest of goodnights as he went into his dressing-room and shut the door.

She lay and looked out into the shadowy room. The bed was a great four-poster, heavily carved. At first sight it had reminded Lisle of a catafalque. She hated it, but when Dale was there and Dale was kind she forgot about that. It was when she was alone and unhappy that all the dark, heavy furniture seemed to belong, not to her, but to the dead Jerninghams who had been born and married and had died here before Lisle Van Decken was thought of. There were three tall windows on her left, two of them curtained and the third with the curtains drawn back. Dale's door faced her, and the moonlight coming in through the uncurtained window laid a pale rectangle upon the floor. The light stretched to the very threshold of the door. If it opened, she would see it catch the light. But it wouldn't open now. Dale wasn't coming. He had said his curt goodnight and left her.

She lay quite still and slowly, steadily, her mind darkened. The moonlight passed from the window and the room darkened too. Some time between midnight and one o'clock Lisle's darkness slid into sleep.

In the next room Dale Jerningham woke up. He came straight from deep sleep into a state of listening alertness. It was his way to sleep from the time his head touched the pillow until seven o'clock. If he waked between these times, it was because something had waked him. He rose on his elbow, heard again what he must have heard already, and throwing back the bedclothes, went barefoot to the door between his room and Lisle's. Frowning in the darkness, he threw the door open and stood there looking in. There was no light except what came from that one uncurtained window—a vague half light, for the moon had run into cloud. The bed, deeply shadowed, looked like a black island in a misty sea. Lisle's voice came out of the shadow, crying his name in a pitifully shaken tone:

"Dale—Dale—it couldn't be Dale—"

He closed the door behind him and came to stand at the foot of the bed between the two black pillars. He could see her now, very dimly, lying high against heaped pillows. She said in a rapid murmur of sound,

"It's no use your giving me your card, because I shouldn't want to use it. I don't see how I could really—because of Dale—Dale wouldn't like it. And it couldn't be Dale. You do see that, don't you? It couldn't possibly be Dale. So I'll just put your card in my bag—but it's no good thinking I could do anything about it, because I couldn't." She flung out her hands in a groping gesture. "She said—lucky because Lydia died. That's what she said—'a lucky accident for Dale'—" The voice went trembling into silence on his name. She fell back. He heard her gasp for breath. She drew herself up in the bed as if she were crouching there. "I nearly had an accident too. She said perhaps I'd have an—accident—like Lydia . . . It couldn't be Dale—" She was going back to that rapid mutter. "Oh, no, no—it couldn't be Dale."

Dale went on listening. When she was quiet he crossed to

a chest between the windows and opened the top right-hand drawer. Lisle had so many bags. She had been wearing a grey flannel coat and skirt when she went down to the Cranes. That meant a grey bag.

He took out the whole drawer, carried it through into his room, and put on the light there. The grey bag was pushed down in a corner. He opened it and sorted through the contents—handkerchief; lipstick; rouge and powder compact; keys. In an inner compartment a snapshot of himself—and a card. He picked it out and turned it to catch the light. The name on the card was completely strange to him, but he looked at it for a long time.

MISS MAUD SILVER

15 Montague Mansions,   Private Investigations
West Leaham Street,   Undertaken.
S.W.

When the time had run out he put the card back into the bag, and the bag into the drawer.

The room was very quiet when he came into it again. He slid the drawer into its place and stood for a moment listening to the stillness, then moved nearer to the bed. She stirred, caught her breath between a sob and a groan, and woke. There was a moment of terror, because the room was dark and someone was there—not speaking, not moving. And then, as he said her name, terror rushed out and joy rushed in.

She said in a warm voice, "Oh, darling, you frightened me," and he came and knelt down beside her and put his arms round her.

"*You* frightened *me*. You were calling out in your sleep. What was it—a dream?"

"Oh, yes—a horrible dream. But it doesn't matter now."

Nothing mattered if Dale was there—if Dale was kind. There were no more dreams, and when she woke up the sun was on the windows and Dale was pouring out tea. Whatever cloud there had been between them, it had gone as completely as if it had never been. He was going over to the aerodrome after breakfast—he was crazy about flying just now. They talked about that, and about flying, and about what a bit of luck it had been getting his own price for the flying-ground. That is to say, he did most of the talking, and Lisle was happy because Dale was pleased.

"I wonder what my father would have said if anyone had told him all that moorland would fetch a fancy price. But there'll be a subsidy worth having on wheat if there's a war— and it's bound to come. In my great-grandfather's time you could stand up there where the aerodrome is and see nothing but wheat, so long as you stood with your back to the sea. Funny if it all came back again. There were big fortunes made then. But that won't happen again, worse luck. They'll skin our profits down somehow, damn them."

He was sitting on the edge of the bed, his hair rumpled and his eyes smiling. Blue and white striped pyjamas set off the clear brown skin. The open collar showed the strong neck. She felt the old hero-worship for him spring up in her.

It was something very primitive, and she was rather ashamed of it. Dale . . . Other women found him good to look at, ran after him. Some of them didn't mind how plainly they showed their feelings. But he wasn't for them—he was hers! She wasn't proud of feeling like that, but she didn't seem able to help it.

He laughed and said, "What are you thinking about?" and when she said, "You," he kissed her and with his arm half round her went on,

"Keep right on doing it, darling, because I want to talk to you."

She said, "What about?" and her heart went cold in her when he said,

"Tanfield."

Dale sat back a little so that he could look at her. His hand slid down from her shoulder and rested against her knee.

"You see, I've got to give Tatham an answer."

"Yes—" She could manage no more than that.

It seemed to her that all their lives hung on the answer which Dale would presently have to make. If he would take Mr Tatham's offer, sell Tanfield, and move those two miles inland to the Manor House, they would be free to live and be happy. But if there was something in him that wouldn't let him sell, then they must stay here, and Tanfield would suck them dry until they were old, grey, dead people dragging an intolerable burden up an unending hill. Her hands came together and held each other tightly, as if they would hold on to something Dale was trying to take away, not from her—not just from her—but from both of them.

Her eyes went to his face and stayed there, dark with apprehension, because whenever they talked about Tanfield something strained between them and was wrenched almost to breaking-point. But today, though he looked serious, he did not frown. He leaned on his hand and said,

"It's a good price. Most people would say I was a fool if I refused it. But you're not most people, Lisle—you're my wife. If I have a son to come after me here, you'll be his mother. That's what I want to talk to you about." His voice changed suddenly and broke. "It's so difficult to make you understand. And I've got a beast of a temper. I get angry, and then I say things, and you get hurt and frightened and we don't get any farther. But I thought—we might—talk about it—differently. I thought you might—try to understand my point of view."

He saw the colour go out of her face. It drained away and left the fair skin white. She said in an almost soundless whisper, "I'll try."

He sat up, looking away from her.

"You don't like Tanfield—you've made that quite plain. No, no, that's all wrong—that's not how I meant to begin. It's so damned hard to make you see, and when I try to get hold of words that will show you how I feel, they're the wrong ones." He turned back to her again. "Lisle, help me by *trying* to understand."

She said, "Yes—yes—"

"Then it's this way. When you've had a place as long as we've had Tanfield, it doesn't belong to you. It's like your country—you belong to it—it comes first. Look at all the pictures in the long gallery. Those people have all lived here, had their time here. Most of them have added something in their time. And they're gone—the whole lot of them. But Tanfield is here, and Tanfield is going to be here when we're gone, and if we have sons, Tanfield will go on being here after their time too. Don't you see what I mean? It doesn't matter about us, and it doesn't matter about our children. We shall go, and they'll go, but Tanfield will go on."

His eye had kindled and the colour had come to his cheek.

Lisle gazed at him with a sort of paralysed horror. He had said, "Try to understand," and she had said, "I'll try." But she didn't have to try. It was easy enough to understand, and the more she understood of it, the more it horrified her. People, human lives, herself and Dale, their children—all of no account in comparison with a great soulless barrack of a house, made uglier and more expensive by the successive sacrifices of each generation. It was a point of view, and she could understand it well enough, but it seemed to her quite mad, quite horrible.

Dale got up, walked to the window, and came back again. He hadn't moved her—he could see that he hadn't moved her. No colour, no response—her eyes watching him.

She said only just above her breath,

"There isn't anything I can do."

He flung himself down beside her.

"Not while you feel like that. Oh, Lisle darling, can't you see? It's no good going to Mr Robson unless you feel different. I know you've asked him to let you put some of your capital into keeping Tanfield, and if you ask him a hundred times, he'll still say no, because he can see that you don't really mean it. If you felt differently, he'd let you do it. It's because he knows you hate Tanfield that he won't help you to save it."

She looked up at him piteously.

"I'll ask him, Dale—I will."

He drew back.

"You asked him before, and he wouldn't do anything. He never will do anything unless he is convinced that you really want him to. You might try to convince him, but unless you really did want him to save Tanfield he wouldn't be convinced. He's as sharp as a knife, and the reason he won't do anything is because he's damned sure you don't really want him to."

He walked over to the window and stood looking out.

Lisle was sitting up clear of her pillows. She was quite rigid with the strain she was putting upon herself—on her body to keep it from shaking, on her voice to hold it steady, on her heart to keep down the cold surge of fear, on her mind and will to make them want what Dale wanted. If she truly and really wanted to keep Tanfield she could persuade Mr Robson. Dale had just said so, and it was true. But no pretending would do—and how can you make yourself want what you shrink from with all your soul?

She was gentle, but she was not pliable. She was unselfish, and she would have given almost anything in the world to please and satisfy Dale. But none of these things shook her conviction that Tanfield would suck them dry and burden them into their graves if it had its way. She thought of it like that—Tanfield's way, not Dale's. Dale was only the mouthpiece. She felt all this too profoundly and instinctively to be able to change. She could go to

Mr Robson again as she had gone to him before, and with the same result, because he would know, as he had always known, that she was saying Dale's words and not her own.

She would have given Dale the money if it had been in her power. Pricking right through the numbed sense of strain came a small, fierce pleasure because it wasn't in her power. Suddenly she relaxed. She leaned back, stopped fighting with herself, and at the same moment Dale turned round and came to her.

"Lisle—darling! What a brute I am! Why do you love me? You do, don't you? But I can't think why. Look here, we're never going to talk about this again. I'll go into everything right down to bedrock, and if I find I can't manage I'll take Tatham's offer. I've got till the end of the week, and I might be able to spin it out beyond that. There's just a chance the Air Ministry may want more ground—there's all this talk of expansion. I'll see if I can't get something definite out of them before I answer Tatham."

He was sitting by her on the bed with his arm round her, his face alive and interested, all the tension gone. He put his cheek against hers and rocked her.

"I can't go up today—I'm flying. Damn! So I am tomorrow too! But I'll tell you what, I'll write to Jarvis and tell him to nose out what he can, and I'll go up tomorrow afternoon. You can drive me in to Ledlington to catch the three-twenty. Then I'll get hold of Jarvis and find out how the land lies, and if it's at all promising I'll go round to the Ministry in the morning. How's that for a scheme?"

She looked at him with a warm, happy smile. Her heart sang. Everything was all right again. She said,

"It's a lovely plan."

He dropped his head on her shoulder.

"Don't stop loving me, Lisle."

NINE

When Lisle looked back on the day that followed she saw it as a bright panel dividing darkness from darkness. It was like a window through which she could see the sun though the room was dark. But as she lived through it, it was just one of those days when everything goes right. The sky was blue and cloudless, the sea was blue and waveless, and the hours just slipped pleasantly by with nothing to mark them. Dale came back from the air-field in high good humour and talked technicalities to her all through lunch. Rafe never got back until the evening, and Alicia had taken herself off for the day, so that they were alone. Later on they bathed and he gave her a swimming lesson. Time just slipped away like light flowing by. That night she slept the perfect dreamless sleep which rests and satisfies.

They were at breakfast next day, when Alicia was called to the telephone. Rafe had finished, and sat with his chair pushed

back, smoking a cigarette. He worked in the designing depart-
ment of the firm which had bought a site for their new aircraft
factory from Dale a couple of years ago. He sat with his eye
on the clock, dallying, as he always did, until the last possible
moment.

Alicia came back into the room with a bright, mocking
smile. She dropped into her chair and addressed herself to Dale.

"That, darling, was Aimée."

"Aimée who?"

She laughed.

"Have you got more than one? I should have thought she
was enough and a little bit over. Aimée Mallam, darling. And
she's staying with the Crawfords, and she wants to come over
to lunch today."

"What fun!" said Rafe. "Devastating for me to have to miss
her. But there'll be all the more for you." He got up lazily and
blew Lisle a kiss. "My child, you don't know your luck. Give
her my fondest love."

"If you don't hurry," said Alicia, "you'll be late."

"Not quite," said Rafe. "I cut it fine, but I don't overstep.
That's what old Mallaby said to me no later than Saturday
morning. Goodbye, children—enjoy yourselves." He went
out, leaving the door open.

Dale got up and shut it. He had a controlled, angry look.

"What did you say to her, Alicia?"

She shrugged her shoulders.

"What *does* one say?" She put on a polite mimicking voice.
"'My dear, how wonderful! We shall simply love to see you—
especially Dale.' That's what I said."

"Don't be a fool, Lal! She can't come here today. I'm flying this morning, and I'm going up to town this afternoon. Lisle's driving me into Ledlington, so unless you want to have Aimée all to yourself—" His eyes met hers, and saw them brighten.

"Oh, no, you don't, darling! Aimée's not my pigeon."

"Then you'll just go back and tell her she can't come!"

Lisle sat there, a little bewildered, a little out of it. Aimée Mallam—For a moment the name stayed on the surface of her mind, then sank into it like a stone. That was the woman who had talked on the other side of the hedge—Rafe's wasp in treacle. A cold, faint shudder went through her. She looked at Alicia and saw her shake an emphatic head.

"I can't do that. The Crawfords are going over to see Joan at her school—she's got into some scrape or other—so of course they don't want to take Aimée." She dropped her mocking manner. "Look here, you'd much better let her come and get it over. She won't be here till one o'clock, and if you're catching the three-twenty—I suppose it is the three-twenty—we can push off at a quarter to."

"*We?*"

Alicia laughed.

"I'm not going to be thrown to the wolves. Besides, I want to fetch my car. Langham said it would be ready any time after three, so I'll do some shopping and drive myself home."

She came round the table to Dale, standing close to him and letting her voice fall to a confidential murmur.

"Honestly, darling, you'd better let her come. She was full of hints about why hadn't she seen you at the Cranes, and why had Lisle gone off in such a hurry—she so *particularly* wanted to meet her. You know the kind of thing—the more you try and put her off, the more determined she'll be. And she'll go away and say you wouldn't let her meet Lisle."

The words were pitched for his ear, but Lisle caught them. They made her feel as if she were eavesdropping. She saw Alicia's look and Dale's black frown. Her cheeks burned as she pushed back her chair and ran out of the room.

Neither Dale nor Alicia noticed whether she stayed or went. There was a struggle between them—or rather, a new version of an old struggle. He frowned, but he couldn't frown her down. The bright malice of her glance said, "Why are you frightened of Aimée? You are. I could have protected you— I'm her match. Why should I protect you? You didn't wait for me. You chose Lisle—let her protect you." The malice melted into soft mocking laughter. "Better make a virtue of necessity, darling—she'll come anyhow," she said, and stood on tiptoe to kiss the point of his chin.

Lisle spent the morning trying to arm herself with a valour which she did not possess. She put on a new dress, straw-coloured linen to match her hair, and was heartened to see how she looked in it. She used a little more colour than she generally did, because whatever happened, Aimée Mallam wasn't going to see her looking pale. After all, what could she do or say at Dale's table and to his very face? She was making herself wretched for nothing at all.

The treacle would probably hide the wasp, and there would be an end of it.

Mrs Mallam arrived in a snappy little car and too smart a dress. It had a very short flared skirt and tight bodice of an emerald green and white striped material. She wore it with green shoes and a twisted emerald hair-band under which her hair showed overpoweringly thick and golden. There was too much hair, and too much gold to be true—a great deal too much. There was also too much bust to be so tightly encased in such vivid stripes. There was too much calf to be so freely displayed. But in curious contrast to all this over-emphasis there was too little of it elsewhere. The eyes, which should have been large and blue, were narrow, rather closely set, and of a light uncertainty of hue. The lips were thin and hardly showed their colour. The cheeks were pale and inclined to heaviness.

She embraced Alicia, put a hand covered with rings on Dale's arm, and said, looking up at Lisle,

"So this is the bride. Which of you do I congratulate?"

It was the voice which had said "A lucky accident for Dale." It drawled, as if clogged with its own heavy sweetness.

For a moment Lisle was numb and dumb. And then, like an automaton, she was shaking hands and saying "How do you do?" Mrs Mallam's hand, plump and warm in a wash-leather glove, clung to hers, pressing it. Her voice drawled,

"I shall congratulate Dale."

Her other hand was still on his arm. She turned to him.

"But I'm about six months too late. I expect you've heard it all hundreds of times."

He smiled down at her.

"The more the merrier, Aimée. I know how lucky I am—I can't hear about it too often."

Aimée Mallam laughed.

"Oh, my dear, but you always were lucky. How *do* you do it? I wish I had the secret."

Lunch went pleasantly enough, at least for Aimée Mallam. She and Dale did most of the talking. Alicia, not in the best of tempers, came darting in when it pleased her. She ate nothing but fruit.

"But, darling, *you* don't have to slim," said Aimée Mallam.

Alicia's eyes rested for a moment upon Aimée's well filled plate. She said,

"My dear, when you have to it's too late. I'm keeping my figure."

Mrs Mallam burst out laughing.

"I can't be bothered about mine. If it wants to go back on me it must. I adore my food, and I don't care who knows it." She turned to Lisle. "You don't know how disappointed I was to miss you at the Cranes'. I couldn't believe my ears when I heard you were gone. You see, I didn't get down there till nearly midnight on the Friday, because I dropped in on my cousin Lady Lowstock on the way, and she insisted on keeping me to dinner. Very naughty of her, and very naughty of me. Marian Crane was furious, but, as I said to her, 'Pamela and I were cousins for about twenty years before you and I ever met, and she simply *insisted.*' You've met the Lowstocks of course?"

"I'm afraid I haven't."

Mrs Mallam looked shocked.

"Whatever has Dale been doing? He ought to have taken you all round and introduced you to everyone. Wanted to keep you all to himself. I suppose. But he must take you over to see Pamela Lowstock. She's such a delightful creature—and a very

old friend of Dale's. In fact there was a time—but we mustn't
rake up old stories now, must we?"

Alicia's light laugh rang out.

"But why not, Aimée? There's no lie like an old one—no
one can check up on it, for one thing."

She got a rap on the arm and a slow, slanting smile.

"Always so amusing, darling." She turned back to Lisle.
"You shall take me round the garden, and I'll tell you about all
Dale's old flames."

This entertainment did not, however, come off. When
lunch was over and coffee disposed of, Dale announced that he
had a train to catch, and that Lisle was driving him and Alicia
into Ledlington. There was no time to go round the garden.

If Mrs Mallam was disappointed she did not show it. She
turned an unruffled smile upon Lisle and asked if she might go
upstairs with her.

"Just a few running repairs, my dear Dale."

If he had intended to prevent a tête-á-tête, he was now
hopelessly at a disadvantage. Alicia, who might have afforded
him some support, merely raised a sarcastic eyebrow and vanished in the direction of her own room. Dale had perforce to
see Lisle and Aimée go side-by-side up the black and white
marble steps. As they came towards him again along the gallery
overhead, their voices reached him—or rather Aimée's voice:

"There isn't any place quite like Tanfield."

Mrs Mallam repeated the remark as she sat powdering her
nose in front of Lisle's mirror. It stood at an angle to the light
and reflected the whole room. In spite of three long windows
the effect was one of gloom. An immense mahogany wardrobe

filled nearly the whole of the opposite wall. Its dark sliding panels, its immense height and depth, gave it the air of a cliff dominating the landscape. It drank the light, and reflected none of it. Between the two doors there was a massive tallboy. The carpet, one of those durable Victorian carpets, was patterned in shades of brown and green, all sunk together now in a general murk. The curtains repeated the same colours in a deep-toned damask. Everything in the room had been very expensive a long time ago, and was now undergoing a dignified decay. Dignified and very gloomy.

Mrs Mallam turned a well powdered nose upon her hostess.

"My dear, why don't you do it all up? It's a beautiful room, but you're not your great-grandmother. Doesn't it give you the pip, all this boiled beef and spinach?"

Lisle found herself jarred, and yet with an inward response. She was getting used to Mrs Mallam's voice. Now that she had heard it say so many other things, the effect of what it had said from behind the yew hedge was wearing off. She thought Mrs Mallam ill-bred and tiresome, but she was glad she had come, because the very fact that she was so obviously just a vulgar mischief-maker deprived what she had said of any real value. She spoke quite pleasantly and easily now.

"It's rather dark and old-fashioned. But don't you think it suits the room? After all, Tanfield Court is old, you know, and I don't think Dale would like to have anything changed."

When Aimée Mallam laughed her lips did not part. They stretched in a thin slanting line and the laugh came gurgling out like water from a close-necked bottle. No, not water—treacle. Rafe's word—and Rafe was right.

"Well, my dear, Dale's made one change for the better anyhow. You didn't know Lydia, I suppose? Oh, no—you couldn't have. You wouldn't have been more than ten or twelve years old when she—died."

Lisle said, "I suppose not." She wanted to say something that would change the subject, but nothing would come.

Aimée looked at her out of narrowed eyes and smiled her tilted smile.

"You know, it really was astounding that he should have married her. Of course she had money, but Dale might have married anyone. My cousin Pamela Lowstock was crazy about him. But you needn't worry about her now, because she's devoted to her Josiah. Lowstock's Peerless Ales, you know. Pots and pots of money. And she hadn't a bean, so it's just as well Dale didn't fall for her, because of course he simply had to marry money. I always say Tanfield is like one of those monsters they used to make offerings to." She laughed her treacly laugh. "The virgin sacrifice, you know. Jerninghams have always married money—they've got to—and Tanfield just swallows it and asks for more."

Something in Lisle was stirred to anger. Something else bowed a weeping head and said, "Yes, it's true."

She turned pale, but she forced her lips to smile. "That sounds rather creepy. Are you ready? Shall we go down?"

TEN

Dale had said that Lisle was driving them into Ledlington. Actually he took the wheel himself. It was Lisle's own car, but, like so many good drivers, to be driven by somebody else fretted him past bearing. Lisle was a good deal relieved to see him get into the driver's seat. She would have left the place beside him to Alicia, but he called out such an impatient "Nonsense—that's your place!" that she slipped into it without further protest.

Alicia shut the rear door a little harder than she need have done. She had thrown on a vivid black and white check coat over her sleeveless linen and bound her dark curls with a white band. Her colour stood high and her eyes were bright. Lisle, weather-wise, took comfort from the thought that she would not have to drive Alicia back.

Dale drove slowly for him. He had pushed Aimée Mallam off by making what she had stigmatised as an absurd fuss about having plenty of time to catch his train, but now that they were on the road, he dawdled up the steep, crooked lane between Tanfield village and the main Ledlington road. The way ran level from there, level and rather high, but the village was tucked into a hollow, with a long gentle slope down from Tanfield Court, and that steep crooked climb to the Ledlington Road.

"Are we going to a funeral?" said Alicia tartly from her back seat.

Dale made no answer. He was frowning over the wheel. After a moment he said abruptly,

"When did you have this car out last, Lisle?"

She said, "Yesterday."

He went on frowning.

"Notice anything odd about the steering?"

"Oh, no. Is anything the matter?"

He was still frowning and intent.

"No—I don't know—I thought it felt odd just now on the hill. You'd better be careful coming back. Get Evans to take her out and test her. That's where we're going to miss Pell—best mechanic I've ever had."

Lisle said "Evans—" and would have done better to hold her tongue.

"Evans is a driver. I don't suppose you know the difference. Women are all damned fools about machinery, and you're worse than most. I was a damned fool myself to let Pell go."

Alicia laughed.

"Oh, darling, you couldn't possibly keep a mechanic who played fast and loose with the village maidens—not with Lisle in the house. Of course he had to go."

Lisle straightened herself. She spoke to Dale, not to Alicia. "It was your own decision. The Coles are your own tenants. You said he must go after Miss Cole came up and saw you about Cissie."

She met a scowling look, but her own held firm. Tanfield and Tanfield's tenants—that touched his pride. And Pell was an outsider from Packham way. Alicia had no business to butt in—it wasn't her affair. He said in a grumbling voice,

"Anything wrong with the steering puts the wind up me."

Lisle said, "It was all right yesterday." The question of the steering did not disturb her at all. Dale was used to driving a much larger car. Small cars irked him, and he never drove hers without finding something wrong—ignition too far advanced, brakes not properly adjusted—there was always something. She was a fair driver, but like most women she knew and cared nothing about the mechanism. She therefore gave no more attention to Dale's remarks about the steering than to hope that he was not going to be vexed.

Alicia said, "Fuss!" in a sweet, provocative voice, but for the second time got no answer.

Dale talked about cars in general and the shortcomings of Lisle's car in particular the whole way to Ledlington station. He was obviously out of humour, not only with the car but with its owner. Quite definitely Lisle received the impression that it was her fault if there was something wrong with the steering. And behind that impression another one—if she had a better car Dale would be better pleased. And why hadn't she a better car? She had plenty of money. If she kept a car which was a reproach to her husband—well, I ask you, doesn't it show a mean streak somewhere? None of these things got into words—Dale's manner said them, not Dale's tongue. But once at least his manner spoke so plainly that Alicia laughed in obvious enjoyment.

When they reached the station, however, there was a change. He put his hand on Lisle's and squeezed it.

"You're such a fool about cars," he said. "All women are, but you're worse than most."

Only the words were harsh. His voice melted to her, and his eyes smiled. She turned to meet them, suddenly radiant.

"I'm *not*!"

"Oh, aren't you just? Now look here, darling, I'm not happy about that steering. Get it looked at. You'd better do it now. Take her round to Langham's."

"Oh, but—"

"You'd better. I should feel happier about it."

He let go of her hand, kissed her lightly on the cheek, and jumped out.

"See you tomorrow," he said. He waved to them both and was gone.

Lisle watched him out of sight before she started the car. Perhaps this was one of the things, all small in themselves, which brought Alicia's temper to the breaking-point. As the car moved, she spoke. There was a sweet, dangerous tension in her voice.

"Well, I suppose you like being babied like that. Pretty sickening, I should have thought. *'Darling, you're a fool'!*" She dropped her voice to mimic Dale's with surprising accuracy. "I'd like to see a man talk to me like that!"

Something inside Lisle said in a whisper, "You'd like Dale to say it to you—oh, yes, you *would*." But her lips said nothing. She turned the car carefully and drove out of the station yard.

Langham's garage was half way down the street on the right. She had to go there anyhow to drop Alicia. Every second counted heavily until she could get rid of Alicia. She mustn't answer back, she mustn't quarrel. It would vex Dale beyond words if she had a quarrel with Alicia. She must drop her at the garage and get away quickly.

But Dale had said wait and have the steering tested.

Oh, no, she couldn't—not with Alicia like this. Evans could see to it at home, and Dale wouldn't really mind as long as it was all right.

And all the time Alicia was talking with a kind of soft fury.

"Can't you stick up for yourself at all—not to Dale—not to anyone? Haven't you got a drop of red blood in you? I don't believe you have! Milk and water—that's what you've got in your veins! How long do you think Dale's going to put up with milk and water?" A little bitter laugh broke through. "Haven't you even got the spirit to damn me for saying that? Upon my soul, I don't believe you have!"

Lisle drew the car in to the kerb. The garage entrance lay just ahead. She opened the door, got out, and stood there, pale but not trembling now. She opened the rear door and waited until Alicia got out.

They stood there together for a moment, and now they were both pale. Alicia without colour was Alicia spoiled. There were marks like bruises under her eyes. She looked her age, and more. But Lisle looked very young—heart-rendingly young, like a child accused of some fault it does not understand. She said,

"Are you sure your car will be ready? I'll wait whilst you find out."

Alicia stared at her.

"Wait? You'll have to wait for your own car, baby. Won't you? You needn't wait for mine—it's ready."

Lisle said nothing. She got into the car and drove away.

ELEVEN

When Lisle had driven about half a mile she stopped by the side of the road and put down the hood. One reason for her obstinate clinging to this little car was the fact that she could open it completely and drive with nothing over her head but the sky—not with either Dale or Alicia, but when she was alone, or sometimes with Rafe. She liked to feel the wind in her hair and see the clouds and the aeroplanes go by, high up and free.

When she got back into the car the beating of her heart had steadied. Thought slowed down. Dale had gone to London. Alicia out of sight was Alicia out of mind. She was Lisle alone, in her own car, with her own road to take. The sun and wind belonged to her, and she belonged to no one. She was free. These were not words. They were hardly thoughts. They were the stuff out of which thoughts are made—escape from authority, the child who gets out of the grown-ups' way, escape into liberty of thought and action—one of the oldest instincts in the world.

Lisle drove slowly along the straight, flat road. There were fields on either side, with here and there a farmstead, a cottage or two, a group of trees. The sky overhead was of a pale, cloudless blue. The wind which she felt in her hair was the wind of her own going. There was no other. The sea came into sight, blue against the blue horizon, a long way off. But when she turned into the steep lane which dropped to Tanfield village the blue glitter was lost behind the high bank and hedgerow of the sunken road. It sloped gently at first, then fell to a hairpin bend, steep above the turn and steeper still below.

It was as she took this bend that she remembered about the steering. The wheels came round, but midway something snapped. The steering-wheel jerked in her hands, wrenched out of them, and was free. The car slewed violently and plunged down the hill, rocking and slipping on the uneven surface. There was a second turn to come, sharp to the right where the side wall of Cooper's barn barred the straight. It had been kept whitewashed ever since someone had driven head-on into it one black night. Lisle's car was driving head-on for it now. The whitewash dazzled her. The man had been killed. His car had been smashed. She had the wheel again, but it was loose and useless in her hands. She let go of it, opened the off-side door, and jumped.

Rafe Jerningham, just round the turn, saw the car smash against the whitewashed wall. He ran forward, and what his thoughts were only he could have told. He had come to that place to meet Lisle, and if there are any certainties in life, he

must have had the certainty that he would find her dead.
He ran to the broken car, and heard the sound of running
feet behind him. Cooper came out of his yard with a purple,
twitching face. The car looked like a toy that has been trodden
on, but the driver's seat was empty. Rafe gave it the one look,
filled his lungs with a deep draught of air, and ran on towards
the hill, the blood pounding in his ears.

She was lying against the hedge where she had jumped,
lying face downwards with her arms flung out. The place where
she lay was where the ditch came in from Cooper's field. There
was a thick growth of grass and wild hemlock, thriving on the
damp. She lay there. And she wasn't dead. The hand which was
clutching a hemlock spray moved. Her head moved.

He took a moment before he touched her. Then he was on
his knees.

"Lisle!"

She was alive. She pushed against the bank and raised herself. They kneeled there facing one another. There was a little
blood on her face. It made the only colour there. Her eyes were
blank and grey. She stared at Rafe, and Rafe stared back at her.

"Are you hurt?"

She said, "No—I don't know—I thought I was dead—"
and Rafe said,

"So did I."

After that the whole village arrived—Cooper and Mrs Cooper, Miss Cole from the post office, her niece Cissie who took
in dressmaking, her brother James who kept the general shop,
Mr Maggs the baker, old Mr Obadiah Crisp, and a crowd of
young Crisps, Coles, and Coopers, all related to each other by

marriage if not by blood, and all shocked, horrified, excited, and full to the brim with curiosity and kindness. It was disappointing to find that Lisle had broken no bones, because it made it less of an accident, but as Mrs Cooper said, "It don't always show at the time."

Lisle, sitting on the grass which had broken her fall, felt herself gingerly all over and repeated in as firm a voice as she could manage,

"I'm all right."

Rafe got hold of Miss Cole.

"Look here, will you telephone to the house. Tell them to send Evans with the other car. And tell them to hurry. I want to get Mrs Jerningham home."

"Whatever could have happened?" said Cissie Cole. She stared after her aunt and then shifted her gaze to Lisle again. "One of those irritating young women who never look at you in case you might take a liberty," was Rafe's quick, impatient thought. He disliked Cissie a good deal—a tall, thin, straw-coloured creature, like Lisle in caricature—untidy too. She pushed a pale wisp of hair behind her ear and said in a flat, lugubrious tone, "Whatever could have done it?"

Rafe Jerningham put the same question in rather different words a couple of hours later. Lisle had refused to go to bed, to have a doctor, or be fussed over. Her dress was torn and stained. She changed it, and came down to sit in a deep chair on the lawn which looked towards Tane Head and the sea. She had tea there alone. It was very peaceful and resting to be alone. She would have used this form if she had spoken, but the thought behind it would have been, "It is very peaceful without Alicia."

Rafe came presently to sit on a stool at her feet and ask his question.

"How on earth did it happen?"

"I don't know. Something went when I took the bend."

"How do you mean, something went?"

"The steering," said Lisle. Her eyes widened. "It just went."

"You didn't notice anything before?"

"Dale did."

He jerked his head aside and looked out to sea.

"Oh, Dale did? What did he notice?"

Lisle caught her breath.

"He'll be angry—because he did notice something. He said there was something odd about the steering—"

He cut in quickly.

"Who was driving—you, or Dale?"

"Oh, Dale. He hates being driven. And he said to take the car to Langham's and get them to test the steering."

Rafe turned back as abruptly as he had turned away.

"Dale told you that, and you didn't do it? Why didn't you?"

She flushed a little.

"I didn't want to."

"Why?"

"Alicia was there. She had to go to Langham's for her car. She was trying to quarrel with me. I didn't want to quarrel, so I didn't wait."

From the time he had turned back, his eyes had been upon her face—bright, watching eyes.

"You'd rather risk a smash than a quarrel—is that it?"

"I didn't think there was any question of a smash. At first Dale said, 'Let Evans see to it.' It was only just as he was going off that he told me to go to Langham's, so when I didn't want to wait I thought it would be all right if Evans had a look at it when I got home." She gave a small hurried laugh. "I didn't really think very much about it."

Rafe hugged his knees. He was in flannels, with a sweater across his shoulders. His skin looked very brown against the white wool. The hair on his temples was ruffled above the pointed ears.

"Why were you and Alicia quarrelling?"

"I wasn't. Rafe—why does she hate me so?"

"Don't you know?" He lifted up his voice and sang mellifluously,

> "'She could not hate thee, dear, so much,
> Loved she not—someone—more.'"

She coloured deeply.

"Don't—that's horrid!"

He laughed easily.

"It's not much of a secret, is it, honey-sweet? Anyhow, in case you haven't noticed it, Alicia hates you for the oldest reason in the world—she's jealous. And if you say 'Don't!' again, I shall tell you why."

Lisle said nothing, only looked distressed, but she met the mockery in his eyes with a certain childlike candour. Rafe laughed at you—he didn't take anything seriously. But in spite of that, perhaps because of it, you could say anything you liked to him.

It was all on the safe, bright surface where the waves splashed, gaily and there were no rocks or quicksands. She said,

"Would you say I was a milk-and-water sort of person?"

He laughed.

"Is that what Alicia said?"

Lisle nodded.

"She said I had milk and water in my veins."

"She would! You should have told her it was better than vinegar."

"But have I, Rafe? Do you think I'm like that?"

He made the oddest face.

"Milk and water? No, I don't think so—more like milk and honey."

Lisle burst out laughing.

"Oh, Rafe—it sounds so *sticky*!"

He hugged himself. At any rate he had made her laugh. She had her colour back, and she was seeing something nearer than the horizon-line. He thought he had done pretty well in the time.

And then all at once she was grave again. It was her own word which drove away the laughter. Sticky—a sticky end—Dale had said that about someone only yesterday— "Oh, he came to a sticky end." That meant smashed, as she had so nearly been smashed with her car against Cooper's barn. Odd to think that instead of sitting here with Rafe in the sun she might have been—well, where? She didn't know. Nobody knew—except God. And if He knew, you were all right.

Rafe said quickly.

"What are you thinking about?"

"If I hadn't jumped—"

He went on looking at her hard.

"What made you jump?"

"I thought it was my only chance."

He nodded.

"So it was. But did you think that, or did you just jump in a blind panic without thinking at all?"

Her eyes darkened.

"I thought—a lot of things—"

"Tell me."

His voice was so urgent that it startled her. She looked surprised. But because it was Rafe, and because it was a relief to speak, she answered him.

"It's very odd what a lot of things you can think about all in one moment when anything happens. I thought about Dale being angry because I hadn't had the steering tested, and I thought Alicia would be pleased because she hates me, and I was glad I had made my will—because of Dale being able to keep Tanfield. And then I saw the whitewash on the side of Cooper's barn, and I thought, 'I'll be dead in a minute if I don't jump,' so I waited for the wet place where the ditch comes in, because I thought that would be the softest place, and then I opened the door and jumped for it as hard as I could."

He made that queer grimace again.

"Clever—aren't you, darling? How do you do it? Too busy thinking to get frightened—was that it?"

"Oh, I was frightened," said Lisle in a matter-of-fact sort of voice. "I didn't want my face to get cut."

"Save, oh, save my complexion! Well, it's worth saving—I grant you that. That scratch on your cheek is only skin-deep—it won't mark you. When did you make your will?"

How like Rafe to go straight from one subject to another without so much as a change of voice. She said,

"Oh, about a fortnight ago, when Dale and I were in town, I ought to have done it before. But, Rafe, you knew—we all talked about it."

He nodded.

"True—I'd forgotten. I'm suffering from overwork and senile decay. That's why I sprained my thumb this afternoon—it's one of the symptoms. And mark you how blessings come disguised! If I hadn't sprained my thumb through catching it carelessly in a door when I was thinking of something else, I should have been drawing lovely, accurate plans of aeroplanes, all hush-hush and confidential, instead of waiting about in the village to cadge a lift home and be deftly on hand to retrieve you from your ditch. By the way, I hope your dress wasn't spoiled."

"Torn," said Lisle.

"Pity about that. It was just the colour of honey—nice with your hair. What sort of will did you make, my sweet? Good old-fashioned everything-to-my-husband kind?"

"Of course."

His eyebrows went up in a quiver of sardonic mirth.

"Why of course? Haven't you any relations?"

Lisle winced stupidly. This was one of the days when she did not want to be reminded of how alone she was.

"There are some cousins over in the States, but I've never seen them. The money would have gone to them under my father's will if I hadn't made one."

"And you didn't leave anything to Alicia? I'm surprised! But I think it would be a really good gesture if you did. Something on the lines of 'My fifth-best pearl necklace to my cousin by marriage, Alicia Steyne.' Like Shakespeare leaving his second-best bed to his wife. I have a feeling that that would go down frightfully well. And what about me? I was rather counting on coming into something in the nature of a competency— enough to keep me off the parish in case my thumb remains permanently sprained. Didn't you leave me anything at all?"

Lisle sat up straight. She looked at the sea and said,

"Did Dale tell you?"

Rafe said, "No." The word came out with a jerk. Where his hands clasped one another about his knees the knuckles showed bone-white.

Lisle got up. Her knees shook a little. She said,

"I did leave you something, but I didn't mean you to know."

Rafe Jerningham sat where he was. He looked on the ground and said,

"I didn't know."

TWELVE

There were two telephone calls about an hour later. Rafe took the first. He was passing through the hall, when the telephone bell rang in the dining-room. He heard Alicia's voice bleak with fury, and nodded a casual dismissal to the young footman who appeared at the service door. Then he said, "Hullo!"

"That you, Rafe? These devils haven't got my car ready yet."

"Darling, why not go and have a nice cup of tea? You sound like a menagerie of furies."

"I feel like one, thank you!"

"And what is the unhappy Langham's place like? A slaughter house?"

She gave an angry laugh.

"I don't think they'll do it again!"

"No survivors? By the way. Lisle had a smash on the way home."

"*What!*"

"Her steering packed up on Crook Hill—on the crook. The car went to glory against Cooper's barn."

There was a dead silence, and then a sharp-drawn breath.

"Lisle?"

"Very nearly a no survivor, but not quite. She jumped lucky."

"She isn't hurt?"

"Not to notice. Small scratch on left cheek, slight wobble about the knees, otherwise intact. Dale won't have to get a black tie this time."

There was another of those sharply taken breaths. It may have represented a last attempt to curb a driven temper. If it was that, it failed. Alicia said with furious distinctness,

"She can't make a job of anything, can she?"

The receiver was slammed down. Rafe Jerningham hung up at his end and walked out of the room.

It was Lisle who took the second call in her bedroom. She was changing for dinner, when the bell tinkled beside the bed. She stood in her peach-coloured slip and heard Dale's voice from a long way off. She hadn't thought of it being Dale. He hadn't said anything about ringing her up, and she wasn't ready to speak because he was bound to be angry about the car, and because she hadn't done as he had told her. She sat down on the edge of the bed and said in a voice which hardly reached him,

"What is it, Dale?"

There was quite a long pause before his voice came in, suddenly loud.

"I can't hear what you say. Who's that speaking?"

"Lisle."

"Who did you say? I can't hear."

A little while ago she would have laughed and said, laughing, "Silly! It's me—Lisle," but somehow the words wouldn't come. Her throat was stiff, and her lips were stiff, though she didn't know why.

She said, "Lisle—it's Lisle," but the voice didn't sound like her own voice at all.

The receiver jarred at her ear.

"Who is it? What are you saying about Lisle?"

She repeated her own name.

"Lisle."

Again that frantic jar of the wires.

"What about Lisle? For God's sake—are you trying to tell me something— has anything happened?"

"The car smashed."

"What?"

"The car."

"What—about—Lisle?"

She found her voice.

"Dale, I can't make you hear. It's me—Lisle. I hope you won't be angry about the car. It's all smashed up."

The loud, urgent voice dropped. He said without any expression,

"The car—you're not hurt—"

"No—I jumped. I had a wonderful escape. I *ought* to have gone to Langham's—but you won't be angry, will you?"

There was a pause before he said,

"You're not hurt at all?"

And at that Lisle began to tremble. How dreadful for Dale if, instead of her own voice saying she wasn't hurt, this had been a stranger's voice, or Rafe's, telling him she was dead.

She said with a rush of warm emotion, "Oh, no, darling—not at all," and heard Dale say her name with a strange break in it. It was as if he had not breath enough for even that one short word. And then the next moment he had too much. The ear-piece crackled with the violence of his anger.

"I told you to go to Langham's! It was the last thing I said! Can't you do anything you're told?"

She was shaken, but she wouldn't show it. It shook her terribly when Dale was angry, but she had begun to learn that she mustn't let him see that she was shaken. She wouldn't be able to live with Dale if he knew that he could shake her like that. The phrase came back to her and trailed away half finished. She wouldn't be able to live with Dale—

His voice leapt at her again.

"Are you there? Why don't you answer me?"

"Dale, you're shouting."

"What do you expect? You've nearly been killed, haven't you? Do you expect me to be pleased? You disobeyed my orders and nearly killed yourself. What do you expect me to say?"

A shudder ran over her. She said, "I don't know," and pushed the receiver back upon its hook.

Sitting there on the edge of the bed, she put a hand down on either side of her and leaned upon the palms, steadying herself. It wasn't Dale's anger she was afraid of. He had been angry before, and she had been afraid before, but not like this. Quite suddenly the fear had come, and she didn't know why.

It was natural that Dale should be angry. Any man would be angry if his wife had nearly been killed because she hadn't done what he had told her to do. And Dale had told her to have the steering tested before she went home. She found herself clinging to that—"He did tell me—he did. I would have done it if it hadn't been for Alicia." There was a moment of relief, and then the fear came closer. He had known Alicia all his life. He knew she meant to pick a quarrel if she could. He knew her car was at Langham's. "Did he know I wouldn't wait to be quarrelled with?"

The shudder came again. She cast back desperately to her first thought —"He told me to have the steering tested."

THIRTEEN

Dale came down next day, and to Lisle's extreme relief he seemed to have left his bad temper behind him, in spite of the fact that he had found out nothing more about a possible government offer for his land. He held her and said, "Oh, Lisle!" and gave her a quick, hard kiss before he turned to Rafe. Alicia got no more than a nod.

"What's happened about the car?" he said. "How much of a wreck is it?"

Rafe made an airy gesture.

"Total, I should say. Chassis all twisted to blazes. Lisle will have to put her hand in her pocket and buy herself a push-bike if it won't run to a new car."

Dale actually laughed, his hand still on Lisle's shoulder.

"Oh, it's not quite as bad as that. Robson's a miser, but he'll let her buy a car if she asks him nicely. But look here, what about the old one? Where is it? The steering ought not to have gone like that. I want to have a look at it."

They were on the terrace, with the sun beating down upon the Italian garden. Rafe, looking down on it, said over his shoulder,

"Evans fetched the corpse home last night. I told him he'd better leave the post mortem till you came."

Later on he strolled into the garage and beheld Dale and Evans very busy with the wreck. But when he came in Dale straightened up and came to meet him.

"It's a most extraordinary thing about that steering. The track rod must have snapped when she came round the bend. It's clean in two. Of course, as Evans says, it's just possible it went when the car hit the barn, but I think that's damned unlikely."

Rafe glanced at Evans, but the chauffeur kept his head down.

"Well, I don't know. You've got to account for the car being out of control. If it hadn't been out of control it wouldn't have run into the barn."

Dale moved away, his hand on his cousin's arm.

"Fact is, Lisle's a damn bad driver. She might have just panicked and let go. I don't mean to say there wasn't something wrong with the steering, because I noticed it myself going into Ledlington—the car seemed inclined to wander. That's what gets my goat, because I told Lisle she wasn't to drive home without having it seen to. I don't know whether she just forgot about it, or whether she couldn't be bothered, but I told her to go to Langham's and have the steering tested, and she didn't do it."

Rafe laughed.

"She was having a row with Alicia—no, the other way about. Lisle doesn't have rows. Alicia was having a row with her."

"Who told you that?"

"Oh, Lisle. That's why she didn't stop at Langham's. She doesn't like rows."

Dale gave an impatient frown.

"I don't know anything about that. I only know I told her to have the steering checked over before she drove the car home."

"Quite a moral tract, isn't it? A Bride's Disobedience or The Fatal Accident." The light bantering voice suddenly hardened. "It came as near being fatal as makes no difference."

Dale's face took on pallor and gravity. He said,

"I know. You needn't rub it in. Look here—" he began to move forward again clear of the garage—"look here, Rafe, Evans is by way of hinting that the steering was tampered with."

He got a sharp sideways glance. No words for a moment. Then,

"How do you mean, *hinting*?"

Dale shrugged a shoulder.

"It's damned unpleasant, and I can't believe it either. I mean, just because you dismiss a man, it's not to say he'll try and engineer an accident for your wife. The thing's absurd, and so I told Evans."

"Meaning?"

"Oh, Pell of course. That's who Evans was hinting at."

Rafe whistled softly.

"Pell—I *wonder*— "

"Why should he?" said Dale. "Even granting he believed that Lisle got him dismissed because he'd been playing fast and loose with Cissie Cole—and it wasn't the case, because I sent him packing myself—well, supposing he believed it was Lisle, it's a nasty risk playing a trick like that. And what had he got to gain? He'd lost his job anyhow, and he was bound to be suspected, so where's the good of it?"

Rafe looked away across the yard. A tortoiseshell cat sat in the sun washing a reluctant kitten. He said,

"Lisle didn't ask you to sack Pell?"

Dale's shoulder jerked.

"She didn't have to. He's got a wife at Packham, and I don't care how many girls he's got anywhere else as long as he doesn't have 'em in Tanfield. Miss Cole came up here to me about Cissie—they'd only just found out he was married—and I came straight out here and sacked him. Lisle didn't come into it at all."

"He might have thought she did."

"Why should he?"

Rafe looked at the tortoiseshell cat.

"She saw Cissie before Miss Cole saw you. Cissie cried and told her all about it. She'd been up with some sewing."

Dale broke in sharply.

"How do you know?"

"I saw her going away. Pell saw her too. She was still crying. He might have thought that Lisle had worked on you to dismiss him. I don't say he did, but he might have."

Dale moved impatiently.

"He'd been here long enough to know that I run my own

show! I don't believe a word of it, and so I told Evans just now! You know how these fellows are. He's got a lift in the world, and Pell's got the boot, so he thinks he can put anything on to him. They're all alike. Any damned thing that goes wrong for the next six months will be Pell's fault. I've told Evans I don't want to hear another word about it!"

The tortoiseshell cat had the kitten by one ear. She licked its face, and cuffed it when it wriggled. Rafe said in a meditative tone,

"Pell was a size too large for his boots. That sort doesn't take kindly to being sacked. Murder's been done for less than that. And you couldn't prove it against him—nobody could because any of us could have done it just as easily as Pell. Have you thought about that?" He did not wait for an answer, but gave a sudden laugh. "Anyone who was fool enough could have done it, which is very incriminating for Pell. Any man who would chuck away a job for Cissie Cole must be a bigger fool than most of us—so if it's got to be anyone, let us by all means make it Pell."

With a squawk the kitten twisted itself free and fled, back arched, tail in a double kink. The mother got up, stretched herself, and came over to Rafe. She rubbed against him, purring. He bent and scratched her behind the ear.

FOURTEEN

They were having coffee on the side lawn after lunch, when Dale plunged a hand into his pocket, brought out a small parcel, and tossed it into Lisle's lap. She looked up, surprised and just a little startled.

"What is it?"

He watched her, very much at his ease in a long chair, at peace with all the world, smiling.

"Open it and see. I've brought you a present."

The colour came up into her face. Why hadn't he given it to her when they were alone? Now she had to open it under Alicia's eye. Not that Alicia was looking at her or at anyone else. She lay in a wicker chair with her feet up watching the faint smoke of her cigarette tremble and fade against the blue of the sky. It was a very perfect afternoon, dead still and hot, with a haze on the sea like the ghost of all the cigarettes that had ever been smoked. On the one side Tane Head and the moors behind it bounded the view. On the other a great cedar swept down in ledges of shade. Lisle sat where the shadow darkened her hair and made a flecked pattern across the green of her dress, but the others basked in the sun.

"Salamanders—aren't we?" said Rafe. He sat cross-legged amongst cushions, his back against Alicia's foot-rest. "The more we bake, the better we like it. The motto is 'Be prepared', because you never know your luck. Personally, of course, I'm expecting a harp and a halo—but then I've got an absolutely snowy conscience compared to Dale and Alicia. My strength is as the strength of ten because my heart is pure—a nice quotation from a poem about the late Galahad by the late Lord Tennyson."

Lisle's fingers slipped on the knot of her parcel. That funny little woman in the train had quoted Tennyson. She wished Rafe wouldn't. Miss Maud Silver—Private Investigations . . . There wasn't anything to investigate.

Alicia knocked the ash from her cigarette and said sweetly, "Bit of a plaster saint—aren't you, Rafe?"

"Not plaster, darling—it's terribly brittle and unreliable. Pure gold—that's me."

Dale was watching his wife. She had very pretty hands— very pretty, and white, and slender, but not clever at things like knots. But the string was off now, and the stiff outer paper with it. A layer of tissue paper came next, and then a jeweller's box fastened with a rubber band. He smiled at her encouragingly.

"Come along—open it."

A strange reluctance possessed Lisle. Dale so seldom gave her a present. He took the eminently reasonable, common-sense view that she had more money than he had, and could buy anything she wanted for herself. This was actually the very first thing he had given her since their marriage. She had felt warmed and touched, but she would have liked to have opened it when they were alone. Her fair skin flushed as she lifted the lid and saw what lay beneath, a piece of rock crystal carved into a grotesque shape. She stared at it, trying to make out what it was . . . Some kind of a squat figure with a face half animal, half human, peering out between leaves—a clawlike hand that clutched a round glistening fruit.

She bent forward. In the sun the crystal went bright and blank. It had no contours. It was just brightness, catching the sun and reflecting it. It dazzled her, and she drew back into the shade. At once the face peered at her again between those crowding leaves.

"Don't you like it?" said Dale impatiently.

She looked at him in a puzzled way.

"What is it?"

"Chinese-rock crystal. I thought you'd like it." His tone hardened. "I'm sorry if you don't."

Something in Lisle quivered. How could she have been so stupid? She ought to have thanked him at once. If they had been alone, she could have flung her arms round his neck. Why did he have to give it to her in front of Rafe and Alicia? She said as quickly and warmly as possible,

"Oh, but I do. I was trying to make out what it was—that's all. It's—it's marvellous."

Alicia blew a smoke ring. She watched it widen out and laughed.

"Dale—*darling!* What do you expect? You give her a jeweller's box, and when she opens it, instead of diamonds there's just a piece of carved rock crystal." She laughed again. "You've a lot of learn—hasn't he, Lisle?"

Lisle flushed to the roots of her hair, but before she could speak Rafe had entered the fray.

"A bit crude, aren't you, darling? Women are of course. To the artist's eye—meaning Dale's and mine—a Chinese carving is worth a pot of diamonds, to say nothing of the fact that Lisle ought never in this world to put a diamond anywhere near her. Pearls of course. Emeralds—sapphires—yes, I'd let her have sapphires. Chrysoprase—and a very pale topaz set in very pale gold. But diamonds—not on your life."

Alicia blew another ring.

"If women wore jewellery because it was becoming, jewellers would die of starvation. Look at the old hags bristling with diamonds at any big show. Did you ever know one who wouldn't wear them if she had a chance?" She sat up and held out her hand. "Here, let's have a look at the substitute."

Rafe took the crystal from Lisle and passed it on.

"Clever," he said, looking at it on Alicia's brown palm. "Rather like something looking at you out of water, isn't it? There one minute, and the next you're wondering whether you've really seen it. Where did you get it, Dale?"

Dale bent forward to look too.

"It was in a second-hand shop in the Fulham Road, in a tray with a lot of other things, mostly junk. I thought Lisle would like it."

He was talking about her as if she wasn't there. She felt young and inexpert. She ought to be able to say, "I love it," but she couldn't. The sly, peering face made her flesh creep.

Alicia balanced the crystal and blew smoke at it.

"Elusive little devil, isn't he?" she said. "Reminds me of the Cheshire Cat's grin."

"Keep it if you like," said Dale. "Lisle doesn't care about it."

Alicia looked at him steadily for a moment. Then she laughed and looked away.

"Do you know, I rather like having my presents chosen for me, not for somebody else. And if you're doing any choosing, I've no objection to diamonds. Hi, Lisle—catch!"

The crystal sparkled in the air. Rafe reached up, caught it deftly, and put it back in Lisle's lap. But before she could touch it Dale got up and came over to her.

"You don't like it?"

"I—Dale—"

"It's a bit sinister," said Rafe.

Alicia laughed. Lisle, tongue-tied and distressed, put out a hand towards her husband.

"Dale—you've got it all wrong. I—it was sweet of you to get it for me—*please*—"

There was a moment of discomfort and strain. The dark colour came up into Dale's face, as it did when he was angry. But before he or anyone else could speak one of the menservants came into the group. Lisle looked at him with relief.

"What is it, William?"

"If you please, madam, it's Miss Cole. She says could you see her for a moment?"

Dale went back to his chair.

"Miss Cole from the post office?" he said.

"Yes, sir."

"I wonder what she wants. You'd better go, Lisle."

Lisle got up and went.

She felt as much in disgrace and as glad to escape as if she had been seven years old instead of twenty-two. She held the crystal in her hand. Alicia's high, floating laugh followed her across the lawn.

FIFTEEN

The one room that Lisle really liked in the big house was her own sitting-room. It was small, and the panelled walls had once been painted white. They had deepened now to the tone of old ivory. It had curtains of faded green brocade, and an old Chinese carpet which had gone away to the colour of grey-green water. Everything in the long slip of a room was old—a bureau of bleached mahogany; a high-back couch; a book-case; a little upright piano with flutings of ash-green silk so tender that it tore at a touch, and a fretwork scroll which displayed the signs of the treble clef on the one hand and the bass on the other. It had a very sweet, faint tone, and when Lisle was quite alone it gave her pleasure to touch the yellow keys and make them sing. There were three windows looking to the lawn, the cedar and the sea.

Lisle came in through the middle one, which was a door, and Miss Cole rose from the edge of an upright chair and advanced to meet her. Nobody would have taken her for Cissie Cole's aunt. Where Cissie was long, limp, and straw-coloured, Miss Cole was small, plump, and brisk. Her eyes were as bright and brown as a bird's. She had a high, fixed colour and a darting way with her head. She began to speak at once, all in a hurry, and as she spoke she got out a handkerchief and dabbed her face and neck.

"How do you do, Mrs Jerningham. Very hot today, I'm sure, isn't it? And I do hope you'll pardon me bringing you in from the garden, and a lovely tree to sit under and all, and the breeze from the sea—most enjoyable, I'm sure. You wouldn't hardly credit how hot it is in the village, but there—we get the shelter in the winter, so where you lose one way you gain the other, and I'm sure we've all got something to be thankful for if we take the trouble to look for it."

Lisle said, "Oh, yes," and, "Won't you sit down?"

Miss Cole sat down on a small Victorian chair worked in cross-stitch with a pattern of roses, thistles, and shamrocks. The groundwork had once been purple but was now grey. A little dull red still lingered about the petals of the full-blown rose, but the shamrock and the thistle were mere wraiths. Miss Cole laid a bright brown handbag on the carpet beside her, smoothed down the skirt of her best dress, a rather lively blue artificial silk, and broke into polite enquiry.

"I hope you're none the worse, Mrs Jerningham. I'm sure I'm as pleased as pleased to find you up and about. I'm not one to go to bed myself. You must have had a shocking turn with the car all smashed to bits like it was, and next door to a miracle you've not been hurt, so it stands to reason it must have been a shock and no saying when it'll come out. My own sister-in-law's sister had a fright with a tramp some time in December, and six months to the day she had to have two good back teeth out, and right or wrong, that's what she put it down to, because all her family had wonderful good teeth, and as she said to me herself, 'Why should I lose mine, if it wasn't for me having a shock?' And I'm sure we must all hope you won't have any effects like that."

Lisle smiled at her.

"Oh, I'm sure I shan't."

"Nobody can't be sure," said Miss Cole briskly. "And of course a shock it's bound to have been. All broken up the steering was, so they say, but of course what everyone wants to know is what call had it got to break. Things don't break of themselves—that's what everyone says, and begging your pardon, I'm sure, for repeating it. There's some that think maybe Pell might know more about it than he's any right to—"

"Miss Cole!"

Miss Cole darted her head like a bird pecking at a worm. She wore a shiny black hat with a bunch of bright blue cherries at the side. Every time she made one of her quick movements they rattled on the brim like hail.

"I'm sure I beg your pardon, Mrs Jerningham, but you can't stop people passing remarks—and when it's an accident right there in the village and that Pell in the bar of the Green Man no more than a week ago letting on that those that went against him never had no luck after. Tom Crisp heard him with his own ears. 'No one never did me down and got away with it'— that's what he said, and, 'Mark my words, there's some that'll get what's coming to them, no matter what high horses they're riding now.' And I'm sure I beg your pardon for repeating such language, but I thought Mr Jerningham ought to know."

"I thought Pell had gone away," said Lisle.

Miss Cole darted again.

"That Pell? Not he! He's one of those that'll hang about as long as there's any mischief to be done—and boasting how he can get a job as easy as kiss your hand!"

Lisle felt an uneasy distaste. She wanted to change the conversation, but found herself helpless. Miss Cole had come here determined to talk about Pell, and talk about him she would. Almost without her own volition Lisle found herself asking the question which Miss Cole intended her to ask.

"Has he got a job?"

"Up at the aerodrome," said Miss Cole portentously. "And in the Green Man every night, talking big about the money he gets, and what a lot they think of him up there." She dabbed at the beads of sweat on her forehead and chin. "And if that was all, he'd be welcome and none of my business—and I'm sure no one can say I've ever been one to push myself into other people's affairs. But there it is and you can't get from it. Cissie's my niece and a poor orphan girl without a father or a mother to stand up for her. And I've not got anything against my brother James, but he's not one to look beyond his own family, and what with the business, and nine children, and Ellen no manager, I'm not saying he hasn't got his hands full. So if I don't look out for Cissie, there's no one else will, and she's not one to look out for herself."

"Is Pell annoying her?" said Lisle.

Miss Cole bridled.

"If he annoyed her, I wouldn't be worrying. He don't let her alone, and it's got so she don't want to be let alone."

Lisle said, "I'm sorry."

"She'll be sorry herself when it's too late," said Miss Cole with a dart. "And how she can—a good girl like Cissie—brought up the way I brought her up! I'll say this for her, if she'd known he was married from the first of it, she'd never have looked his way, but it wasn't but a fortnight ago it come out, as you know. And there she sits and cries, and says she's got herself so fond of him she don't know what to do. That's when I came up to see Mr Jerningham—and most kind he was, I'm sure—a real feeling heart, and might have been the girl's father. And 'Out he goes!' he said, and went straight off and had it out with him. And what I've come up about now is whether Mr Jerningham could get him out of the aerodrome, and I didn't like to trouble him after he'd been so kind and all, but I thought perhaps if you were to say a word—"

Lisle blenched.

"I don't think I could."

It wouldn't be any use. Dale wouldn't. He'd say it wasn't his business—and it wasn't.

"If you would just say a word," said Miss Cole, rattling her cherries. "I'm sure I'll never have a moment's peace while that Pell's anywhere around. I don't say Cissie isn't fond of him, but she's right down frightened of him too. If she says she won't meet him, he tells her she'd best or there'll be something happening to her she won't like, and as long as he's anywhere around there's no telling what he'll be up to. So if you'll just say a word—"

"I don't think I can," said Lisle in a soft, distressed voice. "I don't think it would be any use, Miss Cole—I don't really."

Miss Cole fixed her with a bright, persuasive gaze.

"If you would just mention it. And of course I know what gentlemen are—they take ideas, and then it's no good going on, because it only puts their backs up, but Mr Jerningham's always been so kind, so perhaps if you could bring it in just in the way of talk—"

"Yes, I could do that—but I don't think—"

"You never know," said Miss Cole brightly. "And I won't keep you, Mrs Jerningham, but if you could say a word to Cissie yourself I'm sure she'd think the world of it."

Lisle said "Oh—" and then, "Would she?" in a doubtful tone. She didn't feel old enough or wise enough to give advice to Cissie Cole. And what could she say to her? . . . "You've lost your heart to the wrong man. Take it back again. Don't be sorry any more, because he isn't worth it. Save what you can whilst there is still something to be saved." She might say these things. But would Cissie listen, or would it help her if she did? . . . Faint and far away something whispered, "You might say those things to yourself." It stabbed right through her. She said,

"Is she very unhappy?"

"Cries herself sick," said Miss Cole, for once succinct.

Lisle put a hand up to her cheek. It was a gesture which spoke distress.

"But would she mind? I shouldn't like—"

Miss Cole shook an emphatic head. The cherries rattled.

"She thinks the world of you. There's no one she'd listen to more than what she would to you. I'm sure I was ashamed to think she'd come crying to you the way she did about that Pell, but she couldn't say enough about your kindness, and she took notice of what you said, because she told me some of it You know how it is Mrs Jerningham, if a girl's got a fancy for anyone she'll listen to them, and if she hasn't she won't—and I'm sure Cissie thinks the world of you, as I said before."

Lisle got up. If she didn't say she would see Cissie, Miss Cole would go on talking until she did. It would really be easier to talk to Cissie than to go on talking to Miss Cole. And she could give Cissie her green checked coat. That was a really splendid idea. It would cheer Cissie up, and it would get rid of the coat. Every time she saw it in her cupboard she could hear Alicia say, "That ghastly coat!" But Cissie would love it.

She said quickly, "If Cissie could come up this evening, I could see her. Tell her I've got something for her."

Miss Cole got up too. She picked up her brown handbag, put away her handkerchief, and shook hands. "It's very kind of you, I'm sure," she said.

SIXTEEN

When Miss Cole had gone Lisle stood at the glass door and looked out. The group on the lawn had broken up. The chairs were empty. The shadow of the cedar covered them. If she had to speak to Dale about Pell, she wanted to get it over. If he had come in from the garden, he might be in the study. Nobody ever studied there, but it was by custom and inheritance Dale's own room. Everything at Tanfield was like that. Lisle's little sitting-room was not hers because she liked it, but because the mistress of Tanfield had always had that room. Her great gloomy bedroom was hers for the same reason. If she had wanted another room she would have wanted it in vain.

She came to the study by way of the gun-room next door. Afterwards she wondered why she had not gone straight to the study door. If she had, things might have been different. But think as she would, she could get no nearer to knowing why she had gone through the gun-room. The door was ajar—it might have been that. She crossed to the door which led into the study and found it a hand's-breadth open. There was no sound from the room beyond. She pulled the door a little wider and looked in.

She saw Dale. He had his back to her and his arms about Alicia Steyne. She could not see Alicia's face—only a piece of a white skirt, and her hands locked about Dale's neck and Dale's head bent to hers. She saw no more than she had to see, and turned and came away.

When she reached her sitting-room she sat down on the couch and tried to steady herself. A kiss doesn't mean very much. With some men it doesn't mean anything at all. She mustn't make a mountain out of a molehill or think that the world had come to an end because Dale kissed his cousin. No, she wouldn't cheat herself either—it wasn't a cousinly kiss. But she had hurt his feelings. He had brought her a present. She hadn't liked it, and she had shown that she hadn't liked it in front of Rafe and Alicia. After that, how easy for Alicia to play on the hurt, to use his old feeling for her and blow some spark of passion into a blaze. If she had been there to watch, she could not have been more sure of what had happened. She had a sense of justice as delicate as it was rare. It could divide between Dale's fault and her own hurt. She must not cry, because Alicia would see that she had been crying—and she must not let Alicia see, because Alicia hated her. But Dale loved her. Dale had married her, not Alicia. Dale loved her . . . Her heart turned slowly over. Did he?

Before she had time to answer that Rafe drifted in from the garden.

"All alone, my sweet? Well, that's my luck, isn't it? I've actually missed Miss Cole. Quotation from topical song— 'I miss my miss, and my miss misses me.' I wonder if she does. Alternatively, 'I kiss my miss, and my miss kisses me.'" He made an excruciating face. "A perfectly horrible thought! Do you think she would if I asked her—or rather if I didn't ask her?" He dropped into a chair and declaimed melodiously:

> "'Kisses that by night are stolen
> And by night given back again,
> These are love and these are rapture,
> These are joy and these are pain.'

The poet Heine—my own translation. There wasn't much he didn't know about it, by all accounts. What do you suppose Miss Cole would say if I were to recite that to her?"

Lisle found herself laughing.

"She'd think you were being clever—they all think you're very clever in the village—and she'd say, 'I don't know, I'm sure, Mr Rafe.'"

His glance flickered over her. She had a momentary disconcerted feeling that it showed him everything she most wished to hide. But then, after all, it didn't really matter with Rafe. He took everything so lightly that it didn't matter. He even gave her the feeling that what burdened her was too light and inconsiderable to matter to anyone. Everything went on the surface with Rafe. What the depths held, or whether there were any depths at all, she did not know.

The flickering glance passed on, touching everything lightly and resting nowhere. Then it came back to her.

"Would you have liked to do this room over for yourself—have everything new?"

She looked at him doubtfully.

"I don't think so. It doesn't belong to me."

She didn't say what she had said to Aimée Mallam, "Dale wouldn't like it." And she didn't say it, because there was no need to say it. Rafe's question and her own answer were not on any practical plane, but purely speculative. And that was so well understood between them that Tanfield with its laws and customs irrevocable as those of the Medes and Persians, and Dale, who was their servant, did not come into it at all.

The fleeting gaze was fixed now. It observed her attentively.

"But wouldn't you like to have a room which did belong to you?"

She said again, "I don't know—" And then, "I couldn't—here."

"But you could have your own part in this room. You haven't added anything, have you? Everyone who has had it has added something that was theirs. Why don't you get it new curtains? These will fall to pieces some day."

She shook her head.

"No—they're just right with the room."

She saw him frown, and for a moment the likeness to Alicia Steyne was strong.

"They are right because they are old—is that what you mean? And that makes you a blazing anachronism. Everything in this room is old except us. That's my grandmother's piano—Dale's grandmother, and Alicia's too. The temper comes from her, but she sang like an angel—I can just remember her. And my father brought the carpet back from China—he was in the Navy, you know—and she got the curtains to go with it. My great-great-aunt Agatha worked that cross-stitch atrocity with the roses, thistles, and shamrocks somewhere about the year of the Indian Mutiny. That's her mother in the Empire dress over the mantelpiece—a bit of a beauty in her day. And the bureau was *her* mother-in-law's. So here you are, surrounded by relics of the past and nothing at all to show for your being here—nothing but Lisle in a green linen dress to show that this is Lisle's own room. Something queer about that, isn't there?"

It was just as if someone had touched her with a cold finger. Her hand went up to her cheek. It was cold too. She said,

"Don't! You make me feel like a ghost."

He laughed.

"Rather a fascinating thought, don't you think? Not the old ghosts of a past generation coming back to haunt *us*, but us, all insubstantial and unreal, stepping into their places and haunting them."

He saw her whiten.

"Yes—it feels like that. Tanfield makes you feel like that. That's why I hate it."

There was a sudden change in his face. It had been gently mocking, but now it changed. Something went over it like the shadow that races over water when clouds are blowing—colour dies and sparkle vanishes. He said in a voice that had hardened,

"Yes, you hate Tanfield—don't you? But I don't know that I should talk about it if I were you. For instance"—he was smiling again and his eyes were bright —"I shouldn't say it to Dale."

Lisle's hands went together in her lap.

"Rafe—you won't tell him!"

He laughed.

"I suppose that means that you haven't told him yourself."

"Of course I haven't. I didn't mean to say it just now—it just slipped out. Rafe, you won't tell him! It would hurt him most dreadfully."

"It might hurt you too, my sweet. Have you thought about that?"

She said, "What do you mean?" and met a look which mocked, demanded, and then mocked again.

"Don't you really know?"

She shook her head, looking down at her clasped hands.

He whistled softly.

"Not very bright, are you, honey-sweet? Not too bright and good for human nature's daily food, as the poet Wordsworth said. A perfect woman nobly planned, to warn, to comfort, and command. Only Dale does the commanding in this house, and I'm doing the warning. That leaves you the sweet feminine role of comforter. And if Dale has to let Tanfield go, I don't envy you your job. Have you thought about *that*?"

Lisle said, "Yes."

"Well, I should go on thinking about it. I gather there isn't much prospect of unloading any more land on to the government. Now if you really put your back into it, I feel you might Delilah old Robson into parting with enough hard cash to keep us going for another generation—peace in our time, you know."

She lifted her eyes and saw that he was not looking at her. He was sitting forward, elbow on knee and chin in hand, staring down at the carpet which his father had brought from China.

"I'm not good enough at pretending," she said. "I've tried, and it's no use—he sees right through me."

His eyebrows jerked, the kink in them very apparent.

"Not particularly opaque, are you?" His voice rasped on the words.

"You don't know how hard I've tried."

A shoulder jerked too.

"My poor benighted child! Are you as dumb as you sound? You can't *try* to love, to hate, or to stop loving or hating, or to prevent anyone seeing that you love or hate. I expect Robson's got you taped just about as well as Dale has. And that being so, suppose you listen to the gypsy's warning."

"Rafe!"

He leaned forward, pulled her hands apart, and spread them out palm upwards. They were cold and they quivered.

"A dark man and a fair woman—"

Lisle made herself laugh.

"That's cards and tea-leaves! Hands start with things about the line of life, and the line of heart and all that sort of thing."

His fingers tightened on her wrists. She had the feeling that they were stronger than Dale's for all their slender look.

"Something perfectly frightful happens if you break the psychic spell by talking. There's a dark man and a fair woman, and wedding-bells, and a narrow escape—and then—what's this? . . . Oh, a voyage—a long sea voyage. You're crossing the ocean to the other side of the world—"

"I'm not!" said Lisle. She tried to pull her hands away.

"Well, I think you'd better—it comes out best that way. Besides, it's in your hand."

She glanced up and met a look she could not interpret. It teased, but there was something else. She said on a quick impulse,

"Isn't there a dark woman in my hand?"

"Do you want a dark woman? All right, you shall have one. She can be one of the reasons for the sea voyage."

The colour ran flooding into Lisle's face. She pulled and jerked at her hands to get them free.

"Rafe, let me go! I don't like it. Let me go!"

He released her at once. She got up, and stood drawing long, unsteady breaths whilst he leaned back and watched her. She had fought hard for her self-control, but it had slipped.

"Why did you say that? Do you want me to go away?"

"I thought it might be a good thing if you went."

"To the States?"

"A pleasant family reunion."

She said in a breaking voice,

"I haven't got any family."

"Cousins can be very delightful. I think you said that there were cousins. They would have all the charm of the unknown."

She went over to the glass door. There was an effect of wrenching free and then checking—as if an impetus had spent itself. She said without looking round,

"You want me to go?"

"Yes."

"Why?"

"Least said, soonest mended, my dear."

She did turn round then.

"Why?"

He shrugged his shoulders.

"The family reunion—auld lang syne, and hands across the sea."

Lisle's head came up.

"I am to go?"

"That is the idea."

"And Alicia is to stay?"

"That seems to be Alicia's idea."

Lisle turned and went out through the glass door. There were four steps down on to the terrace. Just before she took the first one she looked over her shoulder.

"I don't think you're very good at telling fortunes," she said.

SEVENTEEN

The events of that evening were to be picked over, sorted out, strained through a sieve, set aside to clarify, and strained again. At the time they seemed quite ordinary, everyday, and dull.

Dinner was at eight, and over at twenty to nine. Rafe and Alicia talked. She was brilliant with a new brilliance. Her beauty shone. She wore a green jewel at her breast. Dale drank rather more than usual. Lisle made a pretence of eating. At a quarter to nine when they were having their coffee on the terrace she was called away to see Cissie Cole. Afterwards she was questioned and re-questioned about this visit of Cissie's, but at the time it was just two girls talking, and both of them unhappy.

Lisle broke the ice by bringing down the green and red checked coat. Even a girl in the throes of an unfortunate love affair can usually extract at any rate a surface pleasure from

a new garment. All Mrs Jerningham's things were expensive
and beautifully cut. The coat had only been worn three or
four times. Cissie put it on, looked at herself in an eighteenth-
century mirror crowned with a gold shell and broke into a
wavering smile. The too vivid checks suited her a good deal less
than they had suited Lisle. They took the last shade of colour
from her face and turned the pale blue of her eyes to a watery
grey. But all she saw was the coat itself, quite new, and smarter
than anything she had ever possessed.

"Oh, Mrs Jerningham—it's lovely!"

She took it off carefully and folded it inside out. She
wouldn't want to be seen walking away in it, not by that William anyway, but she could slip it on as soon as she got clear
of the drive. Some such thought may have been in her mind.

Lisle for her part was thankful for the change in her expression. Cissie had so obviously been sent to see her and was
resenting it. But now that reluctant look had gone. She kept
one hand on the coat and said,

"It's ever so kind of you. Aunt said you wanted to see me."

There was nothing Lisle wanted less. Her heart was heavy
with a sense of Alicia's triumph. She felt beaten and inade-
quate, but she had to find something to say to Cissie. She said,

"I think she's very unhappy about you."

Cissie sniffed and tossed her head.

"She hasn't any call to be! And if she is she's not the only
one."

"You mean you are unhappy too?"

Cissie nodded, gulped, and fished a handkerchief out of the
front of her dress.

Lisle put a hand on her knee.

"Do you think you would like to go away for a little? A friend of mine is looking for a children's maid. She has two little girls, and she wants someone to take and fetch them from school and sew for them. Do you think you would like that?"

Cissie choked into the handkerchief and shook her head.

"You don't think it would make it easier if you went away for a little?"

"And never see him no more?" said Cissie with a sob.

Lisle felt the tears come into her own eyes. Cissie's "never no more" had touched some secret spring of pain.

"What's the good of seeing him?" she said.

"Nothing's any good," said Cissie with another sob. She swallowed her tears, stuffed the wet handkerchief inside her dress, and got to her feet, clutching the red and green coat. "It's no good talking about it anyhow, and I must be getting along. You've been very kind, I'm sure—and thank you for the coat."

Lisle went back to the terrace. Only Rafe was there. He looked over the evening paper at her and said in his lightest voice,

"Dale's gone off to do a spot of night flying. Alicia's driving him. I'm going for a walk. Why don't you go to bed? You look played out."

She had picked up her coffee-cup. She drank from it now. The coffee was cold and bitter.

"Did you know he was going to fly?" she said.

He shook his head.

"A sudden idea. He rang up just now." He went back to his paper. "I think there's going to be a European war, my sweet.

Birds in their little nests agree
Till old enough to fight.
The big uns kick the little uns out.
Sarve the little uns right.

Blessings of civilisation!"

Lisle put down her cup.

"How long is Alicia going to stay here?"

Rafe let the paper fall.

"That sounds as if you thought she had been here too long."

"Hasn't she?"

"Too long—or not long enough." His voice was still light.

Lisle said, "What do you mean by that?" And all of a sudden he was looking at her hard and full.

"Do you want me to say?"

"Yes, please."

His eyebrows went up.

"Have it your own way then. You want Alicia to go. You might have outed her last week. I don't say you could have, because she's in a very strong position. This is her old home, and it doesn't look too good for the new-comer to try and put her out. Then, she had been the unattainable, and is still the unattained. That cuts quite a lot of ice, you know. Still, a week ago you might have had a sporting chance, though I think I'd always put my own money on Alicia, because she hasn't any scruples, and she's definitely a lot tougher than you are. Anyhow that's neither here nor there. Last week has gone and it won't come back again. Now you'll have to wait till the glamour wears thin, and that may be a good long time.

Alicia's a very fascinating woman, and she'd give her eyes to get Dale."

Lisle stood there and listened. His voice was as cold as an east wind. She was so hurt that she felt as if she was bleeding to death, only what was draining away was not blood but hope, and youth, and love. She heard him say,

"It may last a good long time, but it won't last for ever. You don't want to stay and watch it going on, do you?"

He got up and came to her.

"Did you ask my advice, my sweet? Never mind, here it is. Europe's going to be a fairly unpleasant place for the next few months. If I were you I'd go whilst the going's good. Get along out to the States. If Dale wants you he'll come after you, and if he doesn't, well, it's quite a handy country to get a divorce in."

She stood quite still and looked at him, face colourless, eyes dark and wide. After a moment she said in a quivering voice,

"Why do you all hate me? Why do you want me to go?"

His hands came down on her shoulders.

"Isn't hate a good enough reason in itself? Why, what more do you want? Isn't hate enough? Nasty explosive stuff, you know—liable to go off and blow us all sky high. Don't you know when you're not wanted, my dear? Better clear out whilst you can."

She stepped back with a blind shrinking look. His hands fell from her shoulders. She said,

"Do you hate me—like that?"

Rafe Jerningham laughed.

"Oh, like the devil, my dear?" he said, and ran down the terrace steps and across the lawn.

EIGHTEEN

Miss Maud Silver picked up her evening paper and opened it. Her eye, travelling rapidly across the headlines, was caught by the alliteration of "Body on the Beach," and having been caught, remained fixed upon the ensuing paragraph: "Early this morning the body of a young woman was discovered at the foot of a steep cliff in the neighbourhood of Tanfield Court. She had apparently missed her footing and fallen. Tane Head, beneath which the body was found, is a bold and picturesque headland much resorted to by picnic parties and courting couples. Tanfield Court is famous for its Italian garden and a collection of statues brought from Italy and Greece in the late eighteenth century. It is the property of Mr Dale Jerningham. The body has been identified as that of Miss Cecilia Cole, niece of the postmistress of Tanfield village."

Miss Silver read the paragraph twice before she passed to the next column. It was the name of Jerningham in conjunction with Tanfield and the body of a young woman which had arrested her attention. Just for a moment she had feared—yes, really feared . . . But Cecilia Cole—niece of the local post-mistress . . . No, there was nothing in it. Just one of those sad occurrences which evoke a fleeting sigh of pity and are forgotten almost as soon as the sigh is spent.

She began to read about a giant sunflower in a Cornish garden. It was said to be seventeen feet high. Miss Silver's small, neat features expressed a mild incredulity. She reflected that Cornwall was a long way off.

The telephone bell rang sharply. She folded the newspaper, placed it on the left-hand side of her writing-table, and lifted the receiver from the instrument on her right, all without hurry. She heard a voice which seemed to be speaking from a considerable distance. It was a woman's voice. It said,

"Can I speak to Miss Silver?"

"This is Miss Silver."

"Miss Maud Silver?"

"Yes. Who is speaking please?"

There was a pause. Then the voice, faint and hesitant.

"You gave me your card in the train—no, it was afterwards on the platform—I don't suppose you remember."

"Certainly I remember. What can I do for you, Mrs Jerningham?" Miss Silver's tone was pleasantly brisk.

Lisle Jerningham, speaking from a call—office in Ledlington, found herself steadied by it. She said,

"Could I come up and see you—tomorrow? Something has happened."

Miss Silver gave a slight cough.

"I have just seen a paragraph in the evening paper."

Lisle said, "Yes." Then, hurrying and tripping over the words, "I must talk to someone—I can't go on—I don't know what to do."

"You had better come and see me. Shall we say half past eleven? That is not too early for you? . . . Very well then, I will expect you. And please remember that there is always a way out of every situation, and a trouble shared is a trouble halved. I shall expect you at half past eleven."

Lisle came out of the telephone booth. She was very glad that she would not have to drive herself home. In the midst of the horror and the trouble of the day two things had been clear to her. She must have help and advice, and she could not go to Mr Robson, because that would not be fair to Dale. If she went to anyone she must go to a stranger, so that the scales should be even—no more weight on one side than on the other.

Without saying anything to anyone she had gone down to the garage and told Evans to drive her into Ledlington. She couldn't call Miss Silver up from the house, because the line went through the post office exchange, and whatever she might have to say, poor Miss Cole was the last person who ought to hear her say it.

Well, it was done now and she could go home. The police Inspector from Ledlington would be coming over to take a statement from her about Cissie. He would want to see everyone who had seen her—everyone. Well, that was only Lisle herself, and William who had let her in. And what could anyone say? Poor Cissie—she was unhappy—very unhappy. What else was there to be said? There couldn't be anything else. The police were looking for Pell. But what was the good of that? He had made Cissie unhappy. Suppose he had made her so unhappy that she had thrown herself over the cliff—what could the police do about it now? The law doesn't punish a man for stealing a girl's heart or killing her happiness. Only why had the police got to look for Pell? He had his job at the aerodrome. Why wasn't he there?

These thoughts went round in Lisle's head as Evans drove her back to Tanfield.

When she came into the hall Rafe was there. She had not seen him since he had run down the steps the night before. He came to her now without any greeting.

"Where have you been? The Inspector is here. He wants to see you."

"I know—he telephoned. I said I would be back. Where is he?"

"In the study with Dale."

"Dale?"

"He wants to see us all."

"Why?"

"God knows."

She was so pale that it was not possible for her to lose any more colour. The ash-blonde of her hair under a white fillet, the white linen of her dress, the privet whiteness of neck and cheek—all these, with something in the way she stood as if movement as well as colour had been withdrawn, made her seem a statue among the other statues.

They stood there without more words and watched the study door.

NINETEEN

Dale Jerningham sat on the far side of his own writing-table and faced the Inspector across it. They had never met before, but whereas Inspector March knew a good deal about Tanfield and Mr Dale Jerningham, he himself was, as far as Dale was concerned, merely the new Inspector from Ledlington, and until this moment nameless. He sat with formal dignity in Dale's writing-chair with a notebook open before him and a fountain pen in his hand. It was a well shaped, well kept hand, very strong. It went admirably with the rest of him. He was tall and well set-up—a noticeably good-looking man with clear blue eyes and fair hair burnt brown.

When he spoke he used the unaccented English of the English public school.

"Well, Mr Jerningham, I shall be very glad of your assistance. It's a question of this man Pell. I believe he was in your employment?"

Dale said, "Yes."

"And you dismissed him about a fortnight ago?"

"Rather over a fortnight ago."

"Without notice?"

"He had a month's wages."

"May I ask why you dismissed him?"

Dale shifted in his chair. The change of position brought his left arm up over the back of it. He said with a kind of careless stiffness,

"Why does one dismiss anyone? It didn't suit me to keep him."

The Inspector appeared to consider this. In his own study Mr Jerningham could give or withhold information as he chose, but in a Coroner's court he would be obliged to speak. He said gravely,

"Of course if you prefer not to make any statement until the inquest you are quite within your rights."

He saw Dale frown, and thought his shot had gone home.

"I have not the slightest objection to making a statement."

Mr Jerningham could be haughty when he liked. He was being haughty now. Inspector March permitted himself an inward smile.

"Thank you. I am sure you will understand that we want as much information as possible about this man Pell."

Dale nodded.

"Naturally. I dismissed him on this girl's account. I had no fault to find with his work—he is a very good mechanic. But he had been passing as a single man, and when it came out that he was married I had a complaint from the elder Miss Cole about his attentions to her niece."

"Miss Cole asked you to dismiss him?"

"No—she wouldn't do that. But she was very upset. She had just heard of his having a wife over at Packham—he comes from there. The Coles have been tenants of my family for a great many years, and I felt bound to do something about it. I gave the man his money and told him to clear out."

"Did you know that he had got a job up at the aerodrome?" said the Inspector.

Dale's shoulder lifted.

"Yes—it was none of my business. He's an excellent mechanic."

"Miss Cole did not make any further appeal to you?"

Dale shook his head.

"She came to see my wife yesterday afternoon."

"Didn't you see her yourself?"

"No."

"And later in the evening Cissie Cole came here also—to see Mrs Jerningham?"

"I believe she did."

"You didn't see her?"

"No."

The Inspector sat back. Mr Jerningham had found his tongue, but was not very free with it. He said,

"Would you mind telling me what you yourself did during the rest of the evening?"

"Certainly. My cousin, Lady Steyne, drove me up to the aerodrome. I had fixed up to do some night flying."

"Do you remember what time it was when you left the house?"

"About ten minutes past nine, I think."

"Was Cissie Cole still here?"

"I don't know—I suppose she was. We were having coffee on the terrace, and my wife had not come back. She was fetched away to see Cissie."

"You didn't happen to pass the girl in the drive then, or see her later?"

Dale shifted again. His arm came down. He said,

"Certainly not."

"Did you go straight to the aerodrome?"

"Well, no, we didn't. It was a lovely evening, and we drove about a bit."

"Did you go in the direction of Tane Head?"

"Yes—in that sort of direction."

"And did you stop your car and walk up on to the headland?"

Dale made an abrupt movement.

"Look here, Inspector—"

He met a very steady, intelligent gaze. Inspector March said equably,

"Lady Steyne's car was seen standing by the track which leads on to the headland from Berry Lane. You will understand that I am anxious to know who else was on the cliffs last night. How long were you there?"

Dale Jerningham sat forward.

"I don't know—some time—we walked about a bit."

"Did you go right up on to the headland?"

"Yes, I think we did."

"Did you see anyone whilst you were there?"

"There were some children in the lane."

"No one else?"

Dale was silent.

"Mr Jerningham, if you did see anyone, it is a serious matter for you to withhold the fact."

There was a moment of doubt and of something like strain. Then it gave. Dale said,

"I appreciate that. It is just because it may be serious that I hesitate. You see, the person I saw was Pell."

The Inspector looked at him keenly.

"Where did you see him?"

"He was coming down from the headland. He passed us and got on his motor-bike and rode away."

"What time was that?"

"I don't know—somewhere well before ten. There was still some light."

"Did he see you?"

"I don't know. We saw him."

The Inspector was silent for a while. If Pell had a motorbike, there would have been time for him to pick Cissie up at the gates of Tanfield Court or on the road into the village. There would have been time for him to reach the headland with her, leaving his machine in the lane or on the track to the cliff. There would have been time—

He asked suddenly, "Where was the motor-bike?"

"Up along the track," said Dale.

"How far from the lane?"

"Half way to the cliff."

"Was he in a hurry?"

"In the devil of a hurry. That is why I wasn't sure whether

he had seen us. He came running down the track, flung himself on the bike, started up, and went tearing away like mad."

Inspector March wrote that down. He was thinking, "Well—*ce n'est que le premier pas qui coûte*. One minute he won't say anything because the man is a poor devil who's been in his employ, and the next he's positively offering me the rope to hang him with." He looked up and asked,

"You didn't see any sign of the girl?"

"No."

"Or hear any cry?"

"No—nothing. There are always seagulls."

"What did you do after that, Mr Jerningham?"

"I think we walked up towards the cliff."

"And you neither saw nor heard anything of an unusual nature?"

"No."

"And when did you reach the aerodrome?"

Dale leaned back.

"About eleven o'clock."

TWENTY

I should like to see Lady Steyne," said the Inspector. He got up and went towards the bell.

Dale Jerningham stopped him.

"You needn't bother to ring—I'll fetch her. I expect she's on the terrace."

He got a shrewd, straight glance.

"I was going to ask you to wait here till she came." A firm thumb pressed the bell.

Dale said, "Oh, just as you like." He strolled over to the window and stood there looking out.

William came, and went.

Presently the door opened again and Alicia Steyne came in. She glanced first at the Inspector, who had remained standing, and then at Dale, who came to meet her. The Inspector thought her a very pretty woman and much younger than he had expected. Her neck and arms were bare and brown. Her white linen dress showed a slim and pretty figure. There was a carnation colour in her cheeks and her eyes sparkled. He noticed that they dwelt upon her cousin. He said,

"I needn't keep you now, Mr Jerningham. Will you sit down, Lady Steyne?"

Dale got half way to the door. Then he turned and said,

"I had to tell him about seeing Pell on the track. I put it at well before ten. Is that what you would say?"

Alicia sat down composedly. She seemed to consider the question.

"I don't know—I suppose so. Does it matter?"

"It might," said the Inspector. "If you don't mind, Mr Jerningham, I would rather Lady Steyne made quite an independent statement."

Dale said, "Oh, all right," hesitated a moment, and then went out of the room, shutting the door behind him.

The Inspector sat down and took up his pen.

Alicia was lighting a cigarette. When she had got it going she tossed the spent match into the waste-paper basket with an accurate, vigorous aim, and said in her sweet, high voice,

"This is a damnable business, isn't it? Dale's horribly upset about it."

"In what way, Lady Steyne?"

She sketched a gesture with her cigarette.

"Oh, well, you know—the whole thing—this wretched man Pell being in his employment. And Dale swore by him—said he was the best mechanic he had ever had. You know he's mad on flying, and he was going to have his own plane and keep Pell for the ground work. He really was awfully good. I hear he's bolted. Have you got him yet?"

"No, not yet. Did you know this girl Cissie Cole?"

Alicia drew at her cigarette and blew out a cloud of smoke.

"I knew her when she was a child. This was my home till I married. I was brought up here with my cousins, so of course I know everyone in the village. Dale's very feudal, you know. That's why he went off the deep end about Pell. The Coles belong to Tanfield, they've belonged for about three hundred years, and Tanfield belongs to him. Touch one of my people and you touch me. Pell might have committed bigamy in any other village in England, but not in Tanfield. You see?"

March nodded.

"Yes. You say you knew Cissie Cole as a child. Had you not seen her since?"

"Oh, yes—at intervals—as one does, you know. I've bought stamps from her in the post office when her aunt was busy, and said good-morning when I passed her in the village—that sort of thing."

"Did she talk to you about this affair with Pell?"

"Oh lord, no!" She paused, and added, "I believe she talked to Lisle—Mrs Jerningham. I don't live here now, you now—I'm only on a visit."

"I see. Now, Lady Steyne, perhaps you would just tell me what you were doing between nine and eleven o'clock last night."

Alicia sat back. She held her cigarette away and said in a considering tone,

"Nine to eleven—oh, certainly. Dale rang up the aerodrome and arranged to do some night flying—that was just before nine, I think—and then I got out my car and we drove about a bit and went up on to the cliffs—"

"At Tane Head?"

"Yes."

"How long were you there?"

"Well, we got to the aerodrome at eleven. I don't know how long we were up on the moor." She laughed suddenly. "You know, Inspector, this is all damnably compromising—or at least that's what it's going to look like by the time it gets into the papers. Honestly, it's rather hard luck. We go for a harmless evening stroll and before we know where we are we're let in for an inquest, and everybody thinking the worst about us. Dale's fed to the teeth."

The Inspector thought that as far as Lady Steyne was concerned she appeared to be in very good spirits. He reflected that she was a widow and that Jerningham was married, and he speculated for a moment on Mrs Jerningham's attitude towards cousinly strolls on Tane Head. He asked her about the meeting with Pell, and found her answers vague. It was quite light enough to recognise him. It had been a particularly fine evening and the light stayed late on the cliffs. He came running down the track and got on his motor-bicycle and rode away. She couldn't say whether he saw them or not—he might have—they were not on the track, but they were not far away. She agreed that it could not have been much later than a quarter to ten. No, she hadn't heard any cry, and she had never been near enough to the edge of the cliff to look over. No, she hadn't seen anyone else up there. There were some children in Berry Lane.

"And you were up on the headland till about a quarter to eleven?"

"Yes. It would take about a quarter of an hour to drive to the aerodrome."

"If Cissie Cole had been on the headland when you got there, would you have seen her?"

"We might have. We didn't."

"Let me put it this way—could she have been there without your seeing her?"

"Oh, easily. Haven't you seen the place? It's all up and down, with blackberry thickets and gorse—plenty of cover."

"And the light was good enough for you to have recognised her?"

She drew at her cigarette and blew out the smoke.

"That depends on what you mean by recognise. We should have seen if there had been anyone there. We saw Pell—oh, a long way off—but I didn't recognise him till he passed us."

March said, "I see—" And then, "Were you and Mr Jerningham together?"

Alicia laughed.

"You're quite determined to compromise me—aren't you?"

"You were together all the time?"

She laughed again.

"Now what did Dale say when you asked him that? Are you trying to catch me? I believe you are, so I'm going to be on the safe side. We weren't actually holding hands, and I'm not going to swear I never took my eyes off him—you can't expect me to give myself away to that extent, can you?—but—well, I suppose you can guess that we didn't go up there to sit under separate gorse bushes about a quarter of a mile apart. And when you have guessed, I hope you won't think it necessary to tell."

She threw the stub of her cigarette after the match, and with just as good an aim. Then she smiled enchantingly.

"Dale really is frightfully upset," she said. "There's nothing in it, but his wife's that sort of person, and he's got visions of headlines in the papers, and scenes about it with her, and the village simply buzzing. I told you he was feudal, and I do believe it's the village talk he really minds about most." She pushed back her chair and got up. "Is that all? Who do you want to see next —Lisle? She really did talk to Cissie last night, you know."

Inspector Marsh said, "Yes. Perhaps you would ask her to come in."

TWENTY-ONE

Lisle and Rafe were still in the hall when Alicia came out of the study. They had not moved, and neither of them had said a single word either to one another or to Dale, who had gone past them with a black frown.

Alicia Steyne approached them smiling.

"Rather a good-looking policeman—old school tie and all that sort of thing. He's frightfully disappointed because Dale and I didn't actually see Pell push Cissie over the cliff. It must have been quite a near thing, you know." She linked her arm with Rafe's. "Where's Dale? I want to compare notes and see if we have contradicted each other anywhere. By the way, Lisle, he wants you—the policeman, not Dale."

As Lisle came into the study she couldn't help thinking of what she had seen there only yesterday. It felt much longer ago than that—but it was only yesterday that she had looked from the gun-room door and seen Dale and Alicia . . . She put the thought away with a shuddering effort.

Inspector March thought how pale she was. She gave him her hand as if he had been an invited guest, and then sat down and looked at him with the grave attention of a child that has a lesson to say.

"Mrs Jerningham, I believe you saw Cissie Cole last night."

"Yes."

She thought, "He has a nice voice—he looks kind." She relaxed a little.

"Her aunt, the elder Miss Cole, had already been to see you?"

"Yes."

"Will you tell me what passed between you?"

"She was worried about Cissie and—and—Pell. She was worried about his having got a job at the aerodrome. She wanted me to ask my husband to do something about it. I told her I didn't think he would interfere—he wouldn't keep Pell here, but he wouldn't interfere with his getting any other work."

"Yes—go on, Mrs Jerningham."

Lisle looked down at her own hands lying in her lap.

"She was very much upset. She said Pell wouldn't leave Cissie alone. When I said Dale wouldn't interfere, she asked me if I would see Cissie, and I said I would. I didn't think I could do any good but I didn't like to say no."

"And Cissie came to see you last night. Can you remember what time that was?"

"Yes, I think so. We came out of the dining-room about twenty to nine. We were going to have coffee on the terrace.

William brought it out there, but he came back to say that Cissie had come before I had time to drink mine."

"That would make it about a quarter to nine?"

Lisle said, "Something like that."

"And when did she go away?"

Lisle thought before she answered him.

"She didn't stay very long—about a quarter of an hour, I should think. I went up to my room to get a coat I was giving her, and we talked for a little, but I don't think she was there for more than a quarter of an hour or twenty minutes—it might have been twenty minutes."

"That would mean she left you at about five minutes past nine."

"Yes."

"Did you go back to the terrace and drink your coffee?"

A little tremor ran over her.

"Yes. It was cold."

"And your husband and Lady Steyne—were they still there?"

"No, they had gone. She was driving him to the aerodrome."

"Well, they seem just to have missed Cissie Cole. Now, Mrs Jerningham, will you tell me about your conversation with Cissie—everything you can remember. Never mind whether it seems important or not."

Lisle raised her eyes to his face—beautiful, serious eyes of a grey so dark as to seem almost black. The lashes which shaded them were dark also. Under that very fair hair and against the whiteness of her skin they gave her a strange grieving look. She began telling him about the coat.

"It was quite a new one. I chose it in a bad light and it was too bright for me, but Cissie liked bright things and I thought it would please her—"

"Just a minute, Mrs Jerningham. This coat—had it a red and green check on a cream ground?"

Lisle said, "Yes." Her eyes widened with horror as he said, "She was wearing it when she fell."

He saw that faint shudder go over her again, but she went on looking at him. He said gently,

"It's very distressing, but will you tell me just how she took it—the gift of the coat. What I want to get at is her state of mind—and with the probable exception of Pell you must be the last person she talked to."

She put up her hand to her cheek and held it there.

"Yes, I know—I'll do my best." There was a moment's pause. Then she went on, "I gave her the coat, and she said it was lovely. She really did seem very much pleased. She put it on and looked at herself in the glass. Then she took it off and folded it up."

"She didn't go away in it?"

"No—it was still very hot."

"But if Pell had picked her up on his motor-bike, she would probably have put it on."

Lisle's hand dropped from her cheek. It left a faint crimson mark upon the skin. She said in a wondering tone,

"Did he pick her up?"

"We don't know," said March. "He and his motor-bicycle were seen at Tane Head."

He thought this was news to her. And he thought that Dale Jerningham appeared to confide more freely in his cousin than in his wife. He said,

"Yes, Pell was seen there. He rode his motor-bicycle away. But we haven't found anyone who saw him with Cissie. Will you tell me how she talked of him?"

Lisle drew a soft breath.

"She didn't say very much—neither of us did. She said she was unhappy, and I asked her if she would like to go away for a bit. I'd heard of a place which I thought might suit her."

"What did she say to that?"

The mark had faded from Lisle's cheek. She was all white again.

"She said she couldn't go away, because she would never see him again." Cissie's "And never see him no more—" rang in her head. She thought her voice would break under the words. She had to take others.

"Yes, Mrs Jerningham?"

"I said something like what was the use of seeing him, and she said nothing was any use. And then she thanked me again for the coat and went away."

"And that was all?"

"Yes, that was all."

Inspector March sat back in his chair.

"Looking back on that conversation, Mrs Jerningham, would you say that this girl was in a state of mind to commit suicide? You have said she was unhappy. There are a great many degrees of unhappiness. Do you think she was unhappy enough to take her own life?"

For the first time a little natural colour came into Lisle's face. She said without any hesitation whatever,

"Oh no—not when she was talking to me."

March smiled involuntarily. It was just like seeing someone come alive—rather beautifully too. He said,

"You sound very sure about that. Will you tell me why?"

"Oh, yes—it was because of the coat. You could see she was *really* pleased. It didn't suit her very well, but she was terribly pleased with it. We are about the same height, and it fitted her. It was a very good coat. She knew that, and it pleased her. She hadn't ever had anything like it before. All the time we were talking she had her hand on it. I could see her feeling the stuff. A girl who was going to kill herself wouldn't do that—would she?"

"I don't know," said the Inspector. "She might have had a scene with Pell up there on the cliff and thrown herself over. Was she an excitable girl?"

Lisle shook her head.

"No, not a bit. She was the meek, obstinate sort. That's what made it so difficult about Pell. Once she'd got an idea into her head you couldn't get it out again. But she didn't get excited—she just cried."

"You knew her well?"

"Yes, very well. She used to come up here and sew for me." Her voice changed and became unsteady on the last words. Cissie sewing—Cissie talking about Pell—Cissie crying—*Cissie on the rocks at the foot of Tane Head*—

As if he had read her thoughts, Inspector March said,

"Then she had talked to you before about Pell?"

"Oh, yes—quite a lot. We all thought he was courting her, and of course she thought so too. She was very fond of him. And then when she found out that he was married she came up here crying and told me all about it. She seemed afraid I should think it was her fault in some way, poor Cissie."

"Did she ever say anything about taking her own life?"

"Oh, no. I don't really think she was that sort of girl. She was gentle, you know, and quiet—not much go about her—not very bright. She sewed very well, but she took a long time over it. I just can't imagine her doing anything sudden, or violent, or impulsive. She wasn't like that at all. If she had had a scene with Pell she would have sat down and cried about it quite quietly—she wouldn't have thrown herself over a cliff."

As she spoke she had the feeling that she was defending Cissie who was not there to defend herself. The effort brought colour to her cheeks and life into those wide dark eyes. And then quite suddenly, there came the realisation that in defending Cissie she might be accusing Pell. All the strength seemed to drain out of her. A terrible thought came and went. She shut her eyes for a moment, and opened them to see the Inspector looking at her. He was leaning back in his chair. He said in his pleasant voice,

"Thank you, Mrs Jerningham. Now, to come back to last night—you think Cissie went away soon after nine o'clock?"

"Yes."

"And your husband and Lady Steyne had already gone when you got back to the terrace. Where was Mr Rafe Jerningham?"

Lisle looked a little surprised.

"Oh, he was there."

"Did you spend the evening together?"

"No, he went for a walk, and I went to bed. I was tired."

He thought she looked tired now. The long, slim figure would have drooped if it had not been held erect. Its poise was the result of effort. The small fair head was carried with an involuntary pride. This was an ordeal, and she was confronting it with a young dignity as simple as it was touching. He said,

"I'm afraid this is all very trying for you, Mrs Jerningham, but I have finished now. Perhaps you wouldn't mind asking Mr Rafe Jerningham to come here for a moment. I shan't have to keep him very long."

TWENTY-TWO

He opened the door for her and watched her go. She walked slowly. A graceful creature, not over strong. No match at all for Lady Steyne. If she were happy she might be beautiful. No, that wasn't the word—lovely. Yes, that was it—lovely, and sweet, and good.

She came up to Rafe Jerningham, gave him her message, and passed on.

Rafe looked after her as she went, and then took his casual way to the study.

Like Lisle, he gave the Inspector the sort of greeting he would have given to any acquaintance who had dropped in. Unlike the others, he did not sit down, but strolled to the jutting chimney breast, where he stood with his back to the hearth. Overhead, the portrait of the Jerningham who had been Lord Chief Justice of England frowned upon the scene. The crimson of the robes had gone away to the dull glow of a

half extinguished fire, but the frown would endure while there
was paint upon the canvas.

The Inspector, turning his chair to face the chimney-piece,
met it full. The formidable brows beetled over dark eyes which
were very like those of his descendants—more like Dale's than
Alicia Steyne's or Rafe's. But the brown skin was theirs, very
marked against the grey of the wig. The hand grasping a parch-
ment roll was Dale's hand to the life.

Rafe, following the direction of the Inspector's glance, said
with a laugh,

"He was an awful old ruffian—hang you as soon as look
at you. Good old days—weren't they? You'd have been doing
your job with a spot of rack and thumbscrew to get things
going. Life's gone all tame and soft—hasn't it?"

March smiled.

"I can get along without the thumbscrews. Actually, I don't
suppose you can tell me very much, except that I'd like to know
what you thought of Pell when he was here in Mr Jerningham's
employ."

Rafe put his hands in his pockets. He stood easily, one foot on
the stone kerb which guarded the hearth, the knee bent. He said,

"I don't know that I thought of him at all. He didn't come
my way much—I'm one of the toiling millions. I run a small
car, but the other chap, Evans, does anything I don't do myself.
Pell just didn't come my way. You're not asking me what he
looked like, I suppose?"

"I wouldn't mind having that." The Inspector was thinking that you don't describe a man without giving away your
opinion of him.

Rafe's shoulder lifted.

"Short—wiry—tough—not the sort of chap you'd pick for a Don Juan. Very good at his job, I believe. Black hair, lightish eyes—tendency to spread the grease and engine oil about. You know, that's a very funny thing, the other man, Evans, could do the same job and come out comparatively spotless where Pell would be black all over. I couldn't see why Cissie fell for him myself, but I suppose he smartened up a bit when he went courting."

"What sort of temper had he?"

"He never showed any to me, but then, as I say, I hadn't much to do with him. Glum, silent sort of devil, but Dale always says he's the best mechanic he ever came across."

March said, "Thank you." He didn't think Rafe Jerningham had cottoned very much to his cousin's pet mechanic. He said,

"Did you know the girl?"

"I've seen her off and on since she was a baby. I can't say I knew her."

"She didn't talk to you about Pell?"

"Oh, no. I don't think she talked to anyone except Lisle."

"You were not on those terms. But you could hardly have known her for all those years without having your own opinion of her character. Would you say she was the sort of girl who might commit suicide if she was unhappy over a love affair?"

The shoulder lifted again.

"I shouldn't like to say. I suppose anyone might commit suicide if they were pushed too far. I don't know how far she was pushed."

The twice repeated verb made its own impression on the Inspector. He said in his most serious voice,

"Will you give me your impression of the girl."

Rafe frowned. There was a fleeting likeness to the ancestral Lord Chief Justice. He said with distaste in his voice,

"Oh, a long, thin dreep. No guts. The sort that whines and has a perpetual cold when it's a child. But with a kind of obstinacy underneath—you know what I mean."

"Would you expect that sort of girl to throw herself over a cliff?"

"The unexpected does sometimes happen," said Rafe.

Inspector March agreed. He took up his notebook, laid it down again, and said,

"When you left Mrs Jerningham last night it was to go for a walk. Can you tell me in what direction you went?"

Rafe removed his foot from the stone kerb and straightened up. With a careless movement he turned his wrist and took a glance at the watch which was strapped there. He said in rather an absent-minded voice,

"Oh, that—I went down and along the beach."

"In which direction?"

"Oh, round the bay."

"Did you go in the direction of Tane Head?"

Rafe smiled.

"I was forgetting you were a stranger here. If you walk far enough round the bay you get to Tane Head—in time."

"How much time?" said March rather quickly.

"That," said Rafe, still smiling, "would depend upon how fast you walked."

"How long did it take you last night?"

"I'm afraid I didn't get as far as that last night. I turned half way. It would have been too convenient if I had gone on, wouldn't it? Eyewitness's account of—well, I should have been in a position to say whether it was suicide or murder. Or perhaps not? As I don't know exactly where Cissie fell, it's quite possible that I mightn't have been any use as a witness even if I had been on the spot. There are places where the cliff overhangs quite a piece."

"Are you sure you were not there?" said March very directly.

Rafe Jerningham strolled over to the table and stood looking down at the Inspector with his quizzical smile.

"Oh, quite sure."

March returned his look with a searching one.

"I should like to know how long it usually takes you to reach Tane Head from here."

Rafe's tone changed. He said in a perfectly simple manner,

"It is four miles by road—say ten minutes in a car, or on foot just over the hour if you're a good walker. Two miles by the beach, and it takes me three-quarters of an hour."

"Thank you—that is what I wanted to know. But last night you turned back half way?"

"About half way."

"How was the light when you turned?"

"Good enough to see me home."

"That would be about half past nine?"

"A little later than that—but I didn't look at my watch."

"Could you see the headland? Could you have seen if there was anyone moving up there?"

"Until I turned—oh, yes."

"Did you see anyone?"

"Not a soul."

"Or hear anything—either before you turned or afterwards?"

"I'm afraid not. Too bad, isn't it? I'd have been such a convenient witness if I'd only gone on round the bay! But if you'd ever tried walking there after dark you'd know why I turned back."

March said, "I see." And then, "What time did you get in last night?"

Rafe took his hands out of his pockets. He picked up Dale's ruler and balanced it.

"Oh, latish," he said. "If I'd known it was going to matter, I'd have kept count of the time, but I'm afraid I didn't. That's the worst of things like murders and suicides, they drop on you without any warning. If I'd known that the unfortunate Cissie was going to be anything of the sort, I'd have kept an eye on the time, but as it was, I just dawdled along and finished up by sitting down by the sea wall until—well, that's the bother, I don't know when."

"Midnight?" suggested the Inspector.

"It might have been," said Rafe.

TWENTY-THREE

Lisle went out into the garden. Beyond the tennis courts there was a shady place backed by the tall mixed hedge and flanked by old thorn trees. There was a seat against the hedge. She sat down there, leaned back, and let herself relax. She could see the sky, too full of light to be very blue, a grassy slope planted with rhododendron, azalea, syringa, lilac, and the white eucryphia shining like orange blossom in the sun. Lower down a few dark conifers, and hollies—gold, silver, and the old English green. A slender maple fluttered frail pink and white leaves. The air was still, but these translucent leaves were never still. Nothing else moved except the sea, glittering, brightening, changing with its own secret motion.

Lisle saw all these things as one sees things so accustomed that they are part of consciousness and are accepted without thought. Light, shade, sun, air, the scent of growing things in the sun—she opened her mind to them and let them stay there.

She fell into a light sleep, and woke to see Dale looking down at her. He stood between her and the sun. She thought it was his shadow that had waked her. When he moved the sunlight slanted in again between the branches of the old thorn tree. It was warm upon her arm and breast.

He moved, but did not sit down—just stood there frowning a little and looking at her as if there was something he wanted to say but he did not quite know how to begin.

Still not quite awake, she said, "What is it, Dale?" And then all at once the truce of sleep was over and she was broad awake and startled.

He said, "I want to talk to you. This is going to be a most unpleasant business. You've got to help."

She looked at him, her eyes wide and soft, a little colour in her cheeks.

"What do you mean?"

He spoke with a kind of nervous irritation which made the words sound harsher than he meant them to be.

"For God's sake, Lisle, wake up and be your age! I suppose you don't want a lot of talk about this affair any more than I do. Where on earth have you been all day? I wanted to get hold of you before you saw March. What did he say to you? What did you tell him?"

She thought before she spoke. Why did she need to think? His temper flamed.

"What did you say?"

Even then she didn't hurry. If he had known it, she was trying to steady her voice. It was not so very steady as she said,

"He just wanted to know what Cissie had said to me, and whether she was the sort of girl who might commit suicide if she was unhappy. I told him I didn't think she was."

"Was that all?"

"Yes, I think so."

"And what makes you so sure that Cissie wouldn't commit suicide?" His voice was rough with anger. "I should have thought she was just the sort of spineless creature—"

Lisle interrupted him.

"Oh, no—she wasn't like that at all."

"You're very sure."

"Yes, I am—because she was so pleased with the coat I gave her. That's what I told the Inspector, and I think he quite saw it. If you're not too unhappy to be pleased with a new coat, you're not so unhappy that you'd throw yourself over a cliff."

Dale's face had changed suddenly. With a rough impulsive movement he flung himself down beside her and caught her hands in his.

"That damned coat! Why did you give it to her? Do you think I don't keep seeing it—all smashed and stained? Your coat! Horrible!"

"Dale!"

He put her hands to his lips, bending his head down over them, holding them against his cheek, kissing them over and over again.

"Dale!"

"It's a damnable thing! I keep thinking suppose it had been you."

"How could it have been me?" said Lisle in a quiet, empty voice.

He laid her hands back in her lap and slipped an arm about her shoulders.

"That's the sort of trick one's imagination plays. You haven't any, have you? It just got me on the raw—I don't know why. I wish you hadn't given her that coat. I don't like other people wearing your things."

Lisle almost laughed.

"Why, what can I do with them?"

"Burn them."

"Dale—how wasteful! I couldn't!"

"Never mind about that. Are you going to help me?"

A faint uneasiness stirred. She said,

"Of course. What do you want me to do?"

She began to wish that he would take his arm away, but it held her.

"It's this way. You know Alicia drove me up to the aerodrome?"

"Yes."

"Well, we went for a drive first. It was too early for night flying, and we went up on to the headland for a bit. We used to picnic up there when we were children. Lal wanted to watch the sunset, so we went. And we didn't see Cissie, but we saw Pell rushing away in the deuce of a hurry. The worst of it is Lal and I will have to swear to that at the inquest, and if they run Pell in for murder, we shall have to swear to it at the trial. We didn't get to the aerodrome till eleven, and every minute of the time we were together is going to be put under a microscope. It's the most damnable thing that could have happened—you can imagine what people will say. And the only way to stop their mouths lies with you. You've got to go about with Alicia, and you've got to go about with me. We've got to give the best imitation of a honeymoon couple. If everyone sees the sort of terms we're on, and that you and Lal are friends, well, there won't be any more to say."

Lisle sat back into the corner of the seat. His arm fell from her shoulders and lay along the oak rail. She said without looking at him,

"Is Alicia my friend?"

Dale sat back too. His hand came down on the seat with a thud.

"What do you mean by that? She's my cousin—and your cousin."

Lisle said what she had not meant to say.

"Are you in love with her?"

"Are you out of your mind?"

"No. I saw you yesterday—in the study—"

The dark colour rushed into his face. He looked for the moment so taken aback and helpless that her heart smote her. Then anger swept in.

"What are you talking about?"

She shrank back as far as she could go.

"Are you in love with her?"

"I don't know what you think you saw."

She said quite quietly and gently, "I saw you kissing each other. She had her arms round your neck. It was after Miss Cole had gone. I was looking for you to tell you about it. She wanted—no, that doesn't matter—"

"None of it matters," said Dale, in a different voice. He caught her hands again. "Darling, I'm awfully sorry—I really am. I wouldn't have had you hurt for the world. Lal and I haven't the slightest idea of being in love—I give you my word we haven't. We're just awfully fond of each other, and—well, she's impulsive. She'd been on at me to take her up next time I flew, and I'd been saying I wouldn't, and all at once I gave in. She was so pleased she just chucked herself into my arms. Of course you had to come along at that identical moment! I really am sorry, darling. Do be friends." He smiled at her with his eyes, drawing her towards him.

A thin, cold whisper went through her mind like a wandering wind. "It isn't true—it wasn't that sort of kiss—it isn't true—" Why shouldn't it be true? Why couldn't she believe what he said, and believe the smile in his eyes and be happy again? A longing like a sharp hunger came over her to cry away all her fear and doubt and unhappiness in his arms. She mastered it.

Not that way, not because she was so achingly tired and afraid. What she had borne she could go on bearing. If there was more to come she must bear that too, but she would meet it with her eyes open—not drugged and anæsthetised by a false happiness. A line came up out of memory and rang in her ears: "I would hate that death bandaged my eyes, and forbore and crept past." She lifted her head and said gently,

"I'll do anything I can. What do you want me to do?"

"Well, nothing very difficult, darling, though I'm afraid it may be a bit distressing. I thought we might go down and see Miss Cole together. She'd think a lot of it if we did."

He released her hands, and she got up almost with relief. She was physically exhausted and mentally strained. The scene with Miss Cole would be a painful thing to go through, but anything was better than to go on sitting here on this lovely evening—the sea, and sky, and green things praising God, and Dale looking at her as if he loved her with all his heart. Six months ago it was paradise. Now she shrank from it as the last, worst burden she could be asked to bear.

TWENTY-FOUR

They walked down into the village. It took quite a long time to reach the post office, because Dale stopped and spoke to everyone they met. He stood with his hand on Lisle's shoulder or his arm through hers and told young Mrs Crisp who was old Obadiah's grand-daughter-in-law, and his elderly daughter Aggie, and Mrs Cooper, and Mrs Maggs the baker's wife, and quite a lot of other people, how shocked and distressed they both were about poor Cissie's accident.

"I've always said some of those places up on Tane Head ought to be railed off. They're not really safe in the dusk."

Young Mrs Crisp said, "No, that's right," and Aggie remembered her father saying that a boy fell over that very place getting on for seventy years ago, and there was some talk about putting up a railing then, only nothing ever got done. Mrs Cooper was of the opinion that if they railed the whole of the headland off, it would be a good thing and no harm done.

"Never allowed to go up there, my sisters and I weren't, not without it was broad daylight. That sort of lonely place is just putting yourself in the way of trouble—that's what my mother used to say. There were seven of us, and we could go to church with our young men Sunday evening, or we could take a walk along the Ledlington road, but go up on the headland we couldn't, not without it was a party."

Dale laughed a little.

"Are you as strict as that with Mary and Mabel? You know, I'm almost afraid to tell you that Lady Steyne and I went up there to see the sunset last night. My wife had a headache and cried off." He put his arm round Lisle's shoulders for a moment. "You see what you've done, darling—Alicia and I won't have a rag of character left. I ought to have insisted on taking a chaperone. Next time I shall take Mrs Cooper."

That massive lady laughed till all her chins wobbled.

"Funny, isn't it?" she said. "When I couldn't go up on the headland I was always wanting to—and now I can please myself, why, I wouldn't go if you paid me. I should have to go in for some of this slimming first." She sobered suddenly. "Well, it's a shocking thing about Cissie, isn't it? Her poor aunt's taking on something cruel."

Lisle did her part. She said "Darling" when she spoke to Dale, and forced a shy smile when he put a hand on her arm. If she looked pale and distressed, it was put down to the shock of Cissie's death. She was very well liked in the village for her gentle, friendly ways. The present verdict was that she had a feeling heart.

Dale did nearly all the talking as they made their slow progress up the village street. He had a pleasant smile and greeting for everyone. He remembered to ask about Mrs James Crisp's mother who had had a stroke, and young Mrs Crisp's baby who was being christened on Sunday. He knew all about the eldest Cooper boy having got a rise, and he sympathised with the smallest of the Cole tribe who had fallen over its own feet and grazed a chubby knee. And to all and sundry, with Lisle smiling at his side, he proclaimed that he and Alicia Steyne had watched last night's sunset from the top of Tane Head.

"Do you remember how we used to picnic up there, Lucy? Nobody's ever made rock buns as good as yours were. And you're the only woman I've ever met who put enough butter into a sandwich."

Mrs William Crisp, who had been cook at Tanfield eighteen years before, emitted a gratified chuckle.

"Always one for sandwiches, you were, Mr Dale."

The whole thing was very well done. Dale had reason to feel pleased with himself. By the time he and Alicia came to give their evidence at the inquest every soul in the village would already know that they had re-visited their old picnic place to see the sun go down. Robbed of any appearance of secrecy, laughed over in Lisle's presence, the episode would suggest only one possible point of interest, their encounter with Pell.

They found Miss Cole in her parlour behind the shop. One of her brother James' daughters was with her, a pretty, plump girl whose eyes were red with weeping, not because she and Cissie had ever been particular friends, but because it was the first time she had met the violence of passion and death at closer quarters than the cinema screen or the headlines of the penny press.

Miss Cole herself sat in her armchair, rocking herself and weeping aloud. She got up for Mr and Mrs Jerningham, transferred her handkerchief to her left hand, and, pressing it to her eyes, greeted them with a fresh burst of sobbing.

"Such a shock as it's been! Oh, Mrs Jerningham—who'd have thought it—when we were talking so comfortable only yesterday, and poor Cissie so pleased to go up and see you. I'm sure I don't know what I'd have felt if I'd known that was the last I'd see of her. 'It's no good my going. Aunt,' she said. 'Talking to anyone doesn't stop you being fond of a person—I only wish it did,' she said. 'And I wouldn't go, only Mrs Jerningham's that sweet I'd go anywhere if it was to see her.' Oh dear—and I said, 'It's a lovely evening for a walk, and do you good to get a bit of fresh air, slicking indoors the way you do. And don't you be late, Cissie,' I said—and I was thinking of that Pell when I said it. And she stood just over there by the door and looked back over her shoulder, and, 'Who's going to be late?' she said. And that was the last I saw of her." She dabbed fiercely at her eyes, blew her nose, and caught Dale by the sleeve. "Mr Jerningham, they'll get him, won't they—that Pell?"

"I should think so," said Dale. "But you know, Miss Cole, you mustn't make up your mind that he had anything to do with it. She may have fallen."

Her grasp tightened. She stopped crying and her voice took on an angry tone.

"Are you going to tell me you think Cissie would throw herself over? And no call to do it, Mr Jerningham, because she was a good girl, Cissie was, and I'm not going to have anyone saying she wasn't! He made her fond of him, that Pell did, but that's as far as it went. And I don't say she wasn't unhappy, but she'd no call to throw herself over any cliffs. Always after her, that Pell was, and when he couldn't get what he wanted he pushed her over. I knew just such another case when I was a girl over at Ledstock visiting my granny—pushed her in a pond, the man did, because she wouldn't give in to him. And that's what that Pell did to poor Cissie—you can't get from it. All I want is to know that the police have got him." She turned back to Lisle and began to cry again. "I'm sure it's very kind of you and Mr Jerningham, and you must excuse me. They won't even let me have her here, not till after the inquest. I'm sure I never thought anyone in our family would come to be a police case. There's been a gentleman here from the *Ledlington Gazette* wanting her photograph, and I gave him the snapshot Mr Rafe took of her and me when you had the church fête in June. It was the best photo Cissie ever had, so I let the gentleman have it. I'm sure it's wonderful how clever Mr Rafe is with that camera—and no bigger than the palm of your hand. Oh, Mrs Jerningham, it doesn't seem possible when you think about the fête and what a nice time we had! I'm sure it was so kind of you and Mr Jerningham—"

Lisle had very little to say. She held Miss Cole's hand, and sometimes spoke softly to her. She had a saddened sense of what a lonely future the poor thing would have now that Cissie was gone. There were tears in her own eyes when she kissed her and came away.

As they walked back, Dale said in a curious tone,

"You did her good."

"I didn't do anything. I'm so sorry for her."

"That's what she liked. You let her talk, you were sorry for her, and you kissed her when you came away. It was all just right."

Was it? Lisle wondered if it was. Things had left off being right. They were confused, difficult, unendurable, but they had to be endured.

She walked home in silence. Just before they reached the house Dale put his hand on her shoulder.

"Thank you, darling," he said.

TWENTY-FIVE

Lisle went up early to bed. All the way through dinner and whilst the evening was slowly dragging on she had thought of going up to her own room as escape, release, but when she was there with the doors locked it seemed to her that she had evaded one generation of Jerninghams only to find herself surrounded by all those other generations which had gone before. She had never felt that the room was really hers, but never before tonight had she experienced so completely the sense of being a passing guest in this place where so many others had lived, and ruled, and played their fleeting parts.

The heavy curtains had been drawn across the windows. The atmosphere of the room seemed old and stale. The hangings, the carpet, the old-fashioned wallpaper with its embossed design, the massive furniture, all sent out a faint something to taint the air.

She undressed quickly and pulled the curtains back. At once the night was in the room, silver with moonlight and fresh with a breeze from the sea. She stripped back the bed-clothes, leaving only a sheet to cover her. Then she lay against the pillows with her cheek on her hand and watched the tops of the trees below the Italian garden, and the dark, secret glitter of the distant sea. She had come to the end of her strength. She couldn't think any more. From the moment when she had made her appointment with Miss Maud Silver her mind had been in a state of ceaseless conflict. One most terrible thought had come and gone continually. It was so dreadful that she blenched away from it, but as soon as it was out of sight she began to fear it so much that her whole consciousness was in suspense, waiting until the horrible thing should show itself again. Now all that was over. For the moment at least strain had defeated itself. Thought came to a standstill. Out of all the confusion one certainty emerged. Dale had asked her to help him, and she had said she would. She couldn't go and see Miss Silver after all. She would have to go into Ledlington in the morning and ring her up. She needn't give any reason. She need only say that she was sorry she could not come. Her thoughts went no farther than that. She couldn't go and see Miss Silver, because Dale had asked her to help him and she had said yes. She couldn't go and see Miss Silver because it might be hurting Dale. It—wouldn't—help—him. It—might —harm—him.

She fell asleep and had strange dreams. She was in an aeroplane, loud with the roar of its engines and the wind going by like a hurricane. All the winds of the world went by, and the clouds strung out to a thread because of the lightning speed. And there was no pilot. She was quite alone. . . .

The dream was gone. Between sleep and waking she saw the moonlight, turned away from it, and slipped into another dream. There was a place where there was no one at all. Not even Lisle was there. It was the dreadful heart of loneliness, the place when you lost everything, even your own self. She cried out and woke shuddering and cold with sweat.

When she had covered herself she slept again, and dreamed that she was walking in the part of the garden which she liked best. It was a fair evening drawing towards sunset. She came by some unfamiliar steps to the sea-shore. It was not any beach that she knew. There a straight, firm track of golden sand, with the sun shining low down across the sea. Everything was very still and peaceful. The tide was out. It ought to have been a happy dream, but there was a most terrible weight upon her heart. All at once she began to hear footsteps behind her. They were the footprints on the sands of time. They were something inescapable, unalter-able, irrevocable. She could not by any kind of effort turn her head, or go back, or cease from going forward.

And then she saw the rock. It rose up in her path and shut out the light. It was as high as Tane Head. Suddenly it was Tane Head, and at the foot of the cliff Cissie Cole lay broken, with Lisle's coat covering her. The footsteps came on and ceased because they were come to the end. Lisle looked down at the coat. She bent and pulled a fold away from the hidden face. And it wasn't Cissie who was lying there dead—it was Lisle Jerningham . . . Someone put out a hand and touched her—

She woke. The room was dark. She could not tell right hand from left, or up from down. Somewhere in the house there was movement. A door closed. Her sense of direction came back. She got out of bed and went to the right-hand window. A sea mist had come up and blotted out the moon. She could see nothing but its baffling curtain. She stood there a long time looking out.

TWENTY-SIX

The mist was still there when she came down next morning. Dale had breakfasted and gone. Alicia was smoking and sipping orange juice. She waved her cigarette in a greeting which left a queer scrawl hanging in the air between them and said in her sweetest voice,

"Dale says he's broken it to you that we are to be bosom friends. He's horribly afraid of a breath of scandal, isn't he? I don't mind about it myself, but men are such prudes, and, as I told the handsome policeman, Dale is too feudal. He actually minds what all the Coles, and Crisps, and Coopers say in the village. Do you?"

Lisle was pouring herself out a cup of coffee. She said without looking round,

"I don't know."

"And just what do you mean by that, my dear?"

Lisle set the coffee-pot down.

"I shouldn't like the village to say things about Dale, or to think them either. If they were true it would hurt us all, and if they weren't it would be silly to let people go on thinking they were." She turned round as she spoke with her cup in her hand and went to the table.

Alicia laughed.

"How pure that sounds! Well, when do we give an exhibition performance of friendship? What about walking down into the village presently with our arms entwined? We can invent something to do when we get there."

As she spoke, Rafe wandered in, and she broke off to say,

"Hullo! Why aren't you earning your living?"

He went over to the side table and began to lift covers.

"Scrambled eggs—I wonder. Bacon—I don't think. What did you say, darling?"

"I said, 'Why aren't you working?'"

He waved his right hand in her direction.

"I still have a strained thumb, and if you've any idea of pointing out that it is all imagination, I come back at you with 'If I imagine my thumb is strained, I shall also imagine that I can't draw with it.' Vantage to me!"

Alicia blew out a delicate cloud of smoke.

"Do you draw with your thumb?"

"Try drawing without it, darling. Game and set! A kipper— I thought I smelt a kipper. Lisle, what are you having—coffee? That's your American blood." He brought his kipper to the table and sat down beside her. "Good Queen Bess breakfasted off a baron of beef and several bumpers of beer. It's a degenerate age. You are continental—pick your continent. Alicia is definitely decadent—there's something sinister about nicotine and orange juice. I am supporting the herring industry. What is everyone going to do today?"

Alicia stubbed out her cigarette on the edge of his plate.

"Try nicotine and kipper—that's decadent if you like! Lisle and I are walking down into the village all wreathed in friendship."

Lisle looked up.

"I'm afraid I can't this morning."

"Oh?" Alicia stared. "And why not?"

"I've got to go into Ledlington."

Alicia laughed.

"Dale's taken the car," she said.

"Oh—" It was no more than an escaping breath. A feeling of panic invaded her. Suppose Alicia were to offer to drive her into Ledlington. She would have to go—she must telephone to Miss Silver. Suppose Alicia didn't offer. William Crisp had a car which he hired out—she might take that. But then everyone in the village would wonder why she had to hire.

"I think I'm bored with Ledlington," said Alicia. "We can show ourselves there another day. We had better start with the village."

"Obliging creature, aren't you?" said Rafe. "Everyone seems to forget that I possess a car. Lisle and I will go to Ledlington, and you can walk into the village all by yourself. What time do you want to start, honey-sweet?"

Alicia's colour flared.

"That's a perfectly ridiculous name! If I were Dale—"

Rafe burst out laughing.

"You'd eat a proper breakfast. I don't mind betting he went right through everything." He turned to Lisle. "Well, when do we start?"

She looked at him gratefully.

"Could it be rather soon?"

"It could."

"Are you going to buy a new car?" said Alicia in a taunting voice.

"I don't know—I might. It's difficult not having one—"

"Oh, Rafe's at your disposal—whilst he's got a sprained thumb."

Rafe got up to put away his plate. He came back reciting, "'Let me malinger and I'll dare, e'en *that* to drive for thee—' To Anthea who may command him in anything!"

Alicia broke into sudden laughter.

"Are you trying to make Lisle believe you're fond of her? What a hope!"

Rafe smiled.

"She's a credulous creature—she might be taken in. You had better warn her—I can see you are going to anyhow." He turned a laughing look on Lisle. "I'm not a prophet in my own country. Alicia is just going to tell you that I've never been fond of anyone in my life. I'm a philanderer, a specialist in flirtation, an unreliable poacher on other people's preserves. I rob hen-roosts and don't even want to eat the eggs. I throw them away because I like breaking things. It is well known that I have no heart. In fact, You Have Been Warned."

Lisle made herself smile too. Beneath the chaff there ran a swift, secret current. She didn't know what it was, but it made her afraid.

She said as lightly as she could, "Would that be true?" and Alicia laughed again.

"Of course it's true. He's a cold fish. No, fish isn't the right creature—I believe they are quite affectionate."

"Try serpent," said Rafe in an interested voice. "I rather fancy that. 'He sleeked his soul in a serpent's skin, and buttoned it up and buttoned it in.' Strictly original and impromptu effort by Rafe Jerningham. And what she really means, honey-sweet, is, don't trust me an inch, because I might take an ell, and on no account let me drive you into Ledlington, because it interferes with her own plans for this morning."

"I'll go and get ready," said Lisle.

The mist was drawing up as they came on to the Ledlington road. Warmth came through it, and a veiled sunlight prophesying heat. She said suddenly,

"Why does Alicia say that sort of thing?"

Rafe flashed her a quick, enigmatic look.

"Don't you know?"

"No, I don't think I do. She sounded angry."

"Oh, yes, she was angry."

"Why?"

His shoulder lifted.

"Why is anybody angry?"

She left it at that. No knowing where that current would take you if you ventured in too far. She drew back and sat in silence all the way into Ledlington. After a little she found the silence restful.

"Where do you want to go?"

They were amongst houses now, straggling outposts of the town, raw and new, with brightly coloured tiles, unfinished gardens, vivid window curtains, and names like My'ome, Maryzone, and Wyshcumtru.

"Oh, the High Street—Ashley's. I shan't be long."

She heard him laugh.

"When every woman lies! I'll expect you when I see you. Shall I have time to get my hair cut?"

"Oh, yes."

"Several times over, I expect! Don't hurry."

Lisle went up to the ladies' rest room. Ashley's did their customers very well. They catered for women who came in from the country round and made a day of it, shopping in the morning and paying visits in the afternoon. You could have your hair shampooed and waved, you could take a facial treatment, you could rest in a comfortable armchair and look through the latest magazines, you could ring up your friends from a telephone box which ensured privacy.

It was the telephone box which had brought Lisle to Ashley's. She entered it, took care to shut the door, and asked for a London number. Ledlington has not arrived at automatic telephones. The frequently expressed view is that it has no desire to be bothered with them.

Lisle, waiting for her call, was glad to see how empty the rest-room was. A vague attendant just visible through the archway into the dressing-room was polishing a mirror over one of the wash-basins. There was no one else in sight.

The voice of the telephone operator said, "Here you are," and with a little click the prim, reliable voice of Miss Maud Silver took its place.

"Hullo!"

Queer how the one word took Lisle back to the train and a dumpy figure in drab shantung and a brown hat with a bunch of mignonette and pansies. She had no need to ask who was on the line.

"Miss Silver—Lisle Jerningham speaking. I can't come up and see you today. I've had to change my plans."

There was the sound of a faint cough.

"Dear me—that's a pity—really a great pity. You are sure you cannot manage to come?"

Lisle said, "Quite sure," and did not know how the words sounded to Miss Silver's ear.

The prim, reliable voice said, "Dear me!" again. And then, "Could you come up tomorrow?"

Lisle wanted to say yes so much that she began to shake. She wanted to say yes, and she mustn't. She must say no. She said it in a failing voice, and then she said goodbye and hung up the receiver before she could be tempted to say anything more. Then she went quickly back to the car and sat there to wait for Rafe. She had to wait some time.

When he came, her heart knocked suddenly against her side. She thought something had happened, and then wondered what had put the thought into her mind, because he smiled and looked just as usual. But when they were clear of the High Street and drawing away from the town he said in a conversational tone,

"They've got Pell."

Why should that make her heart knock? But it did. She said,

"How do you know?"

"I met March. They're having the inquest tomorrow."

Lisle leaned back and closed her eyes. The mist was gone. The wet road dazzled her under the sun. Her heart beat. She said,

"Did he do it—Pell? Did he push Cissie over the cliff?"

Rafe put his foot down on the accelerator. The new houses streamed away on either side and were gone. The green fields streamed away. He said in his casual voice,

"That'll be for a jury to say. He swears he didn't."

TWENTY-SEVEN

Miss Silver laid down the telephone receiver and picked up her knitting. She was engaged upon a rather elaborate blue jumper designed by herself and intended for her niece Ethel. Purl two—knit two—slip one—purl two . . . It was absolutely necessary to keep the mind unwaveringly fixed on this part of the pattern. But after ten minutes or so the clicking needles slowed down, the pale, plump hands came to rest upon the blue wool. It was always annoying when a client broke an appointment—annoying and unsatisfactory. It indicated a wavering purpose—that much was certain. A purpose might waver because of a naturally unstable character. With some people, to act on impulse provoked an immediate reaction; the impulse was regretted and reversed. Another cause would be fear. The girl who had spoken to her in the train had been quite desperately shocked and afraid. If she had made her appointment then, Miss Silver would not have been at all surprised at its being cancelled later on when she had had time to recover and reflect. But it was after this time for reflection had elapsed that the appointment had been made, and made urgently under some pressure of necessity and fear. Made—and now cancelled. If the reason for making it had been fear, that reason still existed. The voice that had cancelled the appointment had trembled with fear. The girl who spoke was afraid of her own voice. She was afraid of saying too much. She could not stay for the ordinary courtesies. Mrs Dale Jerningham had been gently bred. If fear had not driven her, she would have softened the breach of her appointment with apology and regret. She had not tried to soften anything. There had been no room in her mind for any other thing than her own fear and haste.

Miss Silver considered these points at length. Then she took out of a drawer on her right a bright blue exercise-book with a shiny cover. Opened and laid out flat on the convenient mound produced by Ethel's jumper, it disclosed under the heading "Mrs Dale Jerningham" an account of her conversation with Lisle in the train. There were also a number of newspaper cuttings. To these Miss Silver paid a very particular attention. The room about her settled into silence.

It was a cheerfully Victorian apartment with a brightly flowered Brussels carpet and plush curtains of a particularly cheerful shade of peacock-blue. In front of the empty grate stood a fire-screen with a frame of the same yellow walnut as the writing-table and carved in the same regrettably ornate manner. On the front of the screen was a pattern of poppies, cornflowers and wheat ears worked in cross-stitch upon canvas, with a background of olive green. In front of the fire-screen there was a black woolly mat. The mantelpiece supported a row of photographs in silver frames, whilst above them, against a flowered wallpaper, hung a steel engraving of Millais' "Black Brunswicker", in a border of yellow maple. Similar engravings of "Bubbles", "The Soul's Awakening", and Landseer's "Monarch of the Glen" adorned the other walls. On either side of the hearth there was one of those odd old-fashioned chairs with bow legs profusely carved, upholstered laps, and curving waists.

Miss Silver herself, neat, drab, and elderly, her hair in a knob behind and a fuzzy fringe covered with a net in front, fitted perfectly into these surroundings. The only jarring note was struck by the telephone standing incongruously upon the faded green leather top of the writing-table. New, workmanlike, shiny, without curve, colour or carving, it proclaimed an era removed by nearly four decades from that in which Victoria lived and died.

A small clock wreathed with wooden edelweiss which lurked among the photograph frames on the mantelpiece struck the half hour. Miss Silver put the exercise-book back into the drawer from which she had taken it, laid Ethel's jumper carefully on the left-hand side of the table, and drawing in her chair, proceeded to dial "Trunks". There was a little delay, during which her thoughts continued to be busy. Then a click heralded a booming bass. It said,

"Police Station, Ledlington."

Miss Silver cleared her throat and said precisely,

"Thank you. Good morning. I should like to speak to Inspector March."

"What name, please?"

"Miss Maud Silver."

The bass voice appeared to be allied to extremely heavy boots. They could be heard receding with a measured tread. After an interval other, less resounding footsteps and a familiar voice.

"Miss Silver? How are you? What can I do for you?"

Miss Silver's faint cough travelled along the line. It took Randal March a long way back to a schoolroom where a little inky boy and two much tidier little girls had absorbed instruction in reading, writing, and arithmetic from a Miss Silver who must in those days have been a good deal younger than she was now, but who never seemed to him to have changed in any way with the passage of years. Kind, dowdy, prim, intelligent—oh, very intelligent—and firm. That was Miss Silver twenty-seven years ago, and that was Miss Silver today. They had always kept up with her, his mother, his sisters, and at long intervals himself. Recently however they had been rather closely associated, for it was from Matchley that he had just been transferred to Ledlington, and it was in Matchley that the horrible dénouement of the affair of the poisoned caterpillars had taken place. If it had not been for Miss Silver, he might very well have been occupying a grave in the family plot instead of listening with grateful attention whilst she replied to his questions.

"Thank you, Randal, I am quite well. I hope you are settling down comfortably. Ledlington is a charming, old-fashioned place, though rather spoilt by some of the newer buildings."

"What does she want?" thought Randal March. "She didn't ring me up to discuss architecture. What is she on to?"

"I hope you have good news of your dear mother," pursued Miss Silver.

"Oh, yes—very. She never gets any older."

"And dear Margaret and Isabel?"

"Blooming."

"Please give them my love when you write—but I shall be seeing you."

"Oh, you will, will you?" He did not say this aloud, but he grinned.

Miss Silver went on speaking.

"I thought of taking a little holiday in Ledlington."

"A holiday?" said Randal severely.

"I hope so. And I really rang up to know whether you could recommend me a quiet boarding-house, not too expensive. I am sure you will know what would suit me."

"Well—I don't know—"

"I thought of coming down this afternoon. If you would be so kind as to make some enquiries about a boarding-house—"

"Yes, of course—"

"I could call in at the station, and if you should not be there, perhaps you would leave a note."

Inspector March said that he would. He hung up, wondering what Miss Silver had got hold of. It couldn't be the Cole case—or could it? He felt a pringling in his bones. If Maud Silver was coming to Ledlington, it was because she had got her nose down on a trail. All that about a holiday and "your dear mother," and "dear Margaret and Isabel," and a nice boarding-house, was camouflage. She had just had a holiday with her niece Ethel. Not only did he know that, but he knew that she knew that he knew it. And she didn't throw any dust in his eyes. He knew his Miss Silver. He went off to enquire about boarding-houses.

TWENTY-EIGHT

The inquest took place next day in the village hall. The village attended in force. Miss Cole in black between her brother James and his plump, emotional wife. The party from Tanfield Court. William, uplifted by his own importance as the last person with the exception of Pell, whom he and every one else was already calling the murderer, to see Cissie alive. Inspector March, very smart and upright. The Coroner, old Dr William Creek who had brought Cissie into the world and knew most things about nearly everybody in the room. Pell, sitting beside a stolid young constable, incredibly tousled, sallow and unshaven, with red-rimmed eyes and a jutting, obstinate jaw. He sat there and took no notice of anyone. Every now and then he yawned, showing yellow teeth.

Miss Silver in the third row reflected, not for the first time in her professional career, that girls really did fall in love with the most extraordinary people. A woman beside her said in an indignant whisper, "Look at him sitting there and yawning! Don't care what he done to the poor girl! But he won't get out of it that way. A real murdering face he's got." Someone else said "Ssh!"

Miss Silver was watching Pell's left hand. It hung down beside him and grasped the edge of the bench on which he sat with such a desperate force that the knuckles looked as if they were about to split the skin. She saw it pale, stretched, straining, a mute witness to the man's tortured mind, and then lifted her eyes again to his unwitnessing face.

She looked next at the Tanfield party. After a moment she leaned to the woman beside her and with a faint preliminary cough enquired which of the two gentlemen was Mr Dale Jerningham. On receiving the whispered reply she sat back again and resumed her survey. A good-looking man—oh, yes, very decidedly. He and Mrs Jerningham made a very handsome couple—though of course handsome was scarcely the word one would use to describe anyone so slender and sweet-looking as she was. No—lovely would be a much truer description. And Lady Steyne now—how should she be described? Very pretty—very pretty indeed. Very simply and suitably dressed in white linen, with a black riband round her hat, and black and white shoes. On such a very hot day nothing could be more suitable, and the touches of black would be appreciated by the village. Mrs Jerningham was in white too, but without any black. Of course Lady Steyne, being a widow and a fairly recent one, would have had the black by her, whereas Mrs Jerningham would probably have only a choice between white and some colour, and a colour would not be suitable to the occasion—oh, no, not at all.

Lady Steyne and Mrs Jerningham sat next to each other. A pretty contrast—one so dark and the other so fair. But Lady Steyne had a lovely colour, and Mrs Jerningham was quite dreadfully pale. Of course it did her credit, poor thing—a most distressing occasion. Mr Jerningham was on his wife's other side. Very right and proper, and most natural that he should appear concerned at her looks. He put a hand on hers, bent and whispered to her, and even after receiving what was obviously a reassurance continued to manifest a good deal of affection and concern. The young man beyond him was of course the cousin, Mr Rafe Jerningham. Really they were an extraordinarily good-looking family. Such a graceful person, if one could apply that description to a man. Not so tall or so broad in the shoulders as his cousin Dale, but so very well proportioned. A very mobile, expressive countenance, and such beautiful white teeth. In happier circumstances, Miss Silver judged, he would be a lively and amusing companion. His expression at the moment was decorous in the extreme.

The proceedings began.

Evidence of identification. Medical evidence. Miss Cole's evidence.

The coastguard who had found the body at 7.15. The doctor who had examined it. The time at which death must have taken place, somewhere between 9 p.m. and midnight. Then Miss Cole.

Dr Creek treated her very gently.

"You say that your niece was unhappy."

Miss Cole pressed a clean handkerchief to her eyes.

"Oh, yes, sir," she said with a sob.

"Would you say that she was desperately unhappy—that is, unhappy enough to do some desperate thing?"

Miss Cole sobbed again.

"Oh, no, sir."

"And did she ever speak of doing anything desperate, such as taking her own life?"

"Oh, no, sir. And she never did, and never had any cause to. She was a good girl, Cissie was."

"Yes—that is not in question. You must not feel that there is any slur upon this poor girl's character. She was a good girl, and she was unhappy. We have evidence on both these points. The questions I am asking you are directed to finding out the degree of her unhappiness, and whether she showed any sign of lack of mental balance. Did she show any such sign?"

"Oh, no, sir."

"And you say that she did not at any time threaten to take her life?"

"No, sir."

"Or say that she wished she was dead?"

"No, sir."

William next, uplifted, perspiring, scarlet to the tips of his large ears. He took the oath in a completely inaudible mumble, caught the eye of Ellen Flagg's father amongst the jury, and became convinced that he had done something wrong and would probably be indicted for perjury. He wondered if Ellen was there, gave his evidence in agonised gasps, and retired thankfully to the back of the hall, having established the facts that Cissie Cole had come to see Mrs Jerningham at about twenty minutes to nine, had left again as near as possible to nine o'clock, and had gone away "quite cheerful like." Bad evidence for Pell.

Mrs Dale Jerningham next.

Miss Silver watched her with interest and attention. She took the oath in a faint but perfectly distinct voice, and gave her evidence with great simplicity—the interview with Cissie—the brief exchange of words—the gift of the coat—Cissie's undoubted pleasure.

Everyone was looking at the coat. It lay folded in a brown paper wrapping upon one of the small tables which were used when a whist drive was held in the hall. The paper covered it so that only a small piece showed where the young constable had turned it back. Why was it covered like that? Because of stains too horrible to be seen? The thought was in every mind.

Miss Silver watched the faces, all turned in one direction except her own—interested, frightened, horrified, gloating. Everyone except herself stared at the handsbreadth of woollen stuff showing between the folds of brown paper—a broad green stripe shading into cream, narrow lines of red and yellow crossing the green. Her own eyes rested upon the face of Mr Rafe Jerningham.

Like everyone else, he was looking at the coat in which Cissie had fallen to her death—Mrs Dale Jerningham's coat. He looked at the coat, and then he looked at Mrs Dale Jerningham. In both looks there was a momentary flash of something. Was it horror?

Miss Silver was not sure. The rest of the face was bleakly inexpressive. She felt as if in passing a curtained window she had caught a glimpse of something strange, not meant to be seen by anyone at all—a chink in the curtain, a single fleeting glimpse of what lay behind, seen and gone again in a flash.

There was no interval before the Coroner said,

"Is this the coat, Mrs Jerningham?"

One would not have said that she could be any paler, but she did turn paler as she bent shrinking eyes upon it and said, "Yes."

She went back to her seat.

Dale Jerningham next—very upright, very audible, very straightforward in his plain answers. He and his cousin Lady Steyne had walked up on to Tane Head to see the sunset. They had been for a drive first. He could not be certain of the time, but it would be somewhere about twenty to ten. There was still a good deal of light in the sky—a broad belt of gold where the sun had set.

The Coroner: "The sun had actually set at 9.2, summer time. You were not on the headland then?"

"Oh, no—we were driving. But we saw the light in the sky, and my cousin suggested going up to look at it from the cliff."

"Did you see anyone else on the headland?"

Dale Jerningham hesitated, dropped his gaze, and said in a much lower voice,

"I saw Pell."

"Where did you see him?"

"He was running down the track from the cliff."

"Will you tell us just what happened."

Dale seemed puzzled and distressed.

"Nothing happened, sir. He came rushing down the track and got on his motor-bicycle and rode away. I don't think he saw us."

Miss Silver looked at Pell. His hand still gripped the bench. His face showed nothing. Sweat glistened on his forehead. A lock of black hair fell greasy and unkempt across it. His eyes never shifted from a ragged knot-hole in the boarded floor at a distance of about two yards from his own feet and in a direct line with them.

Dale Jerningham finished his evidence and sat down.

Lady Steyne gave hers. She had been with her cousin. They had seen Pell. She sat down.

Whilst she was giving her evidence, Miss Silver was looking at Mr Rafe Jerningham, who was looking at Lady Steyne. His expression interested her very much indeed. It betrayed admiration, with a kind of mocking sparkle on it which reminded her of the sparkle on some kinds of wine—champagne, or moselle. To a less acute observer it would not perhaps have betrayed anything at all. The village was much too used to Mr Rafe not to take him for granted.

The name of Mary Crisp was called. From the second row of chairs there emerged a thin, lank child with a cropped brown head and a knee-length frock of pink and white cotton. She hung her head and looked shyly at the Coroner as he asked her how old she was.

"Fourteen, sir."

It didn't seem possible. Miss Silver had taken her for no more than ten.

There was a pause, a whispered consultation resulting in the production of Mrs Ernest Crisp.

"Oh, yes, she's fourteen, sir—that's right enough."

Mary continued to hang her head. Only as her mother sat down she darted a bright elfish look at Pell, who had not moved. When the Coroner spoke to her she looked down again, her little brown face quite without expression.

"You were in Berry Lane on Wednesday evening, Mary?"

An only just audible whisper said "Yes."

"With your little brother John aged seven?"

"Yes."

"Did you see anyone go up the track on to Tane Head?"

A pair of bright dark eyes looked up, and down again. The little cropped head was nodded vigorously.

"Who did you see?"

A small, thin finger pointed at Pell.

"Him."

"Was there anyone with him?"

"Yes—Cissie Cole."

"Will you tell us what they did?"

Mary found a shrill, piping voice.

"Rode his motor-bike up on to the track, he did, with Cissie on behind, an' they got off an' walked up on to the cliff."

"Did you see anyone else?"

"Mr Jerningham—an' Lady Steyne. They went up the same way."

"Did you see Pell and Cissie again?"

She shook her head.

"We come home. It was time Johnny was in."

"Now, Mary—are you sure it was Cissie Cole you saw?"

A vigorous nod.

"It was light enough for you to see her quite plainly?"

"Yes, sir. It wasn't only twenty past nine, and Mum said to be in by ha' past, and we was."

From her seat Mrs Ernest Crisp said, "That's right."

TWENTY-NINE

Mary, released, ducked her head and scuttled back to her mother's side. Once there, she directed a long unwinking stare at Pell. His turn had come—Alfred Sidney Pell. But it was not till the young constable put his hand on his shoulder that he lifted first an unkempt head, and then a stiff, unwilling body.

There was a chair for the witnesses, but he did not sit in it. Having got to his feet he kept them, slouching behind the chair, his hands gripping the rail as he had gripped the bench. He took the oath in a deep muttering voice. The words blurred and ran one into the other. They might have been in some foreign language, mechanically repeated without any knowledge of their meaning.

The Coroner put his preliminary questions. The answers came each with its own long pause.

He was Alfred Sidney Pell. He was twenty-nine years of age. He was a married man. He had kept company with Cissie

Cole. She didn't know he was married. Not until a fortnight ago. She was a good girl and nobody need say anything different. He had been in Mr Jerningham's employment as a mechanic. Mr Jerningham had dismissed him on account of his being married.

The Coroner leaned forward with his air of courteous attention.

"Do you mean that literally, or do you mean that Mr Jerningham dismissed you because you had been passing yourself off as a single man in order to court Cissie Cole?"

A rough mumble of something that sounded like "That's right."

"Now, Pell—about Wednesday evening. Had you an appointment to meet Cissie Cole? I believe you admit meeting her."

"Yes—I met her. We'd fixed it up."

"You picked her up on your motor-bicycle as she came away from Tanfield Court."

"That's right."

"But she went there quite unexpectedly, did she not?"

"We'd fixed to meet round about nine o'clock. She was there all right. I didn't know where she'd been."

"You see this coat? Was she wearing it when she met you?"

A pause. Then he said,

"She put it on."

"Did she tell you that it had just been given to her by Mrs Jerningham?"

"Yes."

"Did she express pleasure at the gift?"

Another pause, and a longer one.

"I didn't take that much notice."

"Did she seem in good spirits?"

He repeated what he had just said, doggedly.

"I didn't take that much notice."

Miss Silver thought, "He's uncouth, but he's got a brain. He knows he's in danger. He avoided that cleverly." She missed the Coroner's next question, but not Pell's answer.

"I tell you I'd something else to think about than coats and such."

"Do you mean that you were going to have an important interview with Cissie Cole?"

"I don't know about that."

Yes, he was clever. She looked at the sallow, unshaven cheek and saw how tense was the line of the jaw.

"Will you tell us what happened after you picked Cissie up."

"We went up on Tane Head like that kid said."

"Why did you choose Tane Head?"

The man was waking up. His speech had cleared. He lifted his head.

"I wanted a place where we could talk."

"You had something special to say to her?"

A pause.

"It had got so we had to talk. She was willing."

"Will you tell us what passed between you."

He put up a hand and pushed the hair out of his eyes, then back to gripping the chair again.

"We talked. I asked her would she come away with me and I'd get a job somewhere where nobody 'ud know we weren't man and wife. And she said no."

"Did you quarrel about it?"

"Not to say quarrel."

"You have heard Mr Jerningham's evidence. He says you came rushing down the track alone at about twenty minutes to ten. Is that correct?"

"Something like that."

"You were in an agitated state?"

He swallowed.

"I was upset."

"Will you tell us why?"

"She'd said no—that's why. Wasn't it enough?"

"According to the evidence given by Mary Crisp and Mr Jerningham you had been up on the headland with Cissie Cole for about twenty minutes when you took your motor-bicycle and rode away."

"Something like that."

"And you spent that time trying to persuade her to go away with you?"

"That's right."

"And she continued to say no?"

"Yes."

"What made you break off in the end and leave her there if it wasn't a quarrel? Do you say that there was no quarrel?"

Pell said in a choked voice,

"She wouldn't listen. I'd said all I could."

Miss Silver's eye travelled from him to the Jerninghams. Mr Dale Jerningham was sitting forward watching his ex-mechanic with a full, deep look of concern. Mr Rafe Jerningham was looking out of the open window which framed only a rectangle of empty, cloudless blue. His lifted face seemed to have sharpened. The features had it their own way. There was no expression there. Mrs Dale Jerningham looked down at the hands which were folded in her lap. Lady Steyne looked at the jury. Miss Silver looked at them too—farmers; a retired coast-guard; a couple of small tradesmen; the landlord of the Green Man. They sat there with their country faces blank and tanned, and their minds in all probability already made up. No one could have told what they were thinking about. There was not a face there but could keep its own counsel.

"If it lay with them to hang him, he'd be dead." The thought presented itself to Miss Silver's mind without any credentials whatever, and was immediately accepted.

She went back to Pell. The Coroner was asking,

"Where was Cissie Cole when you left her?"

"Up on the cliff." The chair back groaned with the strain he put upon it.

"You are on oath. Do you say that she was alive when you left her?"

"Acourse she was!" said Pell in a sudden big voice that filled the hall.

"You did not throw her over the cliff?"

"Why should I?"

"No one knows that but yourself. Did you?"

"No, I didn't."

"Or see her throw herself over?"

"She hadn't any call to throw herself over. I never touched her."

"What was she doing when you left?"

Pell's voice dropped again.

"She was sitting on the grass. She'd her handkerchief out, crying into it. I spoke angry to her and made her cry. But I never touched her."

"How near to the edge of the cliff was she?"

"Twenty to twenty-five foot."

"Do you think she could have fallen by accident?"

"I don't know—seems she must ha'd done. How do I know what she did after I come away?"

"Did she say anything to you about taking her own life?"

"No."

"And you swear that she was alive when you came away?"

"She was alive," said Pell.

He went back to his seat, walking heavily with creaking boots. When he had slumped down again his left hand went back to its old position gripping the bench.

The Coroner recalled Dale Jerningham.

"Just a moment, Mr Jerningham. How long had you been on the headland before you saw Pell running down the track?"

"Only a very few minutes."

"Did you hear any cry?"

"No, sir."

"How far were you from that part of the cliff beneath which the body was found?"

"I should think a quarter of a mile."

"Would you expect to hear a scream at that distance?"

He hesitated, and then said, "We could hear the sea-gulls."

"Do you think it is possible that you heard a scream and thought it was the cry of a gull?"

"I don't think so. A gull's cry is different."

"Thank you, Mr Jerningham . . . Lady Steyne—"

He asked her the same questions and received the same answers.

That was all the evidence. Mr Rafe Jerningham was not called.

Miss Silver settled herself in her chair and listened attentively to the Coroner's summing up. Very clear, very fair, very simple. The medical evidence established the fact that the deceased had met with her death by falling from one of the cliffs of Tane Head. The question before them was how that fall had come about, whether by accident, suicide, or murder. There was no evidence as to any intention to commit suicide. There was evidence of unhappiness. Unhappy people did sometimes give way to an impulse to do away with themselves. This possibility could not be excluded. There was no evidence on the score of accident, but this possibility also could not be excluded.

"You have heard Alfred Pell's evidence. If you think that he is speaking the truth and that he left Cissie Cole on the headland alive, you should, I think, bring in a verdict of death by misadventure—there being no evidence to enable you to decide as between suicide and accident."

He dealt with Pell's evidence carefully. Warned them against bias. Directed them as to the law.

The jury retired, remained absent for no more than ten minutes, and returned with a verdict of wilful murder against Alfred Pell.

THIRTY

In the gangway which had been left down the middle of the hall Miss Silver contrived to find herself beside Mrs Dale Jerningham. With her small habitual cough she attracted her attention.

"How do you do, Mrs Jerningham?"

Tall, slender, Lisle looked down at her. There was to the sharp watching eye instant recognition, something that might have been relief, and then quite unmistakably dismay.

"Miss Silver!"

Miss Silver beamed.

"How nice of you to remember me. I am taking a little holiday in Ledlington. Such a relief to get out of London in this heat—really most oppressive, though of course beautiful weather and so good for the harvest. Perhaps you will come over and have a cup of tea with me one day. I was recommended to a very nice boarding-house—Miss Mellison,

Snaith Street—recommended by a friend and really most comfortable."

"I am afraid—"

"Oh, I wouldn't be," said Miss Silver surprisingly.

"Miss Silver—"

Miss Silver smiled and nodded.

"Miss Mellison, 14 Snaith Street, and the telephone number is Ledlington 141. I do hope you will come," she said, and fell back behind Mary and Mrs Ernest Crisp.

As they came out into the hot sunshine, Dale said, "Who was that you were speaking to? I don't know her."

Lisle looked up with a tinge of colour in her cheeks.

"Nor do I really, I just met her in a train. She's staying in Ledlington on a holiday."

Dale was frowning.

"Funny idea of a holiday to come and gape at that poor devil Pell. I don't know what women are made of. Who is she? What's her name? Looks like a governess."

Lisle said, "Yes, she does. Her name's Silver—Miss Silver."

He said nothing at all, and all at once she was nervous. How could he know the name? He didn't know the name. If he didn't say anything, it was because there was nothing to interest him, nothing to say.

Alicia came over to her, slipped a hand inside her arm, and walked along beside her, talking in a low, confidential voice. It was only the voice that was confidential—there was nothing in what she said. A little hot flame of anger burned up in Lisle. The glow of it reached her cheeks. The village was being provided with a demonstration of sisterly affection, and Lisle rebelled. She had said that she would help Dale, but she had not known that it would be so hard. What she wanted to do was to pull her arm away and walk on. She could walk a good deal faster than Alicia if she tried.

Dale's hand touched her on the other side. It was a touch which became a hard, compelling grip. It was no good thinking of what she would like to do. She knew what she had to do. She bent her head and gave a due response to Alicia's talk.

They had only gone a little way, when Mrs Mallam caught them up. She had hurried to do so, and for once in a way her pasty cheeks were flushed. She wore a tightly fitting white dress, a short black and white striped coat, and a solid-looking black bandeau round her thick golden hair. She panted a little as she said,

"I thought I was going to miss you. *Aren't* you in a hurry!"

"Well, we are rather." Alicia Steyne did not trouble to make her voice polite.

Mrs Mallam was not at all easily snubbed.

"My dear, you can't have an inquest and turn me away from your very door. I don't think I've ever been so thirsty in all my life. The atmosphere in there! I really thought I was going to faint."

Dale turned to her with a sudden charming smile.

"We're walking, but I take it you've got your car. Be an angel and go along up to the house. Ring till someone comes and say we all want drinks—with lots of ice. It will be a noble act."

Mrs Mallam beamed.

"Can't I take someone with me? Your wife—she looks all in."

Before Dale could answer Lisle had said, "Oh, thank you." To be saved that hot walk in the sun with Alicia's arm through hers and Dale shepherding them—Real gratitude flooded her heart. And no one could think it strange or say anything. She felt delivered as she leaned back in Aimée Mallam's little car. The air flowed past her, cool and reviving.

Aimée drove slowly. She said in a sympathetic voice,

"Are you all right? It was frightfully hot, wasn't it?"

"Yes, quite all right."

"Horrid business. Nasty for you its being your coat and all. Must have given you a kind of feeling that it might have been you."

Lisle said nothing. There didn't seem to be anything to say.

They reached the house, and when the drinks had been ordered Mrs Mallam asked to be taken upstairs. As she powdered and lipsticked she returned to the charge.

"Do you think that man did it?"

"It looks like it," said Lisle in a weary voice.

"I suppose it does. But do you know, I thought he was fond of her. Of course that mightn't stop him killing her if he was jealous or thought she was going to walk out on him. But I couldn't help thinking suppose he'd come up behind her and just seen the coat and thought it was you, and thought he'd score off Dale by pushing you over—"

Lisle's voice cut in clear and steady.

"Please, Mrs Mallam—that's nonsense. You can't have listened to the evidence. He took Cissie up there with him. He was talking to her after they got there. He couldn't possibly have mistaken her for anyone else."

Aimée Mallam drew a bold cherry-coloured curve with her lipstick. It gave her mouth a queer tilt at the corners—thin, tilted lips, too bright for the pale, plump face.

"Perhaps not—but someone else could. I wonder if anyone did."

Lisle said, *"Please—"*

"Your height, wasn't she, and about your figure? Fair-haired too. When I saw the photograph in the paper I made up my mind to come to the inquest. You see, I couldn't help wondering—"

"There's nothing to wonder about."

Aimée Mallam laughed without amusement.

"Well, I wonder all the same," she said. "I couldn't help thinking about poor Lydia—Dale's first wife, you know. I was only just round a bend of the path when she fell, and I heard her scream. I've never forgotten it. They said she was picking flowers. Anyhow she fell and she was killed. It was only your coat that fell and another woman who was killed, but don't you think there's something odd about it all?" She slipped the lipstick back into her bag and turned round from the glass. "Look here, I'll tell you about Lydia. That place where she fell—it wasn't a dangerous place. She wasn't climbing or anything like that. There was quite a good wide path along the cliff, curving in and out—you know how those paths do. Well, my husband and I were behind. The others had gone on out of sight, and we heard that awful scream. I ran and got round the corner, and there nearest to me, was Dale looking down over the cliff. And a little way on where the path took another bend—there was Rafe, looking over too. And between them was the place where Lydia had gone over. There was a bush, and it was broken. Alicia and Rowland Steyne had been up the hill—there was quite an easy slope above the path. He was a long way up, she was having hysterics on the inner side of the path. They hadn't seen anything, only heard the scream. Rafe said he was round the next curve and came running back. Dale said Lydia was picking flowers along the edge, and she told him to go back and see what my husband and I were doing. He said he had just got to the corner when he heard her scream. He didn't see her fall. He said he was out of sight of the place where he left her. He might have been, you know—the path twisted all the time. *So nobody saw her fall.* Nobody saw this girl fall either, did they? Except the person who pushed he—if somebody did push her."

Lisle stood and looked at her. She had the feeling that her eyes were fixed. She couldn't look away. She said in a stiff, unnatural voice,

"Why are you telling me all this?"

"I wonder," said Aimée Mallam. "And if I were you I should do some wondering too. And there's something else I'd do, and I wouldn't wait about, thinking it over either."

"What do you mean?"

Mrs Mallam gathered up her bag and walked over to the door. With her hand on it—a bare, plump hand with too many rings—she turned.

"I should go back to America."

THIRTY-ONE

Miss Silver had tea in the parlour of the Green Man before walking up Crook Hill to catch the bus into Ledlington. Both before and after the inquest she managed to talk to a good many different people. People will always talk about an accident or a murder. In this case there was but one opinion, voiced with varying degrees of heat and animus. Cissie Cole was a good girl. Not one of your go-ahead ones, but a *good* girl. You couldn't blame her being fond of that Pell when she thought he was a single man. What she had seen in him the dear knows, but once she knew he was married and it come to anything more she wouldn't have it, and he pushed her over out of spite. A dozen times Miss Silver had occasion to say, "Dear me—how very shocking!" or "Really one can hardly believe it." The latter phrase she had always found extremely useful in provoking a flood of corroborative detail.

She used it to Mrs Mottle, the landlady of the Green Man, when she brought in the brown teapot with the bright blue band round it and a plate of rock cakes. The milk-jug and sugar-basin already stood on the parlour table, which was of figured walnut with a single massive leg. The top, much valued, was protected by a number of thick mats crocheted in shades of olive green and salmon pink. An old metal tray with gilt scrolls and a pattern of painted red and blue flowers rested upon two of these mats, whilst a fern in a rose-pink pot had another all to itself in the middle of the table.

Mrs Mottle set down the teapot beside the milk-jug and sugar-basin on the tray, pulled up yet another mat for the rock cakes, and heaved a responsive sigh. She was a buxom woman, short and stout, with a quantity of frizzy black hair only just beginning to be touched with grey, and cheeks as firm and red as Worcester Pearmains.

"Ah—you may well say so!" she said. "And I'm not one that thinks badly of men, because take them all round, well, there's good in them same as there is in most of us. But what I do say and always have said is that some of 'em'll do anything, and you can't get from it."

Miss Silver gave a timid cough.

"Dear me—I suppose so. And of course you must have such opportunities for observing them. Human nature must be quite an open book to you."

"Well you may say so!" said Mrs Mottle. "Men talk free and easy over their beer. Not as I wouldn't soon put a stop to language or anything of that sort, and my husband too—there's nothing of that sort goes on in our house. But human nature, that's another thing—there it is and you can't help noticing it. That Pell now, he'd come in most nights, and how he'd the face after it come out about him being married passes me. But there—some have got face enough for anything, and he'd come in here as bold as brass, and so soon as he'd got into his second glass he'd begin to let himself go and—talk of not believing things—you wouldn't credit what he'd say."

"Really? How very interesting. What sort of things?"

"All sorts," said Mrs Mottle with gusto. "And just as well for him they weren't brought up at the inquest."

"Dear me!"

"Saying what he'd do to anyone that crossed him. Why, I heard him with my own ears—nobody ever came to any good once they got across him. That was after Mr Jerningham give him the sack, and it wasn't only a fortnight later that Mrs Jerningham was as near killed as makes no difference with the steering of her car broke through. And not saying he done it, but there's more than one has their own thoughts about it. And he could have done it easy if he had a mind, and it was only the night before he set down his glass hard enough to crack it and said how he always got his own back on those who got across him. And I told him straight, 'That's not the kind of talk I'll put up with, not while I'm behind the bar.' And he laughed and said, 'You wait and see!' and went out, and a good riddance."

Miss Silver began to pour herself out a cup of tea.

"What a good-looking family the Jerninghams are," she observed. "I was quite struck by it at the inquest. Lady Steyne—really very pretty. She is a cousin, is she not? And Mr and Mrs

Jerningham—such a very good-looking couple. And the other cousin, Mr Rafe Jerningham—"

She heard nothing but good of the Jerninghams from Mrs Mottle. Mr Jerningham had a very feeling heart. There weren't many gentlemen would go with their wives same as he did to see poor Miss Cole, and kindness itself, as she told me with her very own lips. And a pleasure to see him married to such a sweet young lady. "Lost his first wife in an accident in Switzerland a matter of ten years ago, and took him all this time to get over it and put his mind on someone else. Not like some people I could name, and him such a good-looking gentleman and all."

Miss Silver put milk and sugar into her tea.

"Did you know the first Mrs Jerningham?"

Mrs Mottle had got as far as the door. She leaned a firm shoulder against the jamb and shook her head.

"Not to say know—there wasn't many that did. She used to come visiting here when she was Miss Lydia Burrows. That was in old Mr Jerningham's time, but she and Mr Dale went off travelling after they were married. A bit of an invalid she was, and not supposed to stay in England for the winter—and after all she might just as well have stayed as fall down one of those nasty precipices and get herself killed!"

Miss Silver sipped from a cup with a pattern of pink and gold roses, the pink very bright, the gold very shiny.

"How extremely shocking!" she said.

"Picking flowers or some such," said Mrs Mottle vaguely. "And then old Mr Jerningham died and Mr Dale come in for the property. And of course we all thought he'd marry again, so

young as he was and all, but no—seemed as if he hadn't got a
thought for anything except the place. Up early and down late,
and building cottages here and putting on a new roof there.
He come in for a lot of money from his wife, and seemed all
he wanted to do was to spend it on the place—left the girls to
Mr Rafe."

Miss Silver sipped again.

"The good-looking cousin. Yes, indeed—I can imagine that
he would be popular with the ladies."

Mrs Mottle's firm red cheeks wobbled as she laughed.

"All over him like bees in a lime tree," she said. "And what's
a young gentleman to do? He can't afford to get married, and
there isn't a girl anywhere around that'll leave him alone. His
works, you know, up at the aircraft place—clever as they come,
Mr Rafe is. But Saturday afternoons and Sundays it's tennis
games and golf games, and bathing parties and boating parties
and picnic parties. Not that there's any harm in it, and as to
anyone saying there's any harm in Mr Rafe, well, they won't
say it a second time, not to me anyhow! You're only young the
once, and why shouldn't you have a good time—that's what I
say!"

"And Mr Rafe has a good time?"

Mrs Mottle laughed again—a full, jolly laugh.

"It's not his fault if he don't, nor the girls' neither."

THIRTY-TWO

About nine o'clock that same evening Inspector March was enjoying a tête-á-tête with Miss Silver in the small back sitting-room which Miss Mellison had placed at their disposal. It was a very small room, and for its size it contained a surprising variety of objects. Besides the gentleman's armchair in old-gold stamped velvet in which the Inspector reclined, and the lady's ditto upon which Miss Silver sat primly upright, there were two occasional chairs with shiny backs and pseudo-brocade seats finished off with an incredible number of brass-headed nails; a gimcrack table which supported a palm in a bright blue pot; a bamboo plant-stand on the top of which another palm was precariously balanced; two footstools, one crimson and one blue, of the kind found in old-fashioned church pews; a model of the Taj Mahal under glass; two clocks, both wrong; a pair of vases in Mooltan enamel; a row of brown wooden bears from Berne, and a motley collection of pictures. If Miss

Silver lifted her eyes she beheld photographic enlargements of Miss Mellison's parents, he very stout and jolly, she very pinched and fretful, while the Inspector had an excellent view of four faded water-colours and an engraving which depicted the opening of the Great Exhibition of 1851 by Queen Victoria. Blue plush curtains had been pulled back as far as they would go. An inner pair, of Madras muslin, moved gently in the breeze from the open window which was really a door opening upon a small garden gay with hollyhock, phlox, snapdragon, and nasturtium.

Randal March contemplated his hostess with just the hint of a smile and said,

"Well, here we are. May I ask how you are accounting for yourself—and for me?"

Miss Silver was engaged upon the sleeve of her niece Ethel's jumper. She took four needles to a sleeve. They clicked and twinkled in her plump, capable hands as she replied,

"My dear Randal, I am surprised at you. What is there to account for? I used to be your governess. I am taking a little holiday in Ledlington, and what is more natural than that my old pupil, with whose family I have always remained upon the most affectionate terms, should drop in for a friendly chat? Miss Mellison was most interested and most kind. She at once offered me the use of this pleasant little room. I showed her your dear mother's photograph and the group with you and Margaret and Isabel. We agreed that you had really changed very little."

Randal March put his head back and laughed.

"Marvellous!" he said. "What did you get in return—besides the use of the room?"

"She told me all about herself," said Miss Silver. "And you should not laugh, because she is a very brave little woman. Her father was Quarter Master in the Ledshire Regiment, and they were a good deal in India. Her mother lost six children there. Miss Mellison is the sole survivor. Really very sad. And very little capital, I am afraid, but she runs this place extremely well, and I hope will make a success of it. A great-aunt left her the furniture, and she is most hard working." The needles clicked briskly.

"What has brought you down here?" said Randal March. "You might as well tell me and have done with it."

"My dear Randal, I suppose I can take a holiday."

"You've just had one. You came down here to go to that inquest, and I'd like to know why. On the surface, as reported in the press, there wasn't a single point of interest—just a common, sordid village tragedy with nothing, absolutely nothing, to lift it out of the ruck."

"On the surface—" Miss Silver repeated the words in a mild, ambiguous voice.

"*And* as reported by the press. What I want to know is what other source of information you have. It certainly wasn't the press accounts that brought you stampeding down here."

Miss Silver dropped her hands upon the bright blue wool of the jumper in her lap.

"My dear Randal—what a word to employ!"

She got a schoolboy grin.

"Well, you did. Come along—out with it! I saw you go up and speak to Mrs Jerningham. What's behind all this? What do you know?"

Miss Silver resumed her knitting.

"Very little," she said.

"But something. What is it? Is Mrs Jerningham a client of yours?"

The needles clicked.

"That is what I am not sure about."

"That sounds very intriguing."

"She made an appointment with me on Thursday afternoon and rang up to cancel it on Friday morning."

"Thursday afternoon . . . That was after the girl's body had been found . . . Did she mention her?"

"She did not mention anything of a specific nature. She asked if she could come and see me. She said something had happened. She said 'I must talk to someone—I can't go on—I don't know what to do.' She appeared very much agitated."

"There mightn't be much in that. She's a sensitive creature—she knew the girl rather well. It was naturally rather upsetting, especially as Pell had been her husband's employee. But what I want to know is, how did she come to ring you up at all. Where did you come across her?"

"In the train," said Miss Silver, knitting placidly—"on my way back from visiting Ethel. I have given the matter a great deal of thought, and I do not feel that I can take the responsibility of keeping it to myself. There may be nothing in it at all, or—" She paused.

"Well?"

"I think I will tell you just what happened. Mrs Jerningham got into my carriage in an almost fainting condition. I could see at once that she had received some very severe shock.

I could also see that she had come away in a great hurry. I entered into conversation with her, and when I made this remark she said like an echo, 'I came away in a hurry.' When I asked her why, she said, still speaking in this strange way, 'They said he was trying to kill me,' and when I asked her who, she said, 'My husband.'"

Randal March came up out of his lounging attitude with a jerk.

"*What!*"

"That is what she said. Naturally I did not ignore the possibility that she might be suffering from mental illness, but I have some experience and I did not think that this was the case. I encouraged her to go on talking. I thought it would be a relief to her. By piecing together what she told me a little bit at a time I gathered that she had overheard two women talking about her and her husband. I think she was on a weekend visit. She heard these women talking on the other side of a hedge. They were discussing the death of Mr Jerningham's first wife ten years before in Switzerland. She was an heiress and he came in for the money. These people said it saved him from having to sell Tanfield—they said it was a lucky accident for Mr Jerningham. And then they said something about this girl's money—she has a great deal—and one of them said, 'Is she going to have an accident too?' It was a horrible thing for poor young Mrs Jerningham to hear, because, you see, she had narrowly escaped drowning only a very short time before. She told me about it. It must have been just after she had made a will leaving everything to her husband."

"She told you that?"

"Yes, she told me that."

"How was she nearly drowned? What happened?"

"They were bathing—she, and her husband, and Lady Steyne, and Mr Rafe. She says they were laughing and splashing one another when she called to them. She is not a good swimmer and she was finding it hard to get in."

"It might happen very easily."

"It did happen. I don't know who saved her, but it was not her husband. I said to her, 'Well, you were not drowned. Who saved you?' and she answered 'Not Dale.'"

March knit his brows.

"Oh, she did, did she? Well, that's quite an intriguing story. Is there any more?"

"No. We parted on the platform. I gave her one of my cards, and, as I told you, she rang me up on Thursday afternoon. The train journey was on the previous Saturday morning."

"How did you know who she was? Did she tell you?"

"Oh, no. She would hardly have talked so freely if she had suspected that I knew who she was."

"And did you know who she was?"

"Oh, immediately. There was a photograph of her—really a very good photograph—in the magazine which Ethel had very kindly given me to read on the journey. There was one of those ill-mannered gossipy paragraphs as well. It gave me quite a lot of information. Mr Dale Jerningham owned Tanfield Court. He had been married twice, and both his wives had money. It even gave their names. The whole thing was in quite incredibly bad taste."

March said, "I see—" Then, after a pause, "The first wife made a will in his favour and had a climbing accident—the second wife makes a will in his favour and is nearly drowned. Suggestive of course, but—"

Miss Silver said, "Exactly."

"I could bear to know more about the drowning accident."

She nodded gravely.

"It was not the only one, Randal."

"What do you mean?"

"Mrs Mottle, the landlady of the Green Man where I had tea, informs me that Mrs Jerningham had narrowly escaped being killed, I think she said on Tuesday, when the steering of her car broke clean through—I use her own expression— on the hill above the village. I gathered that this is by common consent attributed to a piece of spite on the part of this man Pell, who may have considered that Mrs Jerningham had something to do with his dismissal. He had been heard to utter threats about getting even with those who thwarted him, and it would, I imagine, have been quite simple for him to obtain access to the car and tamper with the steering." She looked up with a faint, prim smile. "You see, Randal, it is not easy."

"Easy! I should say not! And such a nice straightforward case as it looked. Everything points to Pell. Cissie Cole's murder falls into one of the common classes—it all looks as easy as shelling peas. And then you turn up with one red herring— you don't mind a few mixed metaphors, do you?—and I rather think I've got another by the tail."

Miss Silver's needles clicked briskly.

"I think it very probable that the red herrings will have a sufficiently strong flavour to spoil your peas," she observed.

He laughed a little ruefully.

"They've done it already. Look here, I was in two minds whether to tell you or not, but I'm going to—and I won't insult you by telling you that what I'm going to say is strictly confidential and hush-hush."

"That sounds very interesting."

He sat forward and dropped his voice.

"Well, I suppose it is. A little too much if you ask me. The question is, do you really know everything? I used to think you did when I was about eight, and I am beginning to have a horrid suspicion that I was right."

"An exaggerated way of speaking, Randal."

He gave her rather a charming smile.

"Not altogether. But I will come to the point, which is this. Does your omniscience extend to the Hudson processes?"

"I dislike exaggeration," said Miss Silver mildly. "I certainly do not pretend to omniscience. I have a naturally retentive memory and I have cultivated it. I presume that your allusion is to the Professor Hudson who gave evidence in the Hauptmann trial. He had invented an iodine gas process which brought to light fingerprints which under the ordinary method remain invisible. I believe the jury rejected his evidence. Juries are extremely suspicious of scientific evidence—they do not understand it, and therefore they do not like it. But I do not see how the iodine gas process could be applicable to the present case. I believe, however, that Professor Hudson has also made some interesting experiments relating to fingerprints on cloth. If I am not mistaken, there is a process that can be applied to woollen materials. Perhaps that is what you have in mind."

March laughed aloud.

"I was certainly right—you do know everything!"

Miss Silver smiled.

"Silver nitrate is used, if I remember rightly. It changes the salt in the fingerprint to silver chloride. The cloth is soaked in a solution, wrung out, and exposed to the action of sunlight, which turns the silver chloride black, and I believe some quite interesting results have been obtained." She lifted her eyes suddenly to his face. "Am I to understand that you are thinking of having that poor girl's coat submitted to this test, or that you have already done so?"

"I have already done so," said March.

"With what result?"

He got up, pushing back his chair to the imminent danger of the bamboo plant-stand. It creaked, and the palm rocked perilously in its bright blue pot.

"Maddening!" he exclaimed. "Damnably interesting, and completely maddening!"

Miss Silver said, "Dear me!"

THIRTY-THREE

Look here," cried March—"when I went up to Tanfield Court to get their statements I had this business of the coat in my mind—the tests were in fact already being made—so before I came away I got all their handprints. Not that the faintest suspicion attached to anyone except Pell at that time, but the coat having so recently passed out of Mrs Jerningham's possession, the probability of finding her own prints and those of her family were strong, and to be certain of Pell's it would be necessary to identify these others. That was what was in my mind—nothing else. I got the prints and I came away. The whole thing, you must understand, was just an experiment. I didn't in fact—I couldn't in fact—expect it to have any value as evidence, because even if Pell's prints were all over the coat it wouldn't prove that he had done the girl in. He was her lover if he wasn't her murderer. The prints might just as well be there because they had been embracing. In fact I was prepared to play with Hudson's process but not to take it into court, where, as you say, any jury would treat it with contempt, I really expected nothing—nothing."

"And what did you get?" enquired Miss Silver with interest.

"More than I'd bargained for. Look here—here are the prints of the Jerningham family." He picked up a small case, opened it, and took out a sheaf of papers. "We needn't bother about the women. Mrs Jerningham's prints and Cissie's own were on the front of the coat. But it's the back that's interesting. Here is Dale Jerningham's hand from the print I took at Tanfield—here is his cousin Rafe's—and here is Pell's. Well, I can't show you the coat, so you'll just have to take my word for the prints on it. Pell's prints are all over the place. One very clear indeed, right across the shoulder seam up by the collar. He might have had his arm round her neck, or he might have caught her there to push her over the edge."

"Very shocking indeed," said Miss Silver.

"Then, right in the middle of the back between the shoulders, Dale Jerningham's hand—at least I think it's Dale Jerningham's hand. It's not a good print, because it's all messed up with Pell's prints. *But*—though there's no certainty of this—all the three people who have seen them incline to the belief that the Jerningham print is superimposed upon the Pell prints."

"There is no certainty of that?"

He shook his head.

"There is no certainty of anything. It is all very confused, and, as you were about to observe, nothing in the world could be more natural than to find a print of Dale Jerningham's hand on his wife's coat."

Miss Silver said without looking up.

"It is a most shocking idea, but if Mr Dale Jerningham mistook this young woman who was wearing his wife's coat for Mrs Jerningham and pushed her over the cliff, that is in fact where you would naturally expect to find an impression of his hand."

March flung down the papers he was holding and turned from the gimcrack table which supported his attaché case.

"And what do you suppose I should look like if I produced that theory on this evidence—a new-fangled American process which not one person in a million has ever heard about, and the confused and doubtful prints of a man's hand on a coat which only passed out of his wife's possession an hour before the murder took place!"

Miss Silver continued to knit.

"When did Mrs Jerningham last wear the coat?"

"I asked her that—rang up before the inquest. I didn't want the question raised there if I could help it."

"And when did she wear it?"

"Sunday evening," said March.

"Sunday to Wednesday—would a print last all that time?"

"If there were nothing to disturb it—and there wasn't. She put the coat in a cupboard, and Cissie Cole went away with it over her arm folded inside out. Also you've got to consider that the weather has been particularly favourable for making a good print. Everybody's hand would be on the moist side."

"What are you going to do?" said Miss Silver in an interested voice.

He threw himself into his chair again.

"I don't know. Consider my position for a moment. I've just come here with a bit of a feather in my cap for which a good many thanks are due to you. Old Black, the Superintendent here, is away sick. I'm told he won't come back, and I've been given to understand that I'm likely to step into his shoes. I'm a reasonably ambitious man and I've got my foot on the ladder. Well, what happens if I lead off with a set of more or less unsubstantiated accusations and suggestions against one of the leading families in the county? There isn't a jury in the world that would consider that handprint as evidence against Dale Jerningham. There isn't a jury in the world that wouldn't hang Pell on what we've got against him—motive, opportunity, subsequent guilty behaviour—he bolted right away—threats uttered in the presence of witnesses. What have I got to put up against all that—and whistle my prospects down the wind to do it?"

Miss Silver put down her knitting and rested her hands upon it. Her small greyish eyes regarded him in an acutely intelligent manner. From what he had said she plucked one word.

"Family," she said—"you spoke of something against the family. Did you use the expression as a synonym for Mr Dale Jerningham, or in a wider sense?"

He stared at her.

"How did you get at that?"

"It was not at all difficult to see that you were keeping something back. I really think it would be better if you were to tell me everything."

He put up a protesting hand.

"Oh, I was going to, I was going to. But you don't give one time. I just wanted to dispose of Dale Jerningham before we went on to the others. When I spoke of the family I meant the family. Dale and Lady Steyne were together all the evening. If he pushed the girl over that cliff, she *must* know something about it. If she didn't see him do it, she must have the very strongest suspicion. I gather that they are on flirting terms— she was at some pains to make me think so. I wondered why at the time, and it has occurred to me since that she wanted to impress me with the fact that they were too much taken up with each other to notice a little thing like a murder, even if it was happening within a few hundred yards of them. And then there's Rafe Jerningham—"

"The good-looking cousin—yes?"

"I didn't want him called at the inquest, because on the face of it he had nothing to say. His own account for his movements on Wednesday evening is that he talked for a short time to Mrs Jerningham after she had seen Cissie and then he went out for a walk along the beach. He admits that he walked in the direction of Tane Head, but says he turned back half way because the light was failing and the going bad. He did not enter the house until a very late hour—he could not say how late. He accounts for the intervening time by saying that he was down by the sea wall. This is in the grounds of Tanfield Court and affords a fine view-point. He says he was looking at the sea. Sounds a bit queer, doesn't it?"

"People do look at the sea," said Miss Silver in a mild voice.

"Yes—but listen." He leaned forward. "I've been over the ground. There are steps which lead from the sea wall to the beach. It's two miles from there to the place where Cissie was found, and with the sort of going you get there it takes three-quarters of an hour to walk it. Rafe Jerningham put it at that, and that's what it took me. *But*—and this is what he did not tell me—a quarter of a mile from the steps there's a rough track from the beach to what they call the cliff path, and that's a very different affair. It runs right along the edge of the cliffs to the headland, and though it's no shorter than the beach way it's a path with a good hard surface, and an active young fellow could run the distance in about half the time—and if Rafe Jerningham did that, he could have reached the spot from which Cissie fell in time to have pushed her over."

"And why should he have pushed her over, my dear Randal?"

"I don't know. That's one of the maddening things about this case. Threats, motive, opportunity—everything right for Pell. And then you produce Dale as one red herring, and I produce Rafe as another. There's your story—and the evidence of Mrs Jerningham's coat. And whether it's evidence for a jury or not, it's evidence for me, and it's evidence I can't get away from."

"Did you find Rafe Jerningham's prints on the coat?" said Miss Silver.

"Two of them," said March—"and the clearest of the whole blessed lot. And where, I ask you—where?"

"My dear Randal, it is no use asking me."

He gave a short angry laugh.

"Then there really is something you don't know! Well, I'll tell you. On the right shoulder just below the top of the arm a complete print of Rafe Jerningham's right hand, the palm towards the shoulder blade and the fingers coming right round on to the sleeve. On the left side an equally clear impression of his left hand in an exactly similar position. If that doesn't mean that he stood behind her and took her by the shoulders, what does it mean? And if he did that, for what other purpose did he do it than to push her over the cliff?"

Miss Silver sat with her hands folded upon her knitting.

"That," she said, "is very interesting. But have you any idea of why he should want to push her over a cliff?"

The colour came up into March's face, showing plainly under the fair skin.

"Oh, I've got ideas. What I haven't got is evidence. Something may turn up, or it may not. He may have had half a dozen reasons, but the one I fancy is the same as in his cousin's case. Just look at the thing as a whole for a moment. Don't divide the Jerninghams up. Take them as a solid block—as a family. Every enquiry I've made points to their very strong attachment to this property which has belonged to them for hundreds of years. Dale is said to have spent his first wife's money lavishly on improvements. He runs the estate himself, and works hard at it. Rafe contents himself with a modestly paid job at the local aircraft establishment because it keeps him at home. He refused a very much better post in Australia a couple of months ago. Lady Steyne, who had been married ten years, comes back here as soon as she is a widow. Her husband had a place and he left it to her, and a considerable fortune as well, but she comes back here. They stick to each other, these Jerninghams, and they stick to Tanfield. And Tanfield is slipping away from them. As soon as I had those prints I went over to see the old Superintendent at his home. He's got a dicky leg but he can talk all right. He's a Ledstock man and he knows about everyone in the district. He says the Jerninghams have always been like that. 'Close woven yarn' was his expression— touch one of them and you touch the lot. And this is what he told me. They're on the rocks. The first Mrs Jerningham was an heiress, and the money all came to Dale. Most of what he didn't spend on the property petered out in the depression, and there isn't much left. These people talk very freely of their affairs, you know, and Mrs Black had a cousin's daughter in service up at Tanfield Court. Well, the sale of some land for the aircraft establishment and aerodrome tided them over for a bit, and six months ago Dale married again—another heiress. But the talk is that the money is tied up, and that Dale will have to sell. There's a man called Tatham after it—soap-boiler or something of that sort. You say that Mrs Jerningham told you she had just made a will in her husband's favour. Considering the Jerninghams as a family block who will stand or fall together, would Rafe Jerningham have no motive for pushing his cousin's wife over the cliff if he knew about that will? And do you suppose for a moment that he didn't know about it? Add to this that he is Dale's heir, and that Dale has another passion besides Tanfield—flying. I am told he is as keen as mustard and extremely reckless. Tanfield might need an heir at any time. Don't you think that Rafe Jerningham has a pretty strong motive? People have done murder for a good deal less than that."

"There is a motive," said Miss Silver. "But it would only influence a very unprincipled character. And I must confess, my dear Randal, that I think you are straining the probabilities when you contend that, granting a motive, Mr Rafe had the opportunity of committing this murder. You say he talked with Mrs Jerningham after she had seen Cissie Cole, and then went for a walk along the beach. According to your theory he got on to the cliff path and hurried to the headland, where, seeing Cissie Cole in Mrs Jerningham's coat, he took her in the failing light for his cousin's wife and pushed her over the cliff. But why did he go to Tane Head at all, and why, having hurried there, should he think it possible that the person whom he saw could be Mrs Jerningham whom he had just left at Tanfield Court?"

March ran his hand through his hair.

"I can't tell you why he went there, because I don't know. He may have been restless. He may, like Lady Steyne, have wanted to see the sunset, and he may have hurried because the light was failing. But it would have been perfectly possible for Mrs Jerningham whom he left at Tanfield to have reached Tane Head before him. Her own car was out of action, but her husband's car was there, and so was Rafe's. She also might have wanted to watch the sunset. But he wouldn't think of all that. He'd see a familiar figure with its back to him outlined against the sunset. Cissie Cole was a tall, thin girl with fair hair. A back view of her in Mrs Jerningham's own coat might have deceived anyone. I believe it deceived Rafe Jerningham. I believe he came up behind her, took her by the shoulders, and threw her over the cliff, and came back as he went without anyone seeing him. There wasn't anyone to see him except his cousins, Dale and Lady Steyne. If they did see him, do you suppose they would tell? And if that poor girl cried out and they heard her, do you suppose they'd tell that either? No—that's what happened, but unless a witness drops from heaven there isn't enough evidence to risk a sixpence on—nothing but those handprints on the shoulders of her coat."

Miss Silver gazed at him.

"Did you ask Mrs Jerningham who helped her on with her coat the last time she wore it?"

"Yes, I did," said March in an exasperated tone—"and it was Rafe. But I swear those prints were not made then. They're not in the right place, and they're too fresh. You don't put your hands round the top of a woman's sleeve when you help her into a coat. And they're too clear. They couldn't have been made on Sunday. They're the clearest of all the prints."

"It is certainly a very interesting case," said Miss Silver.

THIRTY-FOUR

Miss Silver was walking along the high street next day, when she saw Mrs Dale Jerningham get out of a car and go into Ashley's through the big swing door. The car, which was driven by Rafe Jerningham, moved on again at once and disappeared amongst the traffic. Miss Silver watched it go. She thought it turned down into Market Square, but she wasn't sure. She followed the tall, slim figure in white and came up with it in the Ladies' Outfitting.

"Good—morning, Mrs Jerningham."

Lisle turned from the counter, startled.

"Miss Silver!"

"We do keep meeting, don't we?" said Miss Silver affably.

Lisle said "Yes" in rather a shaken tone. They did keep on meeting—but it couldn't mean anything—if it did mean anything, it would mean . . . She said, hurrying to get away from her own thoughts, "I'm getting a bathing-dress. Mine got torn—" And there her voice faltered and dropped.

Miss Silver gave her little cough.

"Ah, yes—that would be when you were nearly drowned, would it not? I remember you told me. But you did not tell me how it happened, or who saved you. You were bathing with your husband and his cousins, were you not?"

The elderly saleswoman brought a pile of stockinette bathing-dresses and put them down on the counter.

"Perhaps you wouldn't mind looking these through, Mrs Jerningham. We're rather busy this morning." She went away.

There was no one near them at that counter. Lisle picked up a cream jersey tunic and said,

"Oh, I think I made too much of it. I couldn't have been in any real danger."

"It is most alarming to get out of one's depth," said Miss Silver. "I think you mentioned that you were not a good swimmer."

Lisle tried for a smile.

"Oh, not at all. And the others are so good. I went farther out than I meant to and could not get back, and they were laughing, and splashing, and ducking one another, so they didn't hear me."

She looked at Miss Silver with wide, darkened eyes. "It's rather horrid when you call and no one hears you."

"But somebody did hear you," said Miss Silver briskly.

Lisle's golden brown lashes came down and hid her eyes. A bright colour showed in her cheeks and ebbed again. She said in a soft, confused voice,

"I don't know—I don't remember—it was just like drowning—I went down, you know."

"Who saved you, Mrs Jerningham?"

"There was a man bathing off the beach. People aren't supposed to—the ground all belongs to Tanfield—but he had run his car on to the downs and come down by the cliff path. I don't even know his name—nobody thought of asking him. But he heard me call and saw me go down, and swam out and brought me in. I was quite a long time coming round." She stopped and went on again, stumbling over her words. "It—it was dreadful for my—husband and—the others to—to think of my being nearly drowned so—so close to them. Dale was— was dreadfully upset. And my bathing-dress got torn at the neck where the man caught hold of me, so—so I have to get another. I haven't bathed since, but it's no good putting it off, is it? The only way to get over being nervous about a thing is to go on and do it. Don't you think so?"

"Sometimes," said Miss Silver. "But I don't think I should go out of my depth if I were you."

Lisle said, "No." And then, "Rafe said that too. But Dale is such a good swimmer that he wants me to try—Which of these shall I get? Do you like the cream? I have a cream rubber cap."

"I shouldn't go out of my depth," said Miss Silver gravely. "Are you coming to see me, my dear?"

Lisle looked at her for a moment, and then looked away. The look held sadness, but no embarrassment.

"I don't think I can."

Miss Silver came nearer.

"I want to ask you a question. Will you believe that I have a serious reason for asking it, and not think me impertinent?"

Lisle raised her head and looked round quickly. They were alone at the counter. To the right the stocking counter was doing a brisk business. They were as much alone as if four solid walls had closed them in. She said in a young, warm voice,

"I should never think that."

Miss Silver coughed.

"You told me you had made a will in your husband's favour. I want to ask you whether there were any other substantial legacies."

Lisle caught her breath. She had not expected this. Rafe . . . She repeated the name aloud.

"Rafe—there was one for Rafe."

"Does he know that?"

"Yes—I told him—"

"A substantial legacy?"

"Twenty thousand pounds."

Miss Silver leaned towards her and said in the lowest possible voice,

"Mrs Jerningham—will you take my advice? Will you do something?"

"What do you want me to do?"

"Ring up your solicitor—now, at once, from here. Tell him you are not satisfied with your will and you propose to make a new one. Tell him you wish the old one destroyed—now, at once. I do not know whether he will take such an instruction over the telephone. If he knows you well enough to be quite sure that it is you who are speaking, he may do so—it does

not really very much matter. Instruct him to do it and ring
off. Then go home and tell every member of your family what
you have done. Make any excuse you like, but make it quite
clear that you have given instructions to have your existing will
destroyed. Go up to town as soon as you can and make sure
that these instructions have been carried out. Make a provi-
sional will leaving everything to some charity."

Lisle did not look at her. She put out a hand and groped
for Miss Silver's hand. Her eyes were fixed upon the cream-
coloured bathing-dress. She said,

"Why—why?"

"Don't you know why? Come and see me, my dear."

The fair head was very slightly shaken.

"I can't do that." The hand on Miss Silver's wrist withdrew.
Miss Silver looked at her.

"Take my advice and do not go out of your depth."

The saleswoman was coming back.

"I'm out of it already," said Lisle Jerningham in an extinguished voice.

THIRTY-FIVE

Lisle sat silent in the front seat of Rafe's little car. He looked sideways at her when they were clear of the town and said,

"Why so pale and wan, honey-sweet? Didn't the shopping go well? You didn't tell me what you were going to buy."

A brief colour came to the cheek across which his glance had travelled—came, and went again.

"I bought a bathing-dress. Mine got torn—"

He said, "Yes—so it did."

She saw his left hand tighten on the wheel. The knuckles showed bone-white under the brown skin. He might have been remembering twenty minutes of as hot a day as this, with her body limp and cold in a torn bathing-dress, whilst he and Dale and a stranger laboured to make reluctant lungs breathe again.

He laughed suddenly.

"Messed it up properly, didn't you? Are you all set on going bathing again?"

"I shan't go out of my depth." She felt her cheeks burn, and said in a hurry, "Did I keep you waiting? I didn't mean to. I—I met someone."

"So did I—one always does. I hope yours was amusing. Mine was the last girl friend but three—or four—or even more—anyhow there she was, shamelessly buxom, with twins in a double perambulator. I must say I like my lost loves to show a little decent melancholy when they run into me like that."

Lisle could not help laughing. She got a look poignant with reproach.

"Do you know, she married a fat man who jobs stocks. As Tennyson says:

'Oh, my Amy, mine no more!
Oh, the dreary, dreary moorland! Oh, the barren, barren shore!
Is it well to wish thee happy?—having known me—to decline
On a range of lower feelings and a narrower heart than mine?'"

Lisle's eyes danced.

"Perhaps she was afraid your heart was going to be too wide. She might have got lost in the crowd."

He shook his head.

"I don't go in for crowds. I'm highly selective, like the best wireless sets. Only one station at a time—no overlapping, no jamming, no atmospherics—perfect reception. Try our 1939 ten-valve superhet and be happy ever after! You'd think someone would jump at it, wouldn't you? But no—they go off and marry butchers, and bakers, and candlestick-makers and have twins."

"How many girls have there really been, Rafe?"

"I've lost count years ago. It's the quest for the ideal, you know. I always hope I'm going to find it, but I never do. If a girl's got one thing, she hasn't got another. The odds are that the perfect complexion means a perfect circulation and a refrigerating plant instead of a heart, and if they dance like a dream they're no good at soothing the brow when it's wrung with pain and anguish. I don't mind walking out with a hard-hearted Hannah, but I'm damned if I'm going to live with one—and that's not swearing, it's bed-rock fact, because I should probably get up in the night and cut her throat."

Lisle shivered and said, "Don't!"

"Don't worry, darling, I'm not going to. My trouble is that I want too much—beauty, charm, delight, *and* all the moral virtues. And if anyone like that ever existed, someone else would have married her first."

Lisle laughed a little and said,

"What about the girl friends? Perhaps they want an ideal too."

"The girl friends are all right," said Rafe. "As far as they are concerned, I am ideal to flirt with, but when it comes down to brass tacks they're out for someone who can provide a much classier pram than it would run to with me. The female of the species is more practical than *the* male."

"You are a fool, Rafe!"

"The fool died of a broken heart," he said. His white teeth showed in a sudden grin. "I've made you laugh anyway. I had a bet with myself that I would—so I've won, and you owe me sixpence halfpenny."

"What for?"

"Petrol, I expect. What are you going to do when my thumb is all right? I can't keep it sprained much longer or there'll be some harsh words flying. Dale won't let you drive his car, will he?"

"I can get Evans."

"Or Dale?" He waited a minute and then repeated the words—"Or Dale?"

She flushed, and said without looking at him,

"He's busy—you know he is. And he hates shopping."

"I shall have to spin that sprain out. I say, that would make an awfully good tongue-twister, wouldn't it? But to hark back—who was your girl friend? I've told you about mine."

The oddest impulse surged up in Lisle and took charge.

"You'd love her. She quotes Tennyson too."

"The little dumpy woman who spoke to you after the inquest?"

"Rafe! How did you know?"

"A flash of genius. Who is she?"

They had turned into Crook Lane and were slowing for the hairpin bend. She put up a hand to the window ledge and gripped it.

"Mind coming down here?" said Rafe quickly.

"A little."

"Better do it every day until you don't. That's brutal common sense. You're quite safe, you know, honey-sweet."

Lisle said, "Am I?" in a queer flat voice. She kept her hand on the window ledge until they were round the corner where her car had smashed against Cooper's barn. Then she drew a sighing breath and let it fall.

"Go on about the girl friend," said Rafe. "Can't I meet her?

We could swap quotations. Who is she, and why have I never heard of her before?"

Lisle only answered one of the questions. The impulse driving her, she said,

"She's a detective. At least she calls it 'Private Investigations Undertaken' on her card, but I expect that's what it means—don't you?"

Rafe said nothing at all. She looked at him and saw his profile rather as Miss Silver had seen it at the inquest—the brown skin tight across the line of cheek and jaw, the lips without movement, locked and inexpressive. The odd thought went through her head that if she had seen a picture of him like this she might not have recognised it. It was just as if he was not alive.

And then all in a moment the impression broke. His face was the familiar one again, quick with movement and expression. He laughed and said,

"I expect so. Where did you pick her up?"

"In a train."

"And she leapt at you and said, 'Let me privately investigate you.' Was that it?"

The impulse which had carried Lisle as far as this died suddenly. She saw with relief that they were approaching the big stone pillars from which two heraldic beasts grinned down malevolently upon all who came to Tanfield Court. If she waited until they had turned in . . . She measured the distance along the path with her eye. No—she couldn't wait so long as that. She must speak—say something. If she didn't, he would think—what would he think? What did it matter what he thought? It *did* matter.

This was all in one flash of agonised, struggling thought. She made herself laugh and say,

"Wouldn't you like to know?"

They ran smoothly between the pillars and left the grinning beasts behind. Rafe said drily,

"Yes, I should very much. Are you going to tell me?"

"I don't know." Her lips smiled, but her secret thought cried in her with something like despair, "He'll know all the same—he knows now. If I could tell him—I *can't!*"

He said, "Hadn't you better?" and caught the very faint movement of her head which said "No."

As they drew up by the steps leading to the house, he was laughing again.

"Supposing I ask the sleuth herself—do you suppose she'd tell me?"

"There's nothing to tell." She opened the door and got out.

Rafe's voice followed her.

"Shall I try my luck?"

She ought to have laughed and said something light, but she couldn't manage it. She only shook her head again and ran up the steps and into the house.

THIRTY-SIX

The black and white hall was cool and shadowy after the strong heat and light outside. Lisle went up the shallow marble steps past the tortured Actæon on the half-landing, past all those white tormented shapes of death and grief, to her own room. Here the gloom was of another kind. Not stark tragedy but outworn respectability made it a kind of catacomb of Victorian taste. The impression which it always induced came upon her with more than its usual force. The windows stood wide, the middle one a two-leafed door opening upon the narrow parapeted balcony. Lisle threw a cushion on to the sill and sank down upon it, her head against the jamb, her hands in her lap. The sun was on the other side of the house and the breeze was cool from the sea. She stayed like that for a long time. Miss Silver's words came and went in the empty spaces of her mind. She watched them there . . .

Presently she began to think again. It was just as if part of her had gone numb and was coming back to life. She had been able to talk and laugh with Rafe on the way home because the numb thing had not begun to hurt. It was beginning to hurt now. Miss Silver's words kept sounding in her ears: "Change your will. Alter your will. Ring up your solicitor. Change your will. Ring up your solicitor at once. Tell him to destroy your will. Make some excuse. Alter your will. Change your will. Everything to your husband? Any   other legacies? Any other substantial legacies? Twenty thousand pounds to Rafe. Would that be a substantial legacy? Change your will. Alter your will. Tell them that you have changed it. Tell everyone."

She thought about that . . . "Leave all the money to a charity and tell them what I've done . . ." There was nothing to stop her doing it here and now. She had only to cross to the bed, take up the telephone, and call Mr Robson. She could do that and have it done in a quarter of an hour . . . And then go down and tell Dale, and Rafe, and Alicia that she thought one of them was trying to murder her. Because that was what it amounted to. "I'm destroying the will that makes it worth your while. If anyone murders me now they may get themselves hanged, but they won't get any money and they won't save Tanfield." Just exactly that was what it amounted to.

Lisle closed her eyes and wished that she was dead already and out of it. If she was dead she wouldn't mind who had her money. She didn't mind now. She only minded having to think that someone wanted it so much that they would do murder to get it. She thought about that, and she thought about being dead, and it came to her that she couldn't take Miss Silver's advice. If they

were trying to kill her they must try. She couldn't defend herself not that way. Anything that came must come from them. If
her marriage was to be broken—and she thought it was broken
already it must be Dale who broke it. She could not put her own
hand to it. If Rafe . . . Her thought faltered. Twenty thousand
pounds—was friendship worth no more than that? He had said
that he hated her. Perhaps they all hated her. Alicia did, but she
was an open enemy. "The wounds with which I was wounded in
the house of my friends." She thought, "That's in the Bible—but
I have no friends in this house—"

And as she came to that, there was a knocking on the door.
She got to her feet before she said, "Come in"—some feeling
of not being taken at a disadvantage. How far back did that
go—to the jungle? And how much safer was she here among
the trappings of Victorian respectability?

It was Lizzie the second housemaid at the door, a buxom
young thing—bright hair, rosy cheeks, eyes popping with
interest.

"Please, madam, it's the police Inspector. And William told
him Mr Jerningham was out, and he said if he could see you—
and William's put him in the study same as last time if that's
all right."

Lisle said, "Quite all right, Lizzie," and turned to the glass
to smooth her hair. She put colour in her cheeks and touched
her mouth with lipstick. Her white linen dress was crumpled.
She changed it for a soft green muslin, thin and cool. Then she
went down.

Randal March watched her come in with a feeling that he
was here on a fool's errand. This girl—it couldn't be possible

that her husband or some member of his family had tried to murder her. The tears which she had not shed darkened her eyes. When he had seen her before she had been fainting pale. Now, with colour in cheeks and lips, she was lovely, with a delicate, ethereal loveliness which touched and charmed him. She gave him her hand as she had done before and kept her eyes on his face with just that sensitive widening of the dark pupils which told him she was nervous.

He said, "I won't keep you, Mrs Jerningham. I just want to clear up a few points about your coat."

"My coat?" Her hand was cold in his. She drew it away and stepped back.

"The one you gave to Cissie Cole."

"Oh, yes." She went over to the fireplace and sat down there on an old-fashioned backless stool.

"The coat has been tested for prints, and I should be very grateful if you could answer a few questions about when you wore it last, and whether anyone else had the opportunity of handling it then."

"I told you—"

"Yes. Do you mind if we just run over it again? You wore the coat on Sunday evening. Are you sure you didn't wear it again after that?"

Alicia's voice in the hall on Sunday evening—"That hideous coat!"

March saw her wince, and wondered why.

She said in a soft, hurried voice, "Oh, no, I didn't wear it again."

"And where was it between Sunday and Wednesday?"

"In a cupboard in my bedroom."

"No one would have touched it there?"

"Oh, no."

March smiled at her.

"Then we come back to Sunday, when you wore it last. I think you said Mr Rafe Jerningham brought it to you in the garden. Can you remember how he was carrying it?"

"Over his arm."

"Did he help you on with it?"

"I don't remember. I suppose he did."

"I think you said he did."

"Then I suppose he must have." She put up a hand to her cheek. "Does it matter?"

"Well, it does rather, because we want to account for the handprints. You see, if he helped you on with your coat on Sunday evening, we would expect some rather faint prints up by the collar."

She could feel a little pulse beating against her hand. It frightened her. She let the hand fall again into her lap.

"And are there any?"

He nodded.

"Now, Mrs Jerningham, just try and think whether he touched you again after that."

"Touched me?" Her eyes widened.

March smiled pleasantly.

"You were down by the sea wall, weren't you? He didn't take you by the shoulders and swing you round to look at something across the bay, did he?"

"Oh, no!" There was no mistaking her surprise.

"Nothing at all like that?"

"Oh, no."

"Well, that finishes that. Now did anyone else touch you whilst you were wearing the coat—take hold of you, as I said, pat you on the back, or anything of that sort? Your husband, for instance?"

"Oh, no. I came in after we had finished talking. I didn't see Dale. I went straight up to my room and put the coat away. Alicia—Lady Steyne was in the hall, but she didn't touch me."

"Where was the coat before your cousin Rafe Jerningham brought it to you?"

"I think he brought it from one of the chairs on the lawn. It—it turns cold down by the sea as soon as the sun goes."

"That was very thoughtful of him."

Lisle said, "Yes." It rushed into her mind how often Rafe had done things like that. She felt a wave of emotion, a touch of comfort. And on that Rafe himself came strolling in through the window.

"How do you do, March?" he said. "More Third Degree? Just tell me if I'm in the way."

"Not a bit. I have finished with Mrs Jerningham. I was going to ask if I could see you. You couldn't have timed your entrance better."

"Perhaps I was listening for my cue."

Lisle got up and left them. As Rafe opened the door for her she looked up at him and caught a queer crooked smile. It troubled her—a crooked, bitter smile. It robbed her of that newfound comfort. She heard Miss Silver's voice again. "Tell them you've altered your will. Tell them all." The door closed behind her.

Rafe came over to the writing-table and leaned against the

corner of it. He wore a short-sleeved shirt with an open neck and a pair of old grey flannel trousers, and he looked very much at his ease.

"Well?" he said. "What is it now? I thought we'd finished."

"Not yet," said Randal March.

"Because when we have, I was going to say I suppose you're not on duty all the time, and what about coming up for some tennis?"

"Thank you—I'd like to—when we have finished. I'm afraid I'm strictly on duty this afternoon."

"Too much on duty for this?" Rafe offered a battered cigarette case.

"I'm afraid so."

"Oh, very well. I suppose you don't mind if I smoke?"

"Not at all. I've just been asking Mrs Jerningham about the coat she gave to Cissie Cole. We've been trying it out for fingerprints, and we naturally want to know who handled it before it changed ownership."

Rafe struck a match, drew at his cigarette till it glowed, and dropped the match on to Dale's pen-tray.

"*Fingerprints?*" he said. "On that woolly stuff?"

March watched him.

"Yes. It's a new process. Some of the prints are marvellously clear."

Rafe laughed.

"Mine amongst them? I suppose Lisle told you I fetched that coat for her and helped her on with it the last time she wore it—at least I suppose it was the last time."

"Yes, that's what she said."

Rafe blew out a mouthful of smoke. Through the light haze his eyes danced mockingly.

"Too disappointing for you!"

March said, "Perhaps," and then, "Perhaps not." He pushed his chair back, fixed his eyes sternly upon Rafe, and said, "When did you take hold of that coat by the shoulders and upper part of the arms—and who was wearing it at that time?"

Rafe put his cigarette to his lips. Was it to cover them? His hand was steady enough. March thought, "I'd rather trust my lips than my hand if I was in a hole."

The hand dropped. The lips were smiling.

"Well, Lisle has just told you that I put her into her coat."

March shook his head.

"These prints weren't made that way. I'll show you how they were done." He sprang up and came round the table. Standing behind Rafe, he took him by the shoulders, the flat of the palm at the edge of the shoulder-blade, the fingers coming round the upper arm and gripping it. "Like that," he said. And let go, and went back to his seat.

Rafe was still smiling.

"Any explanation?" said March.

Rafe shook his head.

"I can't drink of one—at least not a new one. I did help Lisle on with her coat, you know, but I suppose that's too easy for the modern scientific policeman."

"The prints are too fresh," said March quietly. "They're the freshest prints of the lot. The ones you made on Sunday are a perfectly different affair. These prints were made at a much later time, and they are most unmistakably yours."

Rafe straightened up, still smiling.

"Well, you'll have to prove it, you know. I don't mind your trying, if it amuses you. But just speaking off hand, I should say that none of it would sound very convincing in, let's say, a court of law—or a coroner's court. And perhaps that's the reason no one asked me all these interesting questions at the inquest. I was there, you know."

"You don't offer any explanation?"

Rafe shrugged his shoulders.

"You won't take the obvious one. I'm afraid I haven't any other."

THIRTY-SEVEN

Inspector March got to his feet.

"If you think of one perhaps you'll let me know. But meanwhile I wonder whether you would care to walk along the beach and show me how far you went on Wednesday night."

"Oh, certainly." Rafe's tone was casual in the extreme.

He led the way out by the french window and down through the Italian garden, talking as he would have done to any other guest.

"I don't know if you hate this sort of thing—some people do like poison— Lisle does for one. Too much like a map with all these formal beds. And she doesn't like statues and cypresses either. They're a bit funerary for the climate—as a rule. They need an Italian sky to set them off."

"They've got it today," said March.

"Yes, but you can't turn it on when you want to. The whole thing was a copy of a famous garden at Capua, with statues added by an ancestor who had more money than he knew what to do with. He developed a very pretty talent for chucking it away, so we don't exactly bless his memory."

From the Italian garden they came by way of a tree-planted walk and a long green ride to the sea wall. The bay lay clear before them in the morning sun, Tane Head across the water just softened by the faintest haze. And on the left, cliffs sweeping away from the gap in which they stood, and the black wall of the Shepstone Rocks running down from them to meet the sea and break its surface with a murderous line of jagged points. The tide was full, and everywhere except about the rocks the water lay silken-smooth and blue.

March turned his back on Tane Head and looked towards the cliffs.

"That's a nasty bit of coast. Dangerous, isn't it?"

"Very. There's no real beach after you get round the Shepstone wall. The old story, which was quite strongly believed in my grandfather's time, has it that the bay used to run right round to Sharpe's Point—that's the next headland. There weren't any rocks in those days. It was all smooth hard sand, and the local bad man, Black Nym by name, used to come riding across from the Point at low tide, robbing, murdering, and generally making a public nuisance of himself. Well, one day he came along on a Sunday evening when everyone was at church and drove off a large flock of sheep. He brought them down here and started off across the sands with them, roaring at the top of his great bull voice that those who were fools enough to go to church and serve God should sit up and take notice what much better wages he got from the devil.

There was an old woman in the village nearly a hundred when I was eight years old. She used to tell the tale, and this is how she told it—'And with that, Master Rafe, there did come the most 'orrible great blast of wind and a crack of thunder fit to split the sky. Dark as Christmas midnight it were all at once, and he could hear the sheep crying and the sea roaring, but he couldn't see nothing, not so much as his own hand before his face. He swore worse than ever. There were those as heard him, and some say there was a voice that answered him out of the holy Book—"The wages of sin is death." And some say there wasn't nothing, but only one flash of lightning and a clap after it fit to bring the cliffs about his ears. And that's just what it done—the sea come up in a 'uge unnatural wave and the cliff come down to meet it. And what happened to Black Nym nobody knows but the devil as was his master. Some folks say the sheep was all turned to stone, but I reckon that's a fond saying. Drownded they was, poor things. You won't ever get me to believe as those wicked black rocks was ever anything so 'armless as a pack of soft, silly sheep. Bits of the cliff as come down, that's what they are and you won't get me from it. But whether or no, Shepstone Rocks was the name they got, and that's how they got it'"

March smiled.

"It's a good story. I'd like to have met your old woman."

"She was my nurse's grandmother," said Rafe. He turned and led the way along the wall. "We go down here," he said.

The steps were at the end of the wall on the headland side. At their foot, above high-water mark, was a bathing-hut painted white and green—two rooms and a wide verandah set with chairs and coloured cushions. A track, trodden hard, ran past it skirting the cliff.

It was, as Rafe had said, bad going for a bad light The track soon merged into deep soft sand, with here and there a patch of shingle, and here and there a ribbed line of rock.

When they had come about midway round the half-circle of the bay Rafe stopped and said,

"I must have turned somewhere about here."

March looked at the headland, turned back and sighted the green and white bathing-hut, then faced round to the headland again.

"If your eyes are as good as mine, you'd see anyone on that cliff plainly enough."

"In this light—yes."

"How dark was it when you turned? Could you see those cushions in the verandah of the bathing-hut?"

"No." Then, with a sudden fleeting smile, "They're put away at night."

"Could you have seen them if they had been there?"

"How can I tell?" His smile, the slight lift of his shoulder, the sparkle in his eyes, all said, "I'm not going to tell."

Randal March said, "I want to go on a little farther."

"Just as you like."

"There's a way up on to the cliff path, isn't there, just beyond those rocks?"

"It's a bit of a climb."

"But one that you have often done?"

"Oh, often."

"Did you do it on Wednesday?"

Rafe shook his head.

"I'm sorry to disappoint you, but I didn't leave the beach."

They left it now, and climbed by the roughest of ways to the path which ran like a shelf along the cliff—about half way up at first, but rising gradually until it emerged upon the headland.

Hot sun, breeze cool off the water, a scent of heather, a scent of whin—Tane Head was a pleasant place on a summer morning.

The path became a narrow grassy track and petered out. March walked on, the ground becoming more and more uneven as they made their way along the top of the cliff. Sandy hollows rimmed with dark, scrawny clumps of gorse, great heaped bramble mounds still in bloom but with here and there a cluster of berries for the most part hard and green, low wind-bent trees twisted into every crooked shape.

"This is where she went over," said March, coming to a standstill.

Rafe walked to the edge of the cliff and looked down. There was no sheer drop. If Cissie Cole had been pushed she might have taken the first dozen feet or so at a stumbling run before she went headlong to the rocks below. And just that was what she had done. He said over his shoulder,

"She must have caught at that bush. See where it's broken."

March's voice was a little dry as he answered.

"Yes—we noticed that. I think myself it puts suicide out of the question. If you were going to throw yourself over a cliff you would want to get on with it—you wouldn't choose a place where you had to run down a slope like that before you could get to the edge."

Rafe said, "I suppose not." He stepped back a pace or two. "Well? What's the great idea? Why the personally conducted tour?"

March began to walk away.

"What's the nearest way down to the beach from here?"

"Don't you know?" He laughed suddenly. "I'm sure you do—and I'm sure that even the most suspicious mind can't hold it up against me if I know too. After all, I was born and brought up here. So now we both know that there's a way down the cliff where that path we came by joins the headland. It's a bit of a scramble, but it's a perfectly feasible proposition."

March looked at him.

"Did you go down that way on Wednesday night?"

He got the pleasantest smile in the world.

"You can't go down if you haven't come up. I'm afraid you haven't got a frightfully good memory. I keep on telling you that I didn't leave the beach on Wednesday night."

March opened his lips to speak and shut them again. A forward step had taken him to the top of a small hillock, and as he gained it his eye caught the sun on a moving whiteness, the flutter of a scarf in the wind. He came down off the rise with a run, rounded a high clump of gorse, and found himself face to face with Lady Steyne. Rafe, behind him, said,

"Hullo, Alicia!"

She met them with rather a chilly smile.

"Why, what are you doing up here? My scarf's caught, Rafe. Get it off those thorns without tearing it if you can."

"It was your scarf I saw," said March, and waited while Rafe dealt with it.

"We're taking a walk—if you don't stand still, darling, the darned thing will tear. Pleasure and instruction combined—scene of the tragedy—official observations on it. In fact, a thoroughly profitable morning. There—I'm pricked to the bone, but I don't think I've bled on to your scarf."

"I don't know why I put it on—I'm boiled. I've been looking for my clip." She turned to March. "Oh, Inspector, you will ask your men to look out for it, won't you? I must have dropped it when I was up here with Dale the other night—a big sort of half buckle in emeralds and diamonds. I didn't miss it till this morning, and I must have dropped it up here, because I know I had it on Wednesday, and I haven't worn it since."

"Is it valuable, Lady Steyne?"

"I expect so—emeralds and diamonds, you know. But I don't know what it cost—it was a present. I should simply hate to lose it."

"Well, if you can tell me whereabouts you were—"

She threw out an impatient hand.

"My dear man, we were all over the place! It's the old needle and haystack game. I suppose I had better offer a reward."

"How near the cliff did you go?"

"Not nearer than this. That's why I was looking here. But it's too hot to go on. I've got my car in the lane. Like a lift, Rafe?"

"If the Inspector has finished with me. Perhaps he would like a lift too." He turned to March. "How did you come over—motorbike, push-bike, car?"

"Car. If Lady Steyne will really give me a lift back to Tanfield Court, I shall be very grateful."

Alicia said, "Oh, yes." And then, "And you'll find my clip for me, won't you? I expect I'd better say a fiver for the reward."

THIRTY-EIGHT

Lisle went out into the garden and sat under the cedar. There was always shade there even at high noon. She lay back in the swinging canvas chair and closed her eyes.

Fingerprints on her coat—handprints . . . She felt sick—and not only with distaste. There was a kind of horror about it. All those unseen, unnoticed prints, starting out with their black accusing stains—handprints—fingerprints—everything handled, damaged, blurred. It wasn't only a coat that had been spoiled, it was everything. Six months ago when she had stepped into this new world, how bright, and clear, and beautiful everything had been—love, marriage, home, friendship—a family ready made for a girl who had never had one—there couldn't have been a fairer prospect anywhere. And now it was all dashed and spoiled, the colours faded, the sunlight gone—

A line that she had heard somewhere came into her head:

"Thinned into common air like the rainbow breath of
   a dream."

When had that begun to happen? She looked back, and she
couldn't tell. There had been an imperceptible withdrawal, as
gradual as the ebbing of daylight or the tide.

The tears came up under her eyelids but did not fall, and
presently they dried there. She began to think what she could
do. A wave of terror went over her. Perhaps she could go
away—for a time. But in her heart of hearts she knew that if
she went now she would never come back. She shrank at the
thought. The world was wide, but it promised her loneliness,
not freedom. She found that she was afraid of this promise.

She sat up, and saw Dale coming across the lawn with an
impatient step. He was bare-headed and very good to look at.
All at once the things which she had been thinking seemed
morbid and foolish. She felt sharply ashamed, and the colour
rose to her cheeks.

Dale flung himself into a chair and said in a voice as impatient as his step,

"Where do you get to these days? I want to talk to you."

"I went into Ledlington with Rafe."

He frowned.

"Why Rafe? I would have driven you. Never mind, we'll
talk about that another time. Look here—I've heard from
Tatham, and its take it or leave it. He's got to have an answer
by the end of the month, yes or no, and if Robson won't be
reasonable"—he lifted a hand and let it fall again—"well, it'll
just have to be yes."

Her heart contracted. She said gently,

"I'm sorry, Dale."

"Are you?" He sat up, leaning towards her eagerly. "Are you really? I believe you are. Lisle—what about having one more go at Robson? Will you? He might relent—you never know— and I should feel we'd done everything we could. Don't you see what I mean? I don't want to look back afterwards and think, 'Why didn't we do this?' or 'Why didn't we do that?' or, 'Perhaps Robson would have given in if we'd had one more shot.' Darling, don't you see?"

She nodded. It was easier than speaking. When he looked at her like that, it brought back all the times when the same look had said, or she thought that it had said, "I love you." Now it seemed to her that it only meant, "This is something I want. Give it to me." She had always tried to give him what he wanted. She must go on trying.

He sprang up and pulled her to her feet

"You will? Oh, *darling*! Come along and we'll see what we can do in the heart-melting line! We've got plenty of time before lunch. Everyone else seems to be out. Come along to the study and draft a letter!"

Lisle was to look back on the next half hour with a bewildered sense of strain. What she could not remember was how many drafts she made for a letter which was never to be despatched. Odd phrases, telling arguments, appeals, dispassionate reasoning—Dale swung from one to the other, suggesting, dictating, adding, altering.

"Take another piece of paper! Now try this! No, no,

no—that won't do! Take a fresh piece—that's written on! How does this sound? Take it down!"

"I think it sounds a little exaggerated."

Dale was pacing the room. She remembered how he wheeled round on her when she said that.

"Exaggerated—exaggerated? How do you think I'm feeling about Tanfield? What sort of tepid milk-and-water stuff do you think I'm made of?"

"I only meant—it's supposed to be from me, isn't it? Mr Robson won't think so if I write like that. Oh, Dale, *please*—"

He came over to her and stood there behind her, leaning down to kiss her hair.

"Darling, I'm sorry. It means so much to me. If we can only get this damned letter right . . . That bit's no good! Let's try again. Take another sheet!"

It always came back to that in the end. The table was littered with discarded sheets, some closely written, some with no more than a single sentence. In the end when the lunch bell rang Dale swept them all up with a groan.

"No good going on now. We'll give it a rest. I'll keep these and sort them through. We've gone on at it too long— you look worn out." He put an arm round her and laid his cheek against hers. "Poor tired child—I'm a brute to you, aren't I?"

She said, "No—" in an uncertain voice and slipped away. But his hand dropped on her shoulder, holding her.

"Lisle—don't tell anyone we're having another shot at Robson. I don't want the others to know—I just don't feel like

going over it all. You know how it is—I'm very fond of Lal,
but—she jars sometimes. I don't want to talk about it to anyone but you."

THIRTY-NINE

Inspector March came back to his office, to be told that a lady had been ringing him up—"Wouldn't leave a message, only said she wanted to see you and she'd ring again—a Miss Silver."

March's eyebrows went up.

Ten minutes later the telephone went. A familiar cough came to him on the line.

"Oh, you are back. I am so glad. I think I had better see you for a moment. Would it suit you if I came round now?"

March said "Yes," and hung up.

A constable presently ushered in Miss Maud Silver, neatly dressed in a grey washing silk printed with a design of small mauve and black flowers. Being her last summer's dress, it was quite good enough for Ledlington in the morning. Her hat was of the same date, a rather wilted black straw with a small bunch of mauve and white lilac on the left-hand side. A brooch of bog-oak carved into the shape of a rose fastened her collar. She wore black cotton gloves and black shoes and stockings. Her manner was one of extreme gravity. She took the chair that was offered her, listened to the constable's heavy receding step, and then said without any preliminaries,

"Mr Rafe Jerningham is a beneficiary under Mrs Jerningham's will."

March swung his chair round to face her,

"Oh, he is, is he?"

"To the extent of twenty thousand pounds."

He whistled.

"Well—well—and what do you know about that, as they say across the water?"

Miss Silver coughed.

"I am not entirely up to date in American slang, but if, as I suppose, you would like to know the source of my information, well, that is one of the things I came here to tell you. It came from Mrs Jerningham herself."

"She told you she had left Rafe Jerningham twenty thousand pounds?"

"Oh, yes," said Miss Silver. "You see, when we met in the train and she was so very much upset, she spoke about her will, and I got the impression that she had left everything to her husband. So this morning when I met her in Ashley's I asked her if this was so."

An expression of incredulity appeared upon the well cut features of Inspector March.

"You asked her about her will in Ashley's?" His voice was as incredulous as his expression.

"Oh, yes," said Miss Silver brightly. "She was buying a bathing-dress, and there was no one else at the counter. A shop is really quite a safe place to talk in, because people are thinking about their own affairs—shopping lists, and whether they can match the ribbon they got two months ago—all that kind of thing. We had quite a private talk while the saleswoman was serving someone at the next counter."

March leaned back and contemplated his late preceptress. He was thinking how thoroughly she looked the part—so thoroughly that no matter what she talked about or where she talked about it, no one would dream that her conversation could have the slightest interest for anyone at all. He gave a half exasperated smile and said,

"Go on—tell me all about it."

Miss Silver folded her black gloved hands over a shabby black handbag.

"Well, I think that was really all. I asked her if there were any substantial legacies, and she mentioned Mr Rafe. That was really all, except that I urged her most strongly to ring up her solicitor and instruct him to destroy her will."

March made a movement.

"He would be very unlikely to act on instructions given over the telephone."

Miss Silver coughed in a slightly reproving manner.

"That would be no matter. What I urged Mrs Jerningham to do was to go home and tell the whole family that she had instructed her solicitor to destroy the will. If anyone was contemplating another attempt upon her life, he would naturally hold his hand until he was sure that the will under which he would benefit was still in existence. He could not afford to run the risk of committing murder only to find that the money was now irrevocably beyond his reach."

"That would apply to Dale Jerningham as well as to his cousin Rafe."

"It would apply to Mr Dale Jerningham, to Mr Rafe Jerningham, and also to Lady Steyne."

"And you seriously believe that her life has been attempted by one of these three people?"

"Has been—and will be again." She paused, and added, "Is that not your own opinion, Randal?"

He pushed his chair back.

"Neither your opinion nor mine is of very much value. What we want is evidence, and so far all the evidence in this case is lumped into the scale against the wretched Pell. I went over and saw Rafe Jerningham this morning—that's where I've been—and a more useless, profitless morning I never spent. I saw Mrs Jerningham first. She's a very good witness, and she was quite clear about the coat. She wore it last on Sunday evening. Rafe brought it to her. Rafe helped her on with it—faint prints on the collar all present and correct. He certainly didn't take hold of her by the shoulders in the way he would have had to in order to leave those much clearer, fresher prints. And no one else touched her at all. She went straight in, took the coat off, and hung it up in a cupboard in her bedroom. She wasn't anywhere near her husband. The rather uncertain prints may or may not be his. The one in the middle of the back may have been done at some other time. It's all mixed up with Pell's prints. But Rafe Jerningham did take hold of that coat and whoever was wearing it, and as his prints are the freshest of the lot, he took hold of it on Wednesday night. Only I can't prove that."

"Did he offer any explanation?"

March laughed.

"Oh, yes—slick as you please. He'd fetched his cousin's coat and helped her on with it. And that was that. There aren't any flies on Mr Rafe Jerningham. He knows as well as you and I do just how much of that print stuff would go down with a jury. Can't you hear him in the box? 'Of course I touched the coat. I brought it to Mrs Jerningham and I helped her on with it. I should think my prints would be pretty well all over the place.' I tell you he grinned in my face—and asked me to come up and have a friendly game of tennis when I wasn't on duty."

Miss Silver got up.

"I must not take up any more of your time."

He said, "Wait! About Mrs Jerningham—was she going to take your advice—change her will?"

She shook her head with an air of concern.

"I am afraid not. She did not say, but—I am afraid not."

March went to the door, but stopped there without opening it.

"I've gone as far as I can. The Chief Constable is very insistent that there should be no scandal unless we've got evidence that can be taken to a jury. I've let Rafe Jerningham see that he's under suspicion, and that's as far as I can go. You can't give a girl police protection in her own home. Could you induce her to go away, do you think?"

Miss Silver shook her head again.

"What would be the use of that, my dear Randal? An accident may happen in one place just as easily as in another."

"In fact," said March grimly, "accidents will happen. I have often wondered what proportion of them were really murders."

"A good many," said Miss Silver. She paused, and added, "It is a very shocking thought."

FORTY

It was not until they were having coffee under the cedar after lunch that anyone mentioned the Inspector's visit. It was Lisle who mentioned it and immediately had reason to wish that she had held her tongue.

Alicia yawned ostentatiously.

Rafe—what had happened to Rafe? Something—but she couldn't have said what. She was not looking at him, or he at her, but for a fantastic moment it was just as if a wire ran tightly stretched between them and from his end of it there had come—well, that was just it, she didn't know what. Shock—anger—surprise—fear—a signal—a warning? She didn't know.

It was all over in a flash, and they had emerged into the reality of Dale's anger.

"March? When did he come?"

"This morning, when you were out." She sounded as she looked, a little bewildered, like a child who has offended without quite knowing how.

Dale set down his coffee-cup with a bang.

"And no one told me—no one thought it worth their while to mention it? What did he want—and why wasn't I told about it? Or didn't he want anything at all? A social visit perhaps! Are we going to have that damned policeman walking in and out all day and every day?"

Rafe tilted his head back against the canvas of his chair.

"Probably. But why so heated? It might be worse. He's quite a nice chap when he isn't being a policeman, I should think."

"What did he want?"

"To see me—and Lisle."

"What for?"

Rafe's eyes were half shut. He gazed through his lashes at the heavy green of the cedar overhead.

"Fingerprints," he murmured—"on Lisle's coat, you know—some new process. Naturally the whole thing would be plastered with our prints. That's the worst of being such a united family."

"Mine?" interjected Alicia. There was so much sarcasm in the word that the colour rushed to Lisle's face.

"And mine—and Dale's," said Rafe amiably. "Possibly William's and Evans'—probably Lizzie's. A nice bag of tricks for our modern scientific police. You put 'em in a hat and shake 'em up, and then you put in your hand and pick your murderer."

Alicia said, *"Really,* Rafe!"

Dale laughed angrily.

"Quit fooling and tell me what happened!"

Rafe opened his eyes and sat up.

"Oh, nothing. We're all still here—no gyves on any wrist, though I think he had his eye on mine. You see, I helped Lisle on with that coat last time she wore it, and our imaginative Inspector is all het up over some especially clear prints which I must have left on it then."

Dale stared at him in a kind of horror.

"You don't mean to say the man suspects one of us!"

Rafe Jerningham leaned sideways and stubbed out his cigarette on the short, dry turf.

"He has a nasty suspicious mind," he said. "He'd suspect his own grandmother for twopence."

"But it's insane!" said Dale. "Cissie Cole! Good heavens— what possible motive could any of us have had?"

There was a pause. Lisle didn't look at any of them. She looked down at the dry turf between her feet—short, burnt grass with the colour scorched out of it. It was in the shade now, but presently the sun would reach it again. The shadow of the cedar would shift away from it and the scorching would go on. She heard Rafe say in his pleasant casual voice,

"Oh, one can always think up a motive. In March's place, I could produce half a dozen."

After a moment Dale said in a horrified tone,

"Rafe, you don't seriously mean—"

Rafe got up.

"March does. He hasn't got any evidence of course— he'd never dare take those prints to a jury. He knows that, and he knows that I know it. We had quite a pretty fencing match—honours easy. But we'll have to watch our step, I think. All of us."

Alicia Steyne turned her eyes upon him. He was smiling, a hand in his pocket getting out a cigarette-case. She said, in her high, sweet voice,

"Why have you gone back to that old battered thing? What have you done with the one Lisle gave you for your birthday?"

With the shabby old case in his hand, he smiled at her. Then he snapped it open and took out a cigarette.

"It's gone missing. It will turn up again all right."

"Missing? Since when?"

"Oh, a day or two. Have you seen it?"

Alicia looked at him, then she looked away.

"Perhaps."

"Mysterious—aren't you? Well, I'm not offering a reward, so it's no good your holding on for one." He strolled away.

From where she sat Lisle could see glimpses of his light shirt amongst the trees on the seaward slope. He walked slowly, aimlessly—the perfect picture of an idle young man with the whole summer afternoon to idle in. But there was the funeral—Cissie's funeral—

Suddenly she felt as if she could not sit here any longer between Dale and Alicia. She got up.

Dale said at once, "Where are you going?"

"I thought I would rest for a little before the funeral."

"Wait a minute! You saw March too?"

"Yes."

"What did he say to you—what did he want to know?"

"Very little, Dale—just when I wore the coat last, and whether any of you had touched me when I was wearing it."

"And you said?"

"Rafe helped me on with it—I told him that."

"Well, if it comes to that, I suppose we all touched you."

She shook her head.

"Not whilst I was wearing the coat."

He laughed and looked up at her, all his anger gone.

"Darling, I'd just got home—we'd had a most affectionate meeting."

She began to move away.

"I wasn't wearing the coat then. Rafe brought it to me afterwards."

When she had reached the terrace she looked back. The shadow of the cedar had shifted. Dale was still in it, but the sun touched Alicia. At the instant in which Lisle turned she saw Alicia's hand go up with something bright in it. It dazzled and flew from her to Dale. He reached forward and caught it.

As Lisle went into the house she wondered a little idly what the bright thing had been.

FORTY-ONE

Cissie Cole's funeral was over. With a sigh of relief the little groups about the grave broke up and began to drift away. The Vicar's surplice dazzled under the bright sun. The flowers were wilting already. Black dresses, much too hot for the day, had a rusty look and showed shiny at the seams. Lisle turned back to put a hand on Miss Cole's arm and say a word or two in a low voice, and then it was really over. They got into Dale's car and he drove them home.

There was tea under the cedar, cool drinks as well for anyone who wanted them. A green slope to a blue sea, and the breeze coming off the water. It was all over, and one could set about the uphill business of forgetting.

All over. Lisle said it to herself, but she couldn't make it sound true. She went away up to her room to take off her black dress. Dale came up too, and she could hear him walking about in his room. She slipped on a short-sleeved washing frock, and presently he opened the communicating door and came through in shirt and flannel trousers.

"Well, that's a relief! Darling, you look like a little girl in that silly little dress."

"Little?" She tried to smile. "Do you know how tall I am?"

"Term of endearment, darling." He smiled at her with his eyes. And then quite suddenly the smile went. "Look here, I've got to talk to you, and it's about something so damnable that I've gone on putting it off, only now I can't any longer."

"Dale—what is it?"

"Darling, I'd give anything in the world not to tell you—or even to put it off, but I can't. I would if I could, but—well, the fact is I've got to tell you for your own sake."

"Dale!"

She was sitting on her dressing-stool half turned from the glass. He came to her and took her hands.

"Will you try and remember that I hate what I'm going to do—that I'd give anything in the world not to do it? I've held my tongue all these years, and if I can't go on holding it now, it's because it isn't safe—for you."

She drew her hands away. They were cold. She lifted her eyes to his and said,

"Please tell me, Dale."

"I've got to." He turned away with a groan and began to walk up and down in the room. "It's about Rafe. You mustn't go about with him as you've been doing—it won't do."

Lisle's head came up. She said quickly,

"What do you mean, Dale?"

"Not what you think—I'm not such a fool as that. Rafe makes love to everyone, but it doesn't mean a thing."

"He doesn't make love to me. Do you think I would let him?"

"Of course not. Darling, I didn't mean that—I told you I didn't."

"Then what did you mean?"

He walked to the middle window, and then swung round to face her.

"Lisle, I'm trying to tell you. Will you just listen and not say anything? Rafe—well, he's always been like a younger brother. He, and Lal, and I, we were just like brothers and sister. None of us can remember the time when the others weren't here. Well, Rafe was the youngest. There's not three years between the three of us, but even a year makes a lot of difference when you're children. He was the one who had to be looked after— got out of scrapes and all that sort of thing. Well, we went on here together till Lal and I got married. That broke the thing up. Lal married Rowland Steyne, and I married Lydia. That left Rafe odd man out. I didn't think about it at the time— one doesn't. It was only afterwards I realised that it sent him right off his balance with jealousy. He was eighteen and he was at a loose end between leaving school and going up to Cambridge—and he didn't like Lydia."

He began to walk again, passing her and then coming back to pause and look at her. It was a deep distressed look.

"Lisle—has anyone ever told you about Lydia's accident?"

"Yes." She had to moisten her dry lips before they would say the word.

"Who?"

"Rafe—and Mrs Mallam."

"What did they tell you?"

"Rafe said she fell. He said—"

"Oh, yes, she fell—poor Lydia. It was the most ghastly show. Never mind what they told you—I'm going to tell you the truth. I've never told it to anyone before, but I'm going to tell it now because I've got to. We weren't climbing, you know—Lydia wasn't strong enough. We were just walking along one of those winding paths—Rowland and Alicia, Lydia and I, the Mallams, and Rafe. We got a bit strung out, and the minute you got round a corner you were out of sight of the others—you've got to understand that. You'd be right in the crowd one minute and completely cut off a minute later. Well, we came to a place where the path widened into a sort of bay scooped out of the hill. When you were in the bay you were right out of sight of the people in front and the people behind. Lydia and I and the Steynes were there together. Rafe had just gone on, and the Mallams had fallen a good way back. There was an easy scrambling slope going up from the inner side of the path, but on the outer side there was a most horrible sheer drop. Lal and her husband went up the hill after some flowers. Lydia and I were there together. Well, she sent me back to see if the Mallams were coming. I couldn't have imagined there was any danger, and I went. But I'd hardly got round the first bend—there was a second one just beyond—when I heard her scream—" He broke off. "Lisle, it was horrible! I went on hearing it for months. When I got round the corner again she was gone. There was a broken bush—she must have caught at it, poor girl, but it wasn't strong enough to hold her. And just where she had gone over, there was Rafe, staring down after her."

"Dale!" Her lips hardly framed the word. It came to him as a broken gasp.

He spoke himself, with a calm that appalled her more than any vehemence would have done.

"He pushed her over. I have never had the slightest doubt of it, nor, I think, has Lal. We've never discussed it at all. I don't know if she saw anything. I couldn't ask her—she was completely broken down. Rowland saw nothing, but Alicia—well, I've never been sure—"

Lisle sat there stiff and white, staring at him.

"What are you saying?"

"What I never meant to say to anyone—what I should never have said even to you if—it hadn't happened again."

A moment before she would have said that she was past feeling—too shocked, too frozen. Now she knew that there was something more, something worse. She repeated his last word,

"Again—"

He came nearer, catching her by the shoulders so that she felt the warmth of his hands and wondered at it.

"Lisle—wake up! Don't you realise what has been happening? That accident to your steering—did you think it did itself? I tried to make myself believe that it was Pell who had been playing tricks, and I very nearly succeeded. And then— Cissie Cole—"

Lisle pulled away from him.

"How could it be Rafe? He was here with me after she went away."

"And he went off for a walk along the beach a good half hour before she fell. He says he only went half way and turned back. But suppose he didn't—suppose he went up the track on to the cliff path and saw Cissie standing up there on the headland looking out to the sea. She was standing there with her back to him on the edge of the cliff—like Lydia. It was getting dark. She was wearing your coat. Her hair would show up in the dusk—fair hair, like yours. Wouldn't he take her for you? He'd left you at Tanfield, but why shouldn't you have taken my car or his and driven up there to see the sunset just as Lal and I had done? I tell you he saw Cissie there. He thought he was seeing you, and he pushed her over, just as he had pushed Lydia over and for the same reason."

She moistened her lips.

"What reason, Dale?"

He went and sat down on the bed and put his head in his hands for a moment. Then he looked up again.

"Lisle, you have thought I cared too much for Tanfield—no don't say anything, because it's no good. I've felt you thinking that time and again, and I suppose in a way you were right, because I can see where that sort of thing gets you if you don't take a pull on it. Rafe's always been crazy about the place. Nothing else has ever counted with him. He doesn't love people—he loves Tanfield. I expect you've been taken in by the way he talks about it—most people are. He'll call it a great barrack of a place and say how much better off we'd be if we hadn't got it slung round our necks, but it doesn't mean a thing—it's a cover-up. He's always been like that—if he cares about anything he'll make a joke of it. And what he cares about, and

always has, and always will, is just this place and the fact that
it belongs to us. He'd do anything, sacrifice anyone. You've got
to believe me, because I know what I'm talking about. If Lydia
hadn't died when she did, Tanfield would have had to go. He
saved Tanfield—that's the way it would look to him. What did
Lydia matter? Just one life in all those generations. And then
we come to you—the same situation, the same danger. He
knows I'll have to sell. He knows that if you died, I shouldn't
have to sell. Look back and think about the things that have
been happening. I've had to, and I can't resist the weight of
the evidence. You were nearly drowned. Who was making all
the noise, splashing and ducking us, whilst you were calling
for help? Rafe. The steering of your car snapped on the hill.
Why? Evans said the track-rod had been filed half through. I
shut him up. He thought it was Pell, and that's where I began
to be afraid about Rafe—little things I noticed in his manner
when we were talking about it, and once I saw him look at
you—well, there's no mistaking hate."

Lisle sat there. She had asked Rafe if he hated her, and he
had said yes—on the Wednesday night—just after Cissie had
gone—Dale went on speaking in a deep, troubled voice. "I
can't imagine why that car smash didn't kill you. He was down
in the village waiting for it—do you remember that?—waiting
to see you come down that hill and smash against Cooper's
barn. You know, Lisle, you were born lucky. Just imagine his
feelings when the car went to glory without you. And that
meant he had to try again. He wouldn't give up—not with
Tanfield at stake. Besides, once you start a thing like that, it
gets you and you've got to see it through. He must have been

thinking what he could do next when he saw Cissie on the cliff
and took her for you. It must have looked like the most marvellous chance—and he took it. That's how those prints of his
got on the shoulders of the coat—he took her by the shoulders
and pushed her over. And then he found he'd been tricked
again. He hasn't had much luck, has he? You've had it all. But
you mustn't try it too far—it might turn against you. That's
why I'm telling you this. I must tell him I know and send him
away. And meanwhile you've got to be careful. Don't let him
drive you anywhere. Don't be alone with him. Stick to Alicia or
to me. I couldn't do anything until this funeral was over—we
mustn't have talk. Besides, I only got the proof today."

She had to try twice before she could say, "What proof?"

Dale's hand went into a pocket and came up with something bright. It dazzled as she looked at it, and she remembered the bright thing Alicia had tossed to him when she left
them under the cedar. The bright thing lay on Dale's palm. He
held it out to her.

"Recognise this?"

It was the cigarette-case she had given to Rafe on his birthday, his name on it in her writing—"Rafe."

"When did you see it last?" said Dale.

She knew that answer. All of them sitting on the terrace.
Rafe's case—this case—tossed down on the cushion of a vacant
chair. And William coming out to say Cissie Cole was waiting
to see her.

She said, "Wednesday—just before Cissie came—"

Dale nodded.

"You haven't seen it since?"

"No."

"Nor anyone else. He's been using that old battered wreck we used to chaff him about. Do you know why?"

She moved a very little. The movement said, "No."

Dale threw the case down on the end of the bed.

"Because this one's been lying up on Tane Head where he dropped it when he pushed Cissie over the cliff. Alicia found it there this morning. She missed that diamond and emerald clasp of hers and she went up there to look for it. A complete fool's errand of course. I don't suppose she dropped it there at all—anyhow she didn't find it. But she found Rafe's cigarette-case. It was right on the edge, but it had slipped down into a sort of crack. I suppose that's why the police didn't find it—they must have been all over the ground." He reached out for the case and put it back in his pocket again. "He must have been wondering where he dropped it. He won't show much fight when I tell him—it gives me the whip hand all right. I'll pay his passage, and he can pack off to Australia, and see whether that job he turned down is still going."

Lisle put up her hand to her cheek in a forlorn gesture.

"What about Pell? You can't—you can't let him! Dale!"

Dale got to his feet, came over to her, and put an arm about her shoulders.

"Oh, we won't let Pell hang," he said, and bent to kiss her.

FORTY-TWO

Lisle had the feeling that the day would never end. All this bright sun and blue sky, this inward strain and terror, this numbness dulling something which without it would be agony, seemed to her shocked sense to have neither beginning nor ending. It was like a dreadful travesty of eternity. She felt unable either to look forward or back.

There was a moment when Rafe asked her if she would like to go for a drive—"up over the downs to get some air. You look all in." Dale said, "No—she's too tired," and the numbness was pierced by a jagged stab of pain. Just why that should have hurt so much, she could not have told. Rafe wanting her to go with him, his voice sounding kind. And Dale not giving her time to answer because he was afraid to let her go with Rafe as they had gone so innocently often before their natural world had changed into a nightmare. Afraid to let her go with Rafe . . . But she herself was not afraid. Perhaps that was just because she was too numb to feel afraid—too numb really to take in what Dale had told her. Only she couldn't struggle any more. She let Dale speak for her, and sat there without a word to say.

The endless evening wore on, the four of them together. She thought that it would never end.

When she went up to dress Dale followed her into her room and put his arms round her.

"My poor darling—it's been a horrible day for you, but it's nearly over. And look here—I've got a plan. We'll get away from the others and have a nice peaceful time just by ourselves. I never seem to see you now except in a crowd. I'm very fond of the family, but I do sometimes want my wife to myself. Funny—isn't it?" There was the smile in his eyes which she used to think was for her alone. It had always charmed her, but now she was too tired. Her eyelids fell. She moved a little, but he held her.

"Wait a minute and I'll tell you what I thought we'd do. I'm flying again tonight. I'll say so, and at the same time I'll tell you to get off to bed. That'll be about half past nine, but I needn't really get up to the aerodrome till nearly eleven. It's not dark enough for proper night flying till well after that. And what I thought was this—we could slip down to the beach and get right away from everyone."

Her lashes lay upon her cheek. She said very low,

"I'm so tired, Dale."

"I know, darling, but that's why. It will be cool down there, and right away from everyone—just you and me. Oh, Lisle, I want you to so much! You'll really sleep afterwards."

It wasn't in her to struggle. She said, "Very well," and moved away from him. This time he let her go.

When he spoke again he sounded as pleased and excited as a schoolboy.

"Look here, we won't go off together—that won't do at all. Lal—" he laughed a little—"well, I'm very fond of her, as you know, but she does butt in. I'll get the car and drive out by the back gate. Then I can leave it a bit down the lane and cut through across the park—it's no distance that way—and you can wait for me down by the sea wall." He laughed again. "Rather fun having to make an assignation before you can have half an hour alone with your own wife! Better change into a short dress and put on beach shoes. I thought we'd go down by the rocks and see the tide come in. And you'll have to slip away without being seen, or we'll find we've got the family circle round us again. Will you do it?"

She said "Yes," and was glad not to have to say any more than that.

He dropped a kiss on the top of her head and went off to his own room. She could hear him whistling as he moved about there.

Later, when she was in her room again taking off the dress she had worn at dinner, slipping back into her cotton frock, stripping off thin silk stockings and fastening the beach shoes he had suggested, she could hear him there again, slamming a cupboard door, pulling out a drawer. But this time he didn't whistle.

She sat down on the edge of the bed to wait. Because it was part of the plan that he should get away first, and of course he had to change. He took some time over it, but at last she heard him open the door to the corridor. And then, all in a hurry, he came running back to look in on her with a laughing, mischievous expression and a finger on his lips.

When he had really gone, she stayed where she was for about ten minutes and then made her way down to the sea wall. She saw no one as she went, and as far as she knew, no one saw her go.

FORTY-THREE

It was the first thing that Dale asked her. "Did anyone see you?"

"No."

"Nor me either." He was laughing and breathing a little quickly from his run. "What conspirators we are! Come along quick down by the steps! It's a marvellous evening!"

The sun had been gone for half an hour. The dusk was falling, but the sky still glowed, hyacinth blue at the zenith fading through turquoise-blue to turquoise green. And from turquoise-green to primrose, daffodil, and one deep orange streak. Between the blue and the green the waning moon slipped down the sky, a slender crescent gaining brightness as the light withdrew.

At the foot of the steps Dale turned to the left. He put his arm about her and they walked in silence. Tane Head was behind them, and the Shepstone Rocks ahead. The flowing tide had almost reached and covered the sandy ridge which lay beyond. It was easier walking here than on the side towards Tane Head, because each high tide came up to cover the sand and beat it hard. Easier, that is, until they came among the rocks.

"Where are we going, Dale?"

"Down the ridge. We've just time."

A spit of sand ran down between the rocks. Insensibly the dusk, the cool air, the calm beauty of sea and sky, were having their way with Lisle. The strain of the day relaxed a little. What had been numbness came a shade nearer to being peace. She no longer wished to go back. Dale's arm guided her. It was strong, and he was kind. Her thoughts began to flow in the simplest channels—evening peace and calm—kindness—rest—

Neither of them spoke until they were standing on the ridge piled against the outworks of the Shepstone Rocks by the current which set from Tane Head.

"It's nice here—isn't it?" said Dale.

She said "Lovely—" in a dreaming voice.

"We'll just have time to get round to the far side of the rocks."

"Shall we? Can't we stay here?"

"Just round the point, darling. There's something I want to show you. But we must hurry."

His arm was through hers now. They turned landwards and picked their way down off the sandy ridge to the rock and shingle which lay behind it.

At once the light seemed to have failed. The glow in the sky and its reflection from the sea lay behind them. They faced a flat strand strewn with dark seaweed-covered rocks running back to the steep rise of the cliff. They were in a hollow for the moment, but Dale made for a spit of shingle running up between the main Shepstone wall and another lesser ridge. They had hardly gone any distance before the wall on their left was so high that they could no longer see over it. The Tanfield side of the barrier was gone as if it had never been. Everything familiar was gone. There was only this gathering gloom, the lap of the tide behind them, and a stench of decaying seaweed.

Lisle stopped.

"Dale—I want to go back."

"Why? It's only a little farther." His arm went round her waist again.

"It's getting so dark."

"That's because we've got our backs to the sea. We'll be turning in a minute, and then it will seem quite light again. Look—this is what I wanted to show you, just up here. Give me your hand and I'll pull you up."

He released her as he finished speaking, and scrambled up a long ridged slope, turning to catch her wrist and pull her after him. She came unwillingly but without the energy to resist. When he had shown her what he had brought her here to see he would let her go home again. It was never any good struggling with Dale—he had to have his way. And when he had had it they would go home and she would sleep.

She stood on the flat-topped rock to which he had brought her and looked down into blackness. High rocky walls shut in a roughly shaped triangle of which the base was the stone upon which they were standing. The blackness was a pit which went down and down to a faint gleam of water. The water seemed a long way off. A long way down—how far she did not know. She only knew that her head swam. She would have stepped back but for the arm at her waist—Dale's arm—very strong—and she had thought it kind—

It swung her forward with a sudden jerk. Her feet slipped and lost the rock. She caught at the empty dark and went down into it.

She went down into water, or there would have been nothing more to say about Lisle Jerningham. Down and under, with the scream choked on her lips, and then up again on her knees, sea-water in her eyes, her ears, her mouth. And then with a convulsive effort to her feet again, head and shoulders clear of the water, hands catching at the rock sides of the pit.

Her foothold steadied. She pushed back dripping hair and looked up. Black walls all round her—very black—the sky a still, deep blue—light coming from it. And against the light and the blue of the sky, Dale standing there, black and tall and silent, looking down. She said his name in a gasping whisper.

"Dale—" And then, "I fell—"

It wasn't true. He had thrown her down. She knew that, but she couldn't believe it—not yet—not so soon—it was too dreadful. How do you believe a thing like that about your own husband?

She called his name again and stretched up her hands to him.

"Dale—get me out!"

He moved when she said that. She heard him laugh.

"What a silly woman you are, Lisle! Don't you understand even now? Don't you understand that all the things I told you this afternoon were true—only they weren't true about Rafe, they were true about me? Lydia had to go because her going saved Tanfield. If it's a choice between Tanfield and any woman on earth, Tanfield has it every time. That's what you've been up against all along, my dear. You didn't care about Tanfield, and why didn't I sell it and go and live at the Manor? The very first time you said that to me I thought how much I should like to kill you. But you've had all the luck till now. I thought I'd done the trick the day you were nearly drowned. I heard you calling, but the others didn't—I took good care of that. And if it hadn't been for that damned meddlesome grocer or whatever he was, drowned you would have been, and a lot of trouble saved. You were lucky over the car too. I took a risk there and half tried to back out at the last minute, because somebody might have seen the file marks on the track-rod. Anyhow after my urging you in front of Alicia to have the steering seen to before you went home nobody could have pinned it on me. The disgruntled Pell came in handy there. I thought about that. And considering the way Lal had been chipping you, I didn't really think you'd want to wait about at the garage with her." He gave a sudden contemptuous laugh. "Oh well, you had the luck then, but it's gone back on you now. Clever weren't you, getting that detective woman down to watch me! Miss Silver—Private Investigations! You didn't think I knew about that, did you? You shouldn't have left her card in your bag. It was really very careless. But you needn't think that either she or that damned policeman are going to have anything on me over this, because they're not! You've provided me with a most convincing suicide letter—one of those pieces you wrote to Robson this morning. Do you remember it? I suggested it to you, and you thought it sounded a bit exaggerated. But you wrote it down, my dear, you wrote it down—and it would convince any coroner on this earth that you meant to do away with yourself."

She said in a small, clear voice,

"Did you kill Cissie?"

His tone changed, became rough and unsteady.

"Why did you give her that damned coat?"

Her hair had fallen into her eyes again. She pushed it back. It was getting dark, but she could still see him.

"You took Rafe's cigarette-case and it dropped there when you pushed her over, and Alicia found it. Even if Rafe saw you take it, you knew that he would never say—" Her voice broke suddenly. "Dale—let me out! I won't say either—I promise I won't—only let me out!"

She heard him laugh.

"What a hope!"

And with no more than that he turned and went away. She saw him go, the shortening of the black shadow standing up against the sky, and then the sky without any shadow there.

Dale was gone.

FORTY-FOUR

Dale was gone—all in a moment between one breath and the next whilst she tried desperately for words that would recall the Dale who had loved her and whom she had loved, or move this dreadful stranger to let her go. No words had come and none were needed now, because Dale was gone. Just for a moment his going brought relief. The frantic effort to reach him, the terror of him standing there like a visible presence of evil—these were gone. There was a slow recovery, as from some sudden stroke of pain, but as this passed she began to see what it had left behind—desolation, the breakdown of all she had loved and trusted. He had gone, and he had left her here to die—she was to drown in this rocky pit. How long would it take for the tide to reach her? Perhaps an hour—she didn't know.

Her first relief merged into an agony of fear. She screamed, and heard her voice came back to her from the rocky wall. It was a very hoarse, faint cry from a throat parched with terror. No one would hear it. There was no one to hear—unless the sound reached Dale and brought him back, strong and angry, to finish what he had begun. The thought was so dreadful that she dared not scream again. Not for a long, long time.

She stood there with the water up to her armpits, listening. There was no sound to listen for. The sky was getting darker and she could see the stars. She thought of all the times when she had seen them with a quiet mind. She thought, "I shall never see them like that again," and suddenly her mind was clear and quiet under the stars. Life—She thought, "It goes on wherever you are." She thought, "Dale can't kill me. I shall go on."

She stopped being afraid.

Presently she called again with all her strength, and went on calling. Dale wouldn't come back now. He would be hurrying to the aerodrome. It was all planned. He had taken the car and driven away, and presently he would be at the air-field, taking out his plane, taking off, sweeping up into the sky with a roar. Perhaps she would hear him. Perhaps he would fly overhead and look down to see if the tide was covering her yet.

He would be safe. No one would know that they had been together. She remembered? his "Don't tell anyone, darling. Let's have this time to ourselves." He had betrayed her with a kiss. She hadn't told anyone. No one had seen her go—

She lifted up her voice and called again—and again—and again—desperately.

It was at this moment that Rafe Jerningham came down the steps from the sea wall. After one of the longest half hours of his life he was doing what he had made up his mind that he would never do. Lisle had not gone to her rendezvous as unseen as she had thought. A desperately unhappy young man had stood back among the trees and watched her go down towards the sea. A day or two ago he would have followed her, but now he could no longer trust himself. Something had happened between them, without any words, and it had happened with the horrifying suddenness of a thunder clap. He had driven her into Ledlington. Nothing had happened then, nor at lunch, nor as they came and went about the business of Cissie's funeral. He had had to endure seeing her pale, strained, with that waiting patience in her eyes. He had played the part which he had played so long that no one guessed that it was a part at all. And then something had happened. What? He had no idea, but it was something which set an unendurable barrier between them.

He came down to dinner, and she wasn't Lisle any longer—she was a stranger. She did not look at him. He felt her shrink when he approached her. All that he had ever had of her had been with-drawn, silently, irrevocably, without reason and without relenting.

> "A god, a god our severance ruled,
> And bade between our shores to be
> The unplumbed, salt, estranging sea."

The lines went through his head. They were most bitterly true. He accepted the severance, as he had always accepted it, but that it should become absolute at this of all moments was

the final bitterness. Days of suspicion darkening to a despair-
ing certainty—moments, hours, when these suspicions seemed
a foul miasma from his own corroding jealousy of Dale . . .
There was a voice which talked with him in most unsparing
accents— "You love Dale's wife, and so—Dale is a murderer.
You are eating your own heart, and because of that—Dale is
a murderer. Lisle is the sun and the moon and the stars, and
because they are out of your reach—Dale is a murderer."

Against this a slow damning computation of pros and cons.
Lydia. Lisle—drowning—all but drowned. A smashed car. A
dead girl lying among rocks—a girl who was wearing Lisle's
coat. That poor devil Pell at the inquest. His face. Lisle's coat.
Lisle—Dale looking at her, putting his arm about her, smiling down at her as if she were the sun and the moon and the
stars for him too. Dale—who had been the chief thing in his
life—until Lisle came—

This severance—between himself and Dale—between himself and Lisle—

"The unplumbed, salt, estranging sea—"

He saw Lisle go by, bare-headed in the evening light. At
the moment he could only think that he must let her go. If he
went after her now, his own barriers would not hold.

He let her go, and turning, walked rapidly away in the
opposite direction.

It was perhaps half an hour later that he remembered Lisle's
change of dress. She had worn black lace at dinner, but when
she passed him, going down towards the sea wall, she had on a

light washing frock and beach shoes. *Beach shoes.* Then she was
not just going to sit on the wall as she often did in the cool
of the evening—she wouldn't have changed just for that. She
must have been meaning to go down on to the beach. Why?
In all the time he had known her, when had she ever gone off
to the beach by herself in the dusk? The trouble in his mind
had dulled its natural acute-ness. Suddenly the vague, conflict-
ing fears and doubts, the passionate strivings and repressions
which had made it their battle-ground, fused into certainty.
If Lisle had gone beyond the sea wall, then she had not gone
alone, and if she had not gone alone, then there was only one
person with whom she would have gone, and that was Dale—
Dale who had made a point of telling them all that he was off
to the air-field.

When Rafe's mind had reached this point it took charge of
his body and sent it racing to the house. Not far to go—he had
been on his way there.

He passed Alicia on the terrace.

"Where's Lisle?"

She said, "Gone to bed."

It took him five minutes to make sure that she was not in
her room, to slip into flannels and beach shoes, to snatch up a
torch and be clear of the house again.

When he came to the sea wall he stood there a moment,
listening at first, and then calling her name.

"Lisle—Lisle—Lisle!"

No voice, no answer.

He ran down the steps and switched on his torch. There
was still a little light in the sky. Sea, strand, and sky were still

separate, but like a second and more invisible tide the dusk
flowed out from the land to meet the rising tide of the sea.

He stood irresolute. There was nothing to tell him which
way to go, but if the fear that had brought him here and was
drenching him with its cold sweat sprang from something more
than his own distorted fancy, then it was in the direction of the
Shepstone Rocks that he must look for Lisle. The wildest, the
most dangerous part of the coast, the least frequented—at this
hour solitary as a murderer's heart could wish. By no stretch of
the imagination could he suppose that Lisle would turn that
way alone. And if not alone, where had she been taken, and
how would he find her?

With these thoughts he was questing to and fro, turning
the torch in every direction. Not many people ever came this
way. Once the immediate neighbourhood of the steps was left
behind, the sand was smooth and unmarked as the tide had
left it. The water had not quite reached the wall. The dry sand
at its foot would hold no print. But half a dozen yards along
the torch found what he was looking for—Lisle's footprints
going towards the Rocks, and the larger, bolder prints which
were Dale's.

He had followed them for perhaps half a dozen yards, when
the torch picked up a second set of tracks—Dale's footprints
coming back—alone. They came in at a slant past the out-going
tracks and were lost in the dry sand. It was plain enough and
dreadful enough to read. Two had gone out, and only one had
come back. Within a few short hours the damning evidence
would be smoothed out by the tide, and the sand innocently
blank and bare again. Fate had not given Dale those hours.

Everything in Rafe went cold and still. There was nothing in all the world but to find Lisle, dead or alive, and it came to him that she must be dead, because Dale would not now have left her alive. He could think of this quite calmly, because at the moment when he saw that single returning track all his capacity for feeling died. He was not conscious of distress, and he was not at all conscious of his body. There remained only the capacity for thought—lucid, keen, undisturbed by any hampering emotion.

He followed the footprints to the spit of sand which ran down towards the sea and the ridge beyond the Shepstone Rocks. Half way there he lost them under the first ripple of the tide. The torch went into his pocket and he went on, ankle-deep, knee-deep, breast-deep, and then wading and pushing against the weight of the water, up the side of the long, sprawling ridge. The water was no more than ankle-deep here. He walked along the ridge past the rocky point, and as he turned shoreward he heard Lisle's cry.

It was so faint a sound that at any other time it would have gone by with all the million sounds which are never heard, but at this moment when everything in him was strung to the utmost pitch of expectancy it reached him. His heart jerked against his side. He began to walk towards the sound, coming down off the ridge into the deeper water, and then feeling his way slowly and cautiously so as to avoid the rocks. When the water was at its deepest he heard the sound again. And then his feet were on shingle and he came up the shallow slope of the beach towards the cliff.

As soon as he was clear of the water he called out.

"Lisle—where are you?"

The words beat on the rock wall and came back in a broken echo. And on that, something that wasn't an echo. His name—"Rafe!"

Lisle had gone on calling. There was something in her which wouldn't give up, something which said, "If I drown, it shan't be because I gave up." Giving up didn't just mean dying. It meant letting in the dark, and the loneliness, and Dale's treachery. If she had to die, she wanted to keep those things out, right up to the end. As long as she went on calling it meant that she wasn't letting them in. When she heard Rafe's voice all her courage leapt. She looked up from where she stood and saw the flicker of his torch, high above her like the flash of summer lightning. Only it wasn't lightning—it was light.

She called again, and she said, "I'm here— here—*here*," and went on saying it till the light shone over the edge of the pit and she could see him kneeling there, peering down. The beam of the torch shone suddenly upon her upturned face. White, drenched and drowned, she looked at Rafe. But her eyes were alive. He saw the pupils contract and the lids come down against the glare.

FORTY-FIVE

L isle! What happened? Are you all right?"

She said, "I fell—" and heard his voice with a savage note in it.

"He pushed you!"

Her hands were on the rocky wall, holding it as best she might She hid her face against them and felt how cold they were.

There was a moment, and then he called her sharply.

"See if you can reach me! Stretch up as high as you can!"

The beam of the torch was gone. She could just make out a dark something that was his head. He was lying down on the flat-topped boulder from which Dale had pushed her, reaching down to her at the full stretch of his arms as she reached up. She stood on tiptoe and strained towards him, but their hands did not touch. She heard him move, draw back. The light came again.

"You can't get higher up?"

"No—I'm on the highest bit. The floor slopes down. There's a deep hole. I've been afraid to move."

The beam of the torch went to and fro. It picked up a wide fissure splitting off the flat boulder from a rock wall which joined the main reef. He switched off the light and put the torch in his trouser pocket. Its light and the strength of the battery behind it were pretty well all that stood between them and death. They were not to be wasted. He said,

"I can't reach you. There's a split in the rock—that's why the water is so far down. The pool drains away as the tide goes out. There's nothing to worry about—we'll just have to wait till it comes in, that's all."

"Until the tide comes in!" Her voice was a faint breath of horror. It seemed too dreadful to be borne. Wait till the tide came in and drowned them!

"What's the matter? Don't you see that the water will float you up? Even if I could just reach your hands, I don't think I could get you out of a sheer place like this. There's nothing for me to hold on to, and this rock's as slippery as they're made. But we've only got to wait and the tide will do the trick. Look out—I'm letting my belt down to you. You keep hold of the buckle end. That'll give you something to pull on, and as soon as the water's high enough I'll get you out."

"Will it be long?"

"About twenty minutes, I think—perhaps half an hour. It comes up pretty quick once it's got over the ridge. We're really not much above that level here—that's why I can't risk going back, for help. Evans is the only man about the place who can swim, and he's not much use, and by the time I'd got him and a rope—well, it's not good enough. I'll get you out all right. Have you got hold of the belt?"

"Yes."

"You're not hurt?"

"No."

"Lisle—why did you go with him? Why were you so mad?"

She said, "I didn't know—"

"Why didn't you go away? I tried to make you go away."

"Was that why? I thought you hated me. Was it because you knew—about Dale?"

"I didn't know—I was horribly afraid?"

Strange to be talking like this in the dark, the sky just visible, their faces hidden one from the other. Strange, and easy.

She thought of that, and she thought that it had always been easy to talk to Rafe. She said,

"He killed Lydia. Did you know that?"

He used the same words again.

"I didn't know—I was afraid."

"And Cissie—poor Cissie."

"Lisle, I didn't know anything. I couldn't know. I could only suspect. There was always some way that it might have happened. Lydia might have slipped—she hadn't any head for heights. Pell might have damaged your car, and Pell might have murdered Cissie—things happen like that. But when I found her lying there—"

"You found her?"

"I thought it was you."

"But Rafe—you found her?"

"Yes, I found her—and I thought it was you. I took her by the shoulders to turn her over. That's how my prints came on that damned coat. Lisle, I thought it was you—" His voice shuddered and broke.

She said, "Did you see her fall?"

"No, I just came on her. I didn't hear anything either—the gulls were crying—I was a long way off. I had just been trying to get you to go away, and you asked me whether I hated you—do you remember? I was a long way off from where I was walking. I hadn't thought where I was, or how far I'd gone. I was about a million miles away, and then I came back with a thud that pretty well broke me. And I was right under the Tane Head cliff, with what I thought was your dead body at my feet."

After a long time she said.

"You didn't tell anyone—"

"No, Lisle—it broke me. I came back to the wall and stayed there half the night. It wasn't only the shock of thinking it was you—it was—Dale. If I could think it was you, why so could he. Everything I had been fighting came back and got me down. I didn't know what to do. I made up my mind that unless I was called at the inquest I would hold my tongue. I didn't want to bring you in for one thing. And my finding her proved nothing. It didn't help Pell."

She said in a curious still voice,

"Dale said you killed Lydia—and Cissie. He said you were trying to kill me—because of Tanfield. He said—"

"And you believed him!"

"I don't know—I don't think I believed anything—any more."

"When you came down to dinner you looked at me as if I wasn't there."

Her voice lifted on a sighing breath.

"I didn't feel—as if—any of us were there—really. It was like a horrible dream."

"He'd been telling you then?"

"Yes. He told me. It made me feel—" She stopped as if she was searching for a word, and then said, "stunned."

There was a moment's silence before she spoke again.

"Rafe—what happened to your cigarette-case—the one I gave you for your birthday?"

"Don't you know?"

"Yes, I know. I wanted to know if you did."

He said, "Dale took it—on that Wednesday night. His case was empty. He saw mine lying there on one of the chairs, and he picked it up and put it in his pocket when he and Alicia went off."

"Did he know that you had seen him take it?"

"Oh, yes, he knew. What did he tell you about it?"

"He said Alicia found it up on the cliff where Cissie went over. He said that she was looking for her emerald and diamond clip. And she found your case."

Rafe made a movement.

"And that is very likely! I wondered what she was doing up there this morning." He gave a curious laugh. "It really was only this morning, but it feels like years ago. I don't suppose she dropped her clip at all, but Dale knew he had dropped my case up there, and he sent her to look for it."

The strangest part of all this strange business was the quiet way in which they talked it over. There had been passion and racking fear, the action and reaction of hatred, suspicion, and doubt. There had been first the slow decay, and then the violent death of hope, and faith, and love. There had been flood-tides of emotion. Now all was spent, was gone, was over. They spoke to one another without effort or reserve. Neither could see the other's face, but to each the other's thought was most simple, plain, and clear.

After a long pause Lisle said,

"Alicia—did she know?"

There was no answer. There never was to be any answer to that. Just how much Alicia knew or guessed about Lydia—about Cissie, only Alicia herself could have told, and Alicia would never tell.

The silence spoke. And then Lisle spoke, breaking it.

"The water is rising—"

FORTY-SIX

From the withdrawing of the tide until sundown the pool had reflected and absorbed the light and heat of the day. The water was still warm. It had not seemed so to Lisle, but she became aware of it now when the new cold water brought by the rising tide came eddying in against her breast, against her shoulders, rocking her from her unsteady footing. She held to the belt with one hand and steadied herself against the rocky wall with the other.

The new cold ripple ebbed, came again, rocking, chilling, lifting her—ebb and flow, and ebb and flow again—a tide within a tide, but each flow stronger and colder than the last.

The time came when Rafe's hand, reaching downwards, closed on her wrist. For Lisle the worst was over then. For Rafe all the hardest part was yet to come. The rock on which he lay was slimy with weed. There was nothing to hold to. He had perforce to wait until the water was within three feet of the brink before he could get Lisle over it. She was numb and exhausted. He would have to get her out between the rocks to the sandy ridge, then round the point and in, between the rocks on the other side—just the one possible channel in either case, where the shingle spit ran in on this side and the tongue of sand upon the other. Both were deep under the water now, since the tide, which had been held up by the ridge, was by this time well over it, flooding all the lower levels.

If he had not known every rock on the beach, every twist of the channel, it would have been a very forlorn hope indeed. Even in daylight no one in his senses would have attempted to find his way amongst these formidable and jagged rocks with no real depth of water over them. The worst of them were upon this side of the Shepstone Wall. If he could reach the ridge with Lisle he could bring her in. But he had to reach the ridge. At all times a poor swimmer, she was in no case to help herself or him.

He made her float, and sliding down into the water, began to pilot her towards the ridge, swimming slowly and with extreme caution, one arm about her, his eyes straining to find each landmark.

The summer sky is never quite dark. On a clear July night there is always a faint, mysterious light under which shapes and masses appear without detail but with varying degrees of solidity. To Rafe these vague shapes possessed their unseen contours. There was not one of them which he could not call from its obscurity and see it in his mind as he had seen it unnumbered times under the light of day.

He moved slowly but with the certainty which comes of custom and practice. Lisle lay passive in the water. She might have been unconscious. He wondered if she were. He could see her face as a pale oval.

Lisle was not unconscious, but her consciousness was of a curious kind. It had limits. Within these limits she could think, but beyond them all was as vague, as dimmed as the sea in which she floated. She was not afraid any more. She was quite safe. Rafe said so. She was safe, but she was cold and very tired. She wanted above all things in the world to lie down and sleep. She felt the movement of the water. She felt Rafe's arm. She did not know how time passed. She knew that they moved, but she did not know when they turned the point and began to head towards their own beach. She hardly knew when they reached it.

Rafe's voice calling her—Rafe's hands pulling her up, setting her on her feet—his arm hard about her—

"Can you walk? Better for you if you can. Can you get to the steps? I can't leave you here with the tide coming in. Put your arm round my neck and try."

They got to the steps. They got up them. He was taking most of her weight. At each stage of that journey it seemed as if there was no strength left for the next, yet each stage was accomplished. From the water's edge to the sea wall. From the wall up the long ride, so green by day, so dark and shadowy now. On, and on, and on among the statues and cypresses of the Italian garden. Across the terrace, and at long last to the house.

There was still a light in the hall. To come into it was like coming back from the other side of another world than this. Lisle roused enough to know how cold she was. And then

William was there, and Rafe was telling him that she had had an accident and he must get Lizzie and one of the other maids at once.

The things that happened after that slid vaguely across the dulled surface of her consciousness—Lizzie and Mary being kind—a hot bath—something hot to drink—her own bed. These things slid past like a succession of dreams. They were not so much happenings as impressions. Then, striking through them, something that penetrated the numbness—Rafe's hand on hers—Rafe's voice—

"You're quite safe, Lisle. Lizzie will stay with you. Can you hear me? You're quite safe."

She said, "Yes."

The sense of safety came in like a flood. She sank through it into the deepest waters of sleep.

FORTY-SEVEN

Rafe Jerningham came into the study and shut the door. It was a few minutes short of midnight. He sat down at Dale's table, took the receiver from the telephone, and called the Tanfield aerodrome. The voice which answered was a familiar one.

"Hullo!"

"Hullo, Mac! Rafe Jerningham speaking. Has my cousin taken his plane up?"

Mac's voice came back to him with its Scottish burr.

"Well, I'm not sure. There was a bit of a hold-up. Johnson was working on the plane, and I'm not just sure if he got off or not. Are you wanting him?"

"Yes. Look here, Mac, if he hasn't gone, get hold of him. There's been an accident up here—will you tell him that. Ask him to come and speak to me."

"I hope it's nothing bad—"

Rafe said, "Bad enough."

He heard Mac's footsteps go away, sounding unnaturally loud in the empty, echoing place. They went over the edge of sound and were gone. He waited for those other footsteps—Dale's footsteps—hurrying to hear that Lisle was dead. The room was very still.

The footsteps came at last—the quick, impatient steps of a man who is in no mind to be kept waiting. Then the sound of the receiver being snatched up, and Dale's voice.

"That you, Rafe? What is it?"

"There's been an accident"

"Who?"

"Lisle. I found her."

"Where?"

"In one of those pools beyond the Shepstone Rocks."

"Dead?"

"No—alive."

There was a smashing silence. Not the faintest sound from all those things which that one word must have sent down in ruin. Then, after what seemed a long time, Dale's voice:

"Is she—hurt?"

"No."

"Conscious?"

"Perfectly."

"Has she been talking?"

"Yes."

There was a pause. Then Dale Jerningham said,

"I see." And then, "What happens next?"

"That's up to you."

"Meaning there's no compromise?"

"How can there be?"

There was another pause. Dale laughed.

"Bit of a meddler—aren't you! Why couldn't you leave well alone? Just out of curiosity I'd like to know how you found her."

"Footprints on the sand—two lots going, and only one coming back."

"I see—the odd chance. You can't fight your luck. It's been against me all along. Well? Do you import March into this?"

"Bound to. There's Pell—"

"All right, carry on. There's a letter on my dressing-table in a blank envelope—you might retrieve it. Well, that's all—I'm just going up. You'll hear me come over in a minute. So long!"

The receiver clicked. The line was dead.

Rafe hung up at his end and got to his feet. He stood there for a moment under the light, looking up at the picture over the hearth. Giles Jerningham, sometime Lord Chief Justice of England, looked sternly back at him.

Presently he turned and went out of the room, switching off the light as he went.

Upstairs in the dressing-room, with all the signs of Dale's occupancy about it, he found the letter. It was in a plain envelope propped up against the looking-glass—no address, and the flap not gummed down. Inside, a single sheet with a couple of lines in Lisle's writing. No beginning to them, and no end. Just two lines in a tired, sloping hand:

"I don't feel as if I can stand this strain any more. Please forgive me—"

Rafe saw the words in a blinding flash of horror. Lisle had written them. When? How? There rose before him a brief interchange of words as they came out of the dining-room after lunch. Dale and Alicia had gone on, and he had said to Lisle in the old light way which was dead, "Why so tired, honey-sweet? You look as if you had been through a mangle." And Lisle, half laughing, "Well, I have. We've been trying to concoct a last appeal to my obstinate old Robson. I should think I've spoiled twenty pages and it's no good really." And then, quite suddenly, her hand on his arm. "Rafe, I forgot—Dale didn't want anyone to know. It—it means such a tremendous lot to him." He could hear himself saying, "All right—I won't give you away."

He looked back at the two scrawled lines, and had no doubt that this was one of Lisle's spoiled sheets. Words suggested, perhaps even dictated, by Dale—words which would have been a convincing proof of suicide when Lisle's drowned body came ashore, washed up by tomorrow's tide.

He went over to the fireplace, put a match to the paper, and watched it burn away to a fine ash. Then he opened the long trench window and went out on to the balcony. It was the same upon which Lisle's three windows opened. There was a light in her room, Lizzie would not leave her. The curtains were drawn back. The light made a faint glow upon the stone parapet—a faint yellow glow, perhaps from a shaded candle.

He stood and looked out over the massed woods to the sea. There, between the trees, they had made their faltering way home less than an hour ago.

Faint and far away, coming up out of nothingness, he heard the beginning of the sound he was waiting for. His whole mind and body were so keyed up that the sound seemed to be felt rather than heard.

There was a moment that was not time. Everything that he
had ever felt or known hung in it, suspended between what
had been and what was yet to come. It was sharp, and clear,
and irrevocable.

The moment was gone again, blotted out by actuality. The
insistent drone of an approaching plane clamoured against his
ear, and all at once the sound swept up into a roaring cre-
scendo—the music of flight, a music which he loved and had
always thrilled to. It beat now against every nerve. With its
climax he saw the plane, not overhead but away to the left,
black against the downs—too black to be seen if she had not
cut the dark with so easy and swift a flight. She came round
the house in a great sweep, flying wide and low, and turned out
to sea. She was climbing now—up, and up, and up, black as a
bird against that luminous sky—up, and up. The hum of the
engine dwindled. The bird was lost, and then suddenly, dreadfully found again—falling into sight and sound in a downward
rushing dive towards the sea. The water took her. Sound and
sight were gone.

Dale was gone.

Rafe went on standing there. He leaned on the balustrade
and looked out over the sea. But what he now watched was not
this place which had been Dale's possession or the sea which
was his grave, but the whole procession of their lives, always
linked, always separate . . .

Pictures. Dale in the nursery, lordly and strong at five years
old, all smiles and charm as long as he had his way. Rafe and
Alicia worshipping. Dale at school, strong and big for his age,
carelessly protective to a younger cousin who had a knack of

passing exams but wasn't nearly so good at games. Dale captain of football and cricket. Dale winning the mile. Dale putting the weight. Dale with everything he wanted in the world until Alicia let him down. Too many things coming too easily, and then a knock-down blow. Dale who had had everything he wanted, to have everything taken away.

Was it some sudden temptation which had sent Lydia over the cliff? Or was there even then under all the surface charm and kindness another Dale, perfectly cool and ruthless, who must have what he wanted, no matter what it cost?

Alicia gone and Tanfield threatened. Was that where things began to go wrong? Or had they been wrong all the time? Does a man suddenly become a murderer, or has the cold, ruthless streak been there always? If you matter too much to yourself, if your possession matter too much, then other people's interests, other people's lives, may come to matter so little that they can be sacrificed without a qualm.

Would things have been different if Dale had married Alicia? Outwardly perhaps. There might have been no murder done, because there would have been no advantage in doing it. Why had Alicia thrown him over? Of the two she was the one who had cared—but she married Rowland Steyne. Why? No one would ever know. Alicia kept her secrets. He wondered whether she had come up against that black streak and been scared by it. No one would ever know.

Dale had married Lydia Burrows, quite willingly and cheerfully after a well played scene of renunciation and despair. He had certainly had no love for Lydia, but how perfectly he had played the lover—a really notable performance. At what point had he decided to bring the run to a close and ring the curtain down?

As far as Rafe had ever been able to observe, Dale had had no regrets. Lydia's money made everything easy for him again as long as it lasted.

Give him what he wanted, and no one could be kinder or more generous than Dale. The model landowner, hard-working, public-spirited, careful for his tenants; the good master; the man of many friends—were these all parts which the other Dale had played—easily, enjoyably, savouring them to the full? Did he love Alicia? Had he ever loved Lisle? Had he ever loved anyone at all? Or had he only enjoyed playing the lover, the generous master, the good sportsman? The answer came unwillingly. He loved Tanfield. Not Alicia, not Lisle, not Rafe—nothing human. But Tanfield which was in some sort a projection of himself. His possession which in its turn possessed him utterly.

The pictures went on. The night passed.

When the dawn broke, a low white mist covered the sea. Rafe turned and went back into the house.

FORTY-EIGHT

Inspector March rang the bell of Miss Mellison's boarding establishment late that evening. Miss Mellison herself opened the door in a flowered overall and a string of bright blue beads, her face rather flushed, and her grey hair wispy from the combined effects of the July heat and the kitchen fire.

"I hope I didn't keep you waiting—it's my girl's day out. If you wouldn't mind—my little sitting-room—I'm sure I'm only too pleased. Miss Silver won't be a moment. I think you know the way."

She fluttered towards the stairs, disclosing as she turned a section of a brick-red dress of some woollen material with about two inches of green art-silk petticoat showing at the hem. No wonder she was hot.

March entered the little room in which Miss Silver had entertained him on a previous occasion. The windows were shut and the air thick with the smell of cooking and furniture polish. As he turned round from opening every-thing that would open, Miss Silver came in, cool, and neat, and dowdy.

"My dear Randal—this is very kind! I have naturally been most anxious to see you. Pray sit down. You have dined?"

"Oh, yes."

She settled herself, picked up a new piece of knitting of which only a couple of rows of pale pink wool appeared upon the needles, and said with a regretful sigh,

"So it was the husband after all."

Randal March was so much startled that he was quite unable to disguise the fact.

"My dear Miss Silver!"

She inclined her head in a prim little nod.

"It surprises you that I should know anything about it?"

He gave a rueful laugh.

"I am always expecting you to whip out a broomstick and ride away."

Miss Silver pursed up her mouth in a deprecating manner.

"My dear Randal—"

Before she could say any more the handle turned, the door was pushed open, and Miss Mellison entered with a tray upon which reposed two cups of coffee, a jug of hot milk, a small bowl of sugar crystals, and half a madeira cake.

"Oh, you really shouldn't have troubled."

Miss Mellison said that it was no trouble at all. She had taken off her overall and powdered her nose. The brick-red dress, now fully revealed, was high to the neck and long in the sleeve. The blue beads were of the kind that are sold to tourists

in all the Venetian shops. She fluttered from the room and shut
the door behind her.

"So kind," murmured Miss Silver—"she quite spoils me."
Then, in a brisker tone, "Dear me—what were we saying? Oh,
yes—it is really all very simple. You are wondering how I come
to know about Mr Dale Jerningham having crashed his plane
last night. The young man from the Ledlington Stores—his
name is Johnson—has a brother who works at the Tanfield
aerodrome. When he called with the groceries this morning
he said how upset his brother was. There had been something
wrong with the plane, but they thought they had got it right.
I am afraid I am not sufficiently conversant with such matters
to be able to tell you what the trouble was."

"I'm glad there's something you don't know."

Miss Silver coughed.

"Technical details are always better left to the expert. Well,
Johnson told his brother that Mr Jerningham *would* go up.
He was called to the telephone just as he was starting. There
had been an accident at Tanfield Court, and whether this news
upset him, or whether there was something wrong with the
plane, when Mr Jerningham did go up he seems to have lost
control and his machine crashed in the sea. One of the coast-
guards saw it—a man called Pilkington. They were all very
much upset when he rang up the aerodrome and told them
what had happened. Mr Jerningham was very much liked—
very open-handed and generous, so Johnson told his brother."

March surveyed her with a faint smile.

"How much more do you know?"

Miss Silver sipped her coffee.

"Oh, very little. May I cut you a slice of cake? . . . No? It is a little dry, I am afraid . . . We heard about Mrs Jerningham's accident from the baker who delivers at Tanfield Court. Poor thing—Mr Rafe brought her in at midnight soaked to the skin and in a state of collapse. She had fallen into one of those deep pools among the rocks, and they had been caught by the tide. A most providential escape."

"Yes, I think you may call it that," said Randal March.

"After that," said Miss Silver, "it was really all quite simple. A single accident is quite likely to be an accident—I can believe in it as well as anyone. But four accidents in a row one after another, all connected with the same person, is more than I can bring myself to believe."

"Four accidents?"

Miss Silver sipped her coffee.

"About a fortnight ago Mrs Jerningham was nearly drowned—she only came round after artificial respiration had been employed for some time. Since that her car has been smashed to pieces and she only escaped death by a miracle, a girl who was wearing her coat has been murdered, and she herself has again been within an ace of drowning. She is rescued by Mr Rafe Jerningham, who then has a telephone conversation with his cousin, immediately after which Mr Dale Jerningham takes his plane up and crashes. I must confess that I find it impossible not to connect all these events. Am I wrong in doing so?"

March's smile had gone. He put his coffee-cup back on the tray and said gravely,

"No—you are perfectly right. But look here—this isn't to be talked of."

Miss Silver drew herself up.

"My dear Randal!"

"No, no—I beg your pardon—I didn't mean that. You can know about it—you do know about it—but it's confidential between you and me. I've been with the Chief Constable, and he's most anxious that there shouldn't be a scandal. There's more in it than just the wish to avoid stirring up mud about a well known county family. Rafe Jerningham—look here, this is very hush-hush—is having a couple of inventions taken up by the government. I'm told they are very hot stuff, and that he is considered a valuable asset. He is being given a job under Macclesfield. The last thing on earth that anyone desires is that he should be mixed up with anything that invites publicity. Of course Pell will have to be got out of the mess. The facts will go to the Director of Public Prosecutions, and the case against him will be dropped. Jerningham's dead, and there's nothing to be gained by washing a lot of dirty linen in public."

Miss Silver's needles clicked.

"It is always a very unpleasant proceeding," she observed. "In fact, my dear Randal, there are times when I consider the freedom of the Press a somewhat over-rated blessing. But I am interrupting you. I feel sure you were going to continue your narrative. Pray do so."

He eyed her with the suspicion of a twinkle.

"If there is really anything that I can tell you. Well, this is what happened. Rafe Jerningham rang up at seven o'clock this morning and asked me to go out there. He looked like death, poor chap, and he told me the whole thing. He found that poor girl out beyond the Shepstone Rocks in a regular trap of a pool. Her husband had pushed her into it and left her there for the tide to finish. I've seen the place, and how on earth Rafe got her out of it and back amongst those rocks in the dark beats me."

"A providential escape indeed," said Miss Silver earnestly.

"He got her home, and rang up the aerodrome. As soon as Dale Jerningham heard that his wife was alive he would know that the game was up. Pell was the rock he struck on—they might have held their tongues if it hadn't been for him. But even Dale Jerningham must have seen that he couldn't very well expect them to stand aside and let Pell hang, so he took that dive into the sea."

"Did you see Mrs Jerningham?"

"Yes, I saw her. She made a statement, quite clear and simple. He pushed her in. He's besotted about the place, and her money was tied up so that she couldn't get it. But she had a power of appointment under her father's will, and she had exercised it in his favour. Rafe got twenty thousand, and Dale got the rest. I gather that the rest is a thumping big sum—enough to have kept Tanfield in the family for another generation or two anyhow. Poor girl—I was desperately sorry for her. She didn't attempt to keep anything back. I expect you've noticed that people don't when they have had a really bad shock. It all came out in a gentle, tired voice—no emotion or anything like that. After he had pushed her into the pool he stood there and told her why he'd done it. He complained about her luck—the drowning episode, and the car smash. You were quite right about those. He boasted about how clever he had been. And he admitted to the murder of Cissie Cole, but I don't think he boasted about that. I think that hit him pretty hard. Curious, isn't it—he could kill his wife without a qualm, but I think he was squeamish over having killed Cissie Cole by mistake. The Coles were part of Tanfield, and Tanfield was sacrosanct. I believe he really hated that poor girl his wife because she had given Cissie Cole her coat and let him in for killing her."

Miss Silver nodded.

"I should think that extremely likely. A most shocking story, but of great interest. Did you get a statement from Lady Steyne? It seems to me that she has something to explain. She testified that she and Mr Jerningham were together during the time they were up on Tane Head, did she not?"

"Well, she didn't quite say that. She hedged a little. When I took her original statement I wondered why she was at so much pains to suggest that she and Dale Jerningham were having an affair. It seemed just a little—unnecessary. I remember that when I asked whether they had been together the whole time she laughed in a conscious sort of way and said she wouldn't swear that she had never taken her eyes off him, but—well, what did I suppose they had gone up there for—or words to that effect."

Miss Silver gave a little cough.

"And what does she say now?"

"No more than she can help. It has hit her hard. She says they were together up there, but she missed a diamond and emerald clip she was wearing and they were trying to find it. I ran into her on Tane Head yesterday morning with Rafe Jerningham, and she told us then she had dropped this clip and was looking for it. To go back to Wednesday night—she says they hunted for it for a long time, but the light was bad and they didn't find it From time to time they were out of sight of one another. It's quite plausible, you know—in fact it's quite likely to be the truth—a little stretched perhaps, but near enough. Dale Jerningham would hardly have pushed that girl over the cliff in the presence of a third person unless she was an accomplice. But an accomplice would mean premeditation, and the whole circumstances at this point make premeditation impossible. No—he must have come on the Cole girl unexpectedly. He would see the tall figure, the fair hair, his wife's coat, and he must have acted at once under the first shock of an unforeseen opportunity. With time to think, the improbability of Mrs Jerningham being there must have struck him, and the recollection of Pell rushing from the scene would have suggested his mistake. But I don't believe he had time to think. He had the will to kill his wife. He thought he had the opportunity, and he took it. It was probably all over in a moment. He need not have been out of Lady Steyne's sight for any longer than she says. What she may have thought or guessed about it all afterwards is another matter."

"A very shocking story," said Miss Silver.

FORTY-NINE

Dale Jerningham's body came ashore on the ridge below the Shepstone Rocks. An inquest was held, and a verdict of death resulting from a flying accident was duly returned. Mrs Jerningham was not present. She was said to be prostrated with grief. When she had recovered she went away to stay with friends in Devonshire. Devonshire is a long way off.

Mr Tatham renewed his offer for Tanfield Court and the estate which went with it. Rafe Jerningham, who succeeded to the property, accepted the offer. Completion of the purchase would naturally have to be deferred until probate had been granted.

Miss Maud Silver returned to London, where her whole attention became immediately concentrated upon the case of Mr Waley and the Russian ikon—Waley was of course not his real name. The storm-clouds began to pile up higher and higher on the European horizon. July slipped into August, and

August slipped into war. The deaths of Cissie Cole and Dale Jerningham were left behind upon the farther side of world-shaking events. Nobody thought about them any more.

On a day when winter had begun to turn towards the spring Rafe Jerningham came into a room in a London flat. He was there to see Lisle, whom he had not seen since she left Tanfield. As has already been remarked, Devonshire is a long way off. And Lisle was a long way off, removed from him by tragedy, by kinship, by all the things which at once emphasise distance and obliterate it. He had written to her, and she had written to him. He knew what drives she had taken, when she first began to walk abroad again, how kind the Pearses were to her, and how there were violets in bloom against the south wall on New Year's day. Such things do not stay the hunger of a man's heart, and presently even these would be gone, because Lisle herself would be gone. It was natural and inevitable that she should go back to America. Once there, she would stay. She would marry again. Her letters would drop off, dwindling to a few lines at Christmas, and presently not even that—a card perhaps, with her new signature slanting across it.

The door opened and she came in.

She was in grey with a little bunch of violets—not the kind you buy. She must have brought them up from Devonshire. They were small, and dark, and very sweet. There was one white one. He looked at the violets because for the moment it wasn't easy to look at Lisle.

They touched hands. The only other time they had ever shaken hands was when Dale first brought her to Tanfield. It seemed strange and formal to be doing it now—so strange that he hadn't a word to say. He was out of his own key, and not sure of hers.

She thought, "Why does he look like that? Oh, Rafe, are you ill? Or do you really hate me? Oh, Rafe, *why?*"

But this was in her heart. Her lips began to speak at once, saying obediently all the things which people say when they have not met for a long time —"How are you?" and, "What have you been doing?" and, "Isn't it kind of Margaret Cassels to lend me this charming flat? The Pearses have been angels, but I am quite well now, and Mr Robson wants to see me."

"So do I," said Rafe. He looked at her then. "Are you well?"

"Don't I look well? The Pearses thought I did them great credit."

He went on looking. The strained patience was gone from her eyes, but it had left a shadow there. She was not so thin as she had been. There was colour in her cheeks, but it came and went in a breath. She had done her hair a new way. It shone like very pale gold, like winter sunshine. He said,

"The sale has gone through. Tanfield's gone to Tatham."

Lisle looked away. She caught her breath and said softly,

"Do you mind?"

"Mind? I'm thankful!" He pushed back his chair and got up. "I thought he'd cry off when the war came, but not a bit of it—the moment the probate was through, there he was, just itching to sign a cheque and move in."

There was a pause. He walked to the window and stood there with his back to her. A wet pavement, a row of houses opposite, a pale blue sky. He said abruptly,

"I've kept the Manor."

"Oh, I'm so glad!" said Lisle in a pleased voice.

Still with his back to her, she heard him say,

"You liked it."

"I loved it. There was something friendly about it, as if nice people had lived there and been fond of each other."

"My father and mother lived there. They were—very fond of each other."

There was another pause.

Extraordinary for Rafe to have no words.

He turned a little, and said simply,

"You know they've given me a job?"

"Yes. Is it interesting?"

"Oh, very. I could live at the Manor, but—I don't suppose I shall."

Lisle said, "Oh—"

None of this seemed to be getting them anywhere.

Rafe picked up the cord of the blind and began to twist it about his wrist.

"I don't suppose you would ever want to see the place again."

Lisle said, "Why?"

"I should think you would hate the sight of anything or anyone who reminded you of Tanfield."

"Why should I?"

She saw his eyebrows lift with that queer crooked tilt. An odd smile just touched his lips and was gone again.

"Plenty of reasons, my dear."

It was the old light voice for a moment. Then it quivered and broke. He untwisted the cord about his wrist and threw it back against the window. The ivory acorn rattled on the glass.

"Oh, Lisle—I love you so much!"

She felt the kind of surprise which stops thought. Thrown back on something simpler, she could only say,

"Do you?"

"Didn't you know?"

She shook her head.

"You said you hated me."

Rafe laughed. It was a queer jerky sound.

"I had to try and get you to go away. You weren't safe. Did you really think I hated you?"

She put her hand to her cheek—the old gesture which had always caught at his heart. It said, "I'm defenceless—I don't know what to do."

He came over to her, pulled a chair up close to hers, and sat down on the arm.

"Let's talk about it. I want to. I've been wanting to ever since—but—I can't get the right words."

She was looking up at him, her grey eyes dark, her colour now there, now gone.

"Why?"

"Because I've used them all up. I've made love to dozens of girls, but it's all been a game—very pleasant at the time and no feelings hurt when it was over—love all and vantage all. But none of that's any use now. It didn't mean a thing—it was just a game. Now it's—well, for the last twelve months it's been hell."

Her hand fell into her lap. She didn't speak.

"Naturally you must hate the very sight of anyone connected with Tanfield. I said that to you just now, and you said 'Why?' I've been saying that to myself ever since July, and I've never got any further than 'Why not?' But I have got to the point where I want to know how we stand, and whether there's ever going to be any hope for me. And before you say anything I want you to listen to me, and I want you to tell me the truth—the real truth. And you needn't bother about wrapping it up—it won't be any good."

Lisle caught her lip between her teeth. Something in her was quivering. Her lip quivered too. She tried to hold it steady.

Rafe leaned forward. He put a hand on the arm of her chair.

"How do you feel when you're with me?"

She was silent.

"You must know. You needn't mind about hurting my feelings. We used to go about together a lot. What did you feel then?"

She said, "Safe," and saw the colour run up into his face, darkening and changing it. Some of that haggard look was gone when the flush died down.

He said, "It that true?" and she gave a grave little nod.

"Yes—quite true. I don't tell lies. I always felt safe when you were there. Even when I was in the pool I felt safe—after you came."

He drew back with a jerk.

"A kind of super policeman! By the way, I've made great friends with March. He's a good chap."

What had she said? Why had he suddenly drawn away like that just when the strangeness was melting away between them? Was it what she had said about the pool? She didn't know. All she knew was that she couldn't bear it if he went away and became a polite stranger again—Rafe, who had always been so lightly and cheerfully free with his tongue. Her colour rose. She looked at him in distress.

"Do you mind if we talk about it? I think we must—just this once. Because if we don't, it will always be there—between us."

The odd crooked smile again, changing to a sudden gravity.

"Go on then. What do you want to talk about?"

"Dale."

The new bright colour went out as suddenly as a candle in the wind. It was as if a cold, dark wind out of the past had rushed between them.

He said, "Very well."

She kept her eyes on his face.

"Did he ever love me—at all? It makes a difference, you see. I want to know the truth. Sometimes I think he did—at first. And then he got angry—about the money—and about Tanfield. I oughtn't to have let him know I hated Tanfield. That was one of the things that made him want to kill me—he said so down at the pool. I keep on going over and over it in my own mind. That is why I want to know the truth. Do you think he did love me at all?"

Rafe didn't look at her. He said in a strained voice,

"Dale didn't love people. Sometimes he wanted them. He wanted Alicia. I don't know what would have happened if he had married her. He wanted Lydia because of her money. He wanted you—not altogether because of the money, though he wouldn't have married you if you hadn't had it. That's the truth, Lisle."

There was a silence that went on, and on, and on. He looked at her at last and broke it.

"Does it hurt so much?"

She said, "Not now." And then, "It feels as if it was all very far away and a long time ago—a little as if I really had died that night and all those things had happened in another life—as if I'd left them a long way behind—" Her voice faltered and stopped.

He leaned forward again.

"Am I one of the things you have left behind?"

She said, "I don't know—that's for you—"

All at once he was on his feet with her hands in his, pulling her up to face him.

"Why are we talking like this? I've told you I love you! It's been hell, but it might be heaven. I don't want to keep you safe—I'm not asking for a resident policeman's job. I want you to love me—I want you to marry me. I want you to come and live at the Manor with me. I don't want to talk about the past or think about the past any more. I want to know whether you love me. Do you? *Do you?*"

Her voice trembled into laughter. It was the sweetest sound he had ever heard.

"I wondered when you were going to ask me that."

ABOUT THE AUTHOR

Patricia Wentworth was one of the masters of classic English mystery writing. Born in India as Dora Amy Elles, she began writing after the death of her first husband, publishing her first novel in 1910. In the 1920s, she introduced the character who would make her famous: Miss Maud Silver, the former governess whose stout figure, fondness for Tennyson, and passion for knitting served to disguise a keen intellect. Along with Agatha Christie's Miss Marple, Miss Silver is the definitive embodiment of the English style of cozy mysteries.

THE MISS SILVER MYSTERIES

FROM OPEN ROAD MEDIA

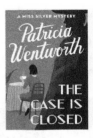

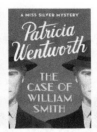

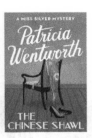

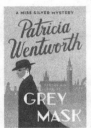

OPEN ROAD

INTEGRATED MEDIA

OPEN ROAD
INTEGRATED MEDIA

Find a full list of our authors and
titles at www.openroadmedia.com

FOLLOW US
@OpenRoadMedia

CPSIA information can be obtained
at www.ICGtesting.com
Printed in the USA
JSHW021935060223
37371JS00002B/307

9 781504 047869